REASONS OF THE HEART

A NOVEL BY HENRY GINIGER

Reasons of the Heart

FRANKLIN WATTS   NEW YORK   TORONTO   1987

Library of Congress Cataloging-in-Publication Data

Giniger, Henry.
Reasons of the heart.

I. Title.
PS3557.I487R4 1987   813'.54   86-29024
ISBN 0-531-15047-X

REASONS OF THE HEART

CHAPTER

One

In a house in Tangier one night, David Becker thought he was about to die. No, he was sure of it. Part of him was already on its way, floating dazed and helpless on a cloud of hashish. It is too soon, he thought bitterly. I am a twenty-year-old student, and now I am at my last lesson on earth. This was what hashish did but, sadly, he would have no time to leave word for the unwary. Hovering uncertainly in midair, anxious to start the journey toward the unknown, his soul impatiently contemplated his body, stretched out on a satin couch, awaiting a shroud. It should be blue. He looked good in blue. His mother had always told him that. She had not told him much about life but, thanks to her, he would know how to be at his best in death. The final moment, he was amazed to discover, was a kind of sound-and-light show. The flickering light of a small candle glowed brilliantly over his supine form while muffled moans entered from offstage.

Companions so close only a few hours before, now selfishly absorbed in themselves, had put a wall between them and him. Some companions! It was they who had administered the instrument of his death, then perversely abandoned him to his last agony. He anguished alone through the night, mind stubbornly split from body, until at last, day came to rescue him. Sunshine streamed into the room, overwhelming the candle of death, bringing the living world back to him. He felt whole and in control again, ready to go on a while longer. He peeked into the room where the companions lay entwined, their moans long silenced by exhaustion and sleep, then quietly tiptoed out of their lives. He had hoped it would be forever. But he had stopped counting the times over half a century when they had peopled his thoughts as he rambled through the longest night of his life. The scene could come back anywhere: while he clung to a pole on a crowded bus, or waited in line at a movie, or now on a balmy morning of his seventieth June, as he sat, plump, round-shouldered, and gray, on a half-broken bench on upper Broadway.

His reverie was impervious to the roar of buses and cars or to the aimless chatter of neighbors like himself, jowly men in flowered sport shirts and baggy pants, and women with dyed hair and, he thought, grotesque makeup for their age. In Riverside Park the air was better, but the benches there were often solitary places. More frequently than he liked to admit, he felt the need for people, a man who liked to be left alone but who often went out of his way to avoid loneliness. Sometimes he did not get much companionship on the Broadway benches either. Many of those he found himself wedged among were Jews who knew each other from the neighborhood temple. Becker had not been in a synagogue since his bar mitzvah. With an eye toward beefing up a congregation uncomfortably thinned by age and illness, and paying off an increasingly burdensome mortgage, the people on the benches had tried to recruit him. When he refused, he came to be looked on as something of a renegade, who got a nod or a curt greeting but was rarely brought into their conversations. He did more than refuse; he made jokes. Exasperated one day by yet another discussion of why God had allowed the Holocaust, he butted in.

"It would be much simpler," he said, "if you accepted the idea that there is no God. Then you wouldn't worry about things like that. Just think of the Holocaust as the work of man at his worst. You see how easy the problem becomes?"

His listeners could not believe their ears. Jews without God? At the first opportunity, over a little schnapps after Friday night service, they mentioned Becker's outrageous observation to the rabbi. He smiled. "The man is a fool or a wise guy," he said. "In either case, ignore him."

Which most did. He would not have improved matters, he imagined, if he had explained that he really had nothing against God, didn't even wish to dispute His existence, but had no particular use for Him. He had trouble explaining it to himself. Was his standoffish attitude toward God a kind of rebellion against his father, who had always sought to rule over him like a stern deity?

Yet his rejection of higher authority, his yearning to be free to do what he wished, even to flout conventional morality, was a puzzle when he considered that his whole life had consisted of dogged adherence to convention, order, and predictability. He liked to attribute that to his mother, as gentle as his father was grim, but so protective that a scraped knee would send her into a frenzy of tearful solicitude.

It was as if he were at war with himself, a war the night in Tangier had intensified to the point that he had never since been sure who he was. Today he listened like a good though silent neighbor to stories of little businesses long since liquidated or gone to seed under incompetent heirs, of flawed husbands or wives, of successful children with half-acres in Westchester, and of trips to Florida and other adventures. One gossiper added a fillip—a nephew found half-crazed one night on something called angel dust. "You have no idea," the man said, "what drugs can do to you."

"Tell me about it," Becker muttered. But it was no invitation to prolixity. Becker's eyes were half-closed, his mind already tumbling back through the years to the least predictable moment of his life.

He had gone to Tangier in 1934 after spending his junior year studying French language and civilization in Paris. His reluctant parents had allowed him to escape abroad on condition he be quartered with a respectable French family rather than live by himself. The family turned out to be so straitlaced they would make a fuss when he returned late from classes and seemed to worry as much about his morals as about his grammar. The worry was unjustified. He had little disposition to run wild, even at that age. Still, he found his foster parents as oppressive as his real ones. Paris was not the great love affair he had anticipated.

To compensate, he took an unauthorized foreign fling, his last before returning to his senior year at Columbia. Unable to spend much money in Paris, he had enough left to go to Morocco, not telling his parents until he got there and could fend off their indignant telegrams.

Tangier began with a chance meeting on a crowded café terrace at the aperitif hour. "Do you mind?" asked a stocky young man with an American-sounding accent, who pointed to the empty chairs at Becker's table, then gestured toward the terrace as if to say, "You are my only hope."

The American, who had a tall, slim, handsome Moroccan in tow, turned out to be a Canadian living in Tangier as a writer. David exulted in the tourist's delight at not falling in with tourists. As inexperienced as he was, he had at least heard of the literary colony that thrived on the outskirts of the city on cheap rents, drugs, and liquor and even produced some well-considered books. The Moroccan's function was unexplained. Looking hardly out of his teens, he talked little, mostly asides in French that Becker had trouble catching. But he smiled at Becker often, a smile so warm and gracious Becker found himself responding in kind, almost ignoring the Canadian until the latter, after another word in his ear from the Moroccan, asked if he would care to spend the evening with them. At twenty, Becker was dazzled by the prospect of a close look at local exotica.

What happened afterward in a small cluttered villa, Becker tried hard to recall, but parts remained murky. Perhaps he wanted it that way. If he really wanted to discover something about himself, he could go to some West Side Freudian who would explain, for $100 an hour, about the deliberate though unconscious suppression of memory. But before the layers of consciousness could be peeled off to reveal some inner truth, he was likely, he thought, to get up from the couch and walk out. Some things he would rather not examine.

They stopped at a store to pick up things for dinner. He remembered the last item on the order—50 grams of hashish. It could have been cornflakes, so casually was it requested and laid on the counter. At the stucco villa, on a hillside overlooking the sea, they first sat in a little garden. Becker began to feel tipsy from the strong Moroccan red wine on top of the anise he had drunk at the café. He was also vaguely disturbed by the strong scent of the flowers that bordered a small, closely cropped lawn. In the middle was a raised clump of earth shaped into something he could not make out. He took a closer look. The forms were unmistakable. Within a frame of gracefully flowing 69's two men were performing fellatio on each other. Becker stared at it and flushed, then retreated silently back to his chair. He threw a side glance at his hosts and sought to cover his confusion with a quick sip from his glass.

The Canadian grinned. "Beshir is a sculptor," he explained matter-of-factly. At the sound of his name, the young Moroccan grinned too. "When he doesn't have clay," the Canadian continued, "he works with earth. Down at the beach, he plays around with wet sand." Becker acknowledged this with a weak smile and continued sipping. He tried to imagine Beshir applying his talent to Jones Beach, protesting to the cops as they dragged him away that they knew nothing about art. Working in a private, closed-in garden in Tangier seemed to Becker brazen enough. Were all their guests assumed to share their tastes, or was this a show of defiance, at least until the next rainstorm destroyed all traces? He nodded politely at the artist.

"C'est bien, très bien," he said and looked away, wary of exploring Beshir's talents further, indeed, wondering how he could escape without fuss. But curious or titillated, he had never been sure which, he followed them like a docile child into the house. They had eaten, then sat cross-legged on cushions in dim candlelight, drinking brandy and listening to records of mournful Arab music and, in a more cheerful mood, Charles Trénet. Silently, the writer—Becker had forgotten even his first name, although the Moroccan's had stayed with him—stuffed hashish into a little pipe and handed it around as if it were chocolates. It was Becker's first meeting with what the French aptly called a *stupéfiant* and he did not reject it. How many times he accepted the pipe when it came his way he could not remember. Increasingly flushed and woozy, he felt hands softly caressing him. Had he accepted them too? He could not remember that either. He wanted to believe he had pushed them away, and perhaps he had. After a while he found himself lying alone on a couch on the other side of the room, then woozily watching as, hand in hand, his companions walked out, the Moroccan looking back once or twice as though longing to stay.

He returned to New York breathing not a word to his parents or anyone else of the night in the villa. He was still shaken, almost frenzied in his need to prove he was like anyone else. After virtually ignoring them through high school and most of college, he dated girls with a vengeance, getting them to bed with a kind of grim determination, even when they did not particularly appeal to him.

A year later, on Commencement Day, he rebelled against his father once again by rejecting law. Law school would be too much work, but his father was angry enough, and he kept his lack of ambition to himself. He had a facility for French; it would make a career. Teaching largely uninterested high school students for forty-odd years had not been exciting, but Morocco had convinced him that he was not really cut out for excitement. Perhaps he had died a little in that house in Tangier if living meant taking risks. Along with the hashish pipe had come a dare, which he accepted mostly because he did not know how to refuse. After that night he went out of his way to avoid dares.

Two years after he got his first teaching post, the spinsterish school nurse, three years older than he, found him vulnerable after daily taking his pulse for a month when he remarked feeling faint one day. Her caring interest flattered his self-esteem as well as his sense of what was right and normal. He found himself proposing. She accepted and without resistance, almost enthusiastically, he embraced matrimony. Passion had not launched their relationship and seldom intruded afterward, but things had worked out well, he felt. They had been affectionate and faithful to each other during thirty years of untroubled marriage. It had been very boring, he often reflected later. But what could he expect? His one fling he had put definitively behind him.

The world during that time moved on in ways that distressed him. Experiments in drugs and sex were commonplace. They had become industries, in fact, which, along with the excitement, engendered merciless violence and heartache. To his own little experience, he perversely clung like a shipwrecked sailor to a rock; it was the only moment that stood out in the gray, featureless ocean of his life. If anyone wanted to discuss "alternative life-styles," he was prepared. He could answer, carefully adopting a with-it way of expressing himself, "Hell, I was into that a long time ago." In his fifties, he had actually said it, while his wife was out of earshot, to some young people at a party when their talk had moved to the drug and sex gap between generations. But nobody said, "Hey, far out!" They stared silently at the lumpy little man in the gray suit and dark tie until he flushed and sheepishly retreated to the bar for another cognac.

He had to admit to himself he really wasn't with it at all and didn't dare to be. Of all the examples of changing mores, the gay liberation movement appalled him the most. Watching one evening a fifteen-second television sequence of a homosexual parade in San Francisco, he was both fascinated and sickened. Not only letting their demons out, they were flaunting them! Well, if he had any demons of his own—and he was not admitting anything—at least he had the decency to keep them within himself. Yet, one day in the school where he was teaching, he had come upon two students embracing in the washroom. He simply lectured the boys for being out of class! He could not bring himself to denounce their behavior, let alone report them. He tossed for hours that night wondering whether he had been unconsciously sympathetic with them, even a little envious of their uninhibited display, before falling asleep.

Now, his head was being nudged, and he awakened to upper Broadway. Beside him, a smiling young black leaned back nonchalantly against the broken slats of the bench and said, "What's happenin', man?" David stammered an apology for falling against him.

"Hey, no problem, man." The black's long, slim body was stylishly draped in tan flannel slacks and a violet sport shirt. His polished slip-ons sported gold-flecked tassels. Expensive but a little loud, Becker thought. Not quite wide awake, he could not keep from staring, entranced with the bizarre notion that Beshir had come back exactly as he had been fifty years before. The youth Becker gazed on now with such fascination was slightly darker, and his nose and mouth were broader than the Moroccan's, but he had the same smiling grace and beguiling look.

The black seemed not to notice the interest he had stirred. He took what looked like a homemade cigarette out of his shirt pocket, lit it, and inhaled deeply. If Tangier had taught Becker anything, it had been to identify the heavy, sweetish odor that surrounded the smoker. He looked around nervously to see who might be watching. The others had left, except for an elderly woman in a housedress at the end of the bench. She looked up from her Yiddish newspaper to sniff the air, then glared at the black. She, too, seemed to know the difference between tobacco and marijuana. The young man looked relaxed and unconcerned.

"You wanna puff?" he asked, extending the cigarette.

Becker shook his head. "Only on a dark cushion in a dim room," he said.

"Huh?"

"Just a joke. I've given the stuff up."

"Anything you say, Pop."

He bridled. "My name's not Pop. I'm Mr. Becker, David Becker."

The black extended his hand. "No offense. I'm Sam."

"Maybe you shouldn't be doing that around here, Sam," Becker said in a soft, avuncular tone. "I mean, I know all about it, but somebody might take offense." He looked toward the other end of the bench where the elderly woman was folding her paper. She stuffed it in a shopping bag, rose, and walked slowly off. *"Shvartzer,"* she muttered as she passed in front of them. A frown flitted across the black's face, then it resumed its smile. In the silence that followed, Becker took out a cigarette and tried to look casual as he lit it. Sam broke the tension. "You live around here?"

Becker nodded and felt obliged to return the question.

"Nah, just got a business appointment in the neighborhood." He looked at his watch, stubbed out his cigarette, and put the rest back in his pocket. "I guess I gotta go. Ya get to feelin' like havin' a drag, lemme know. I'm around."

Becker watched him take long, graceful strides across the avenue, his eyes lingering on the small, round buttocks. What kind of business? he wondered.

Becker felt something close to jealousy that the black should have someone waiting for him. He looked at all the others pacing purposefully along Broadway or rushing by in taxis and cars. Somewhere, someone was expecting them too. He got up with the tiredness that comes from sloth and shuffled through litter toward the supermarket, skirting little tables where one signed petitions to end rape, porno, vivisection, or landlord greed. Nobody was being mobilized against ennui, he noted. Too bad. He would sign up in a flash.

"Defend women's rights, take a stand against pornography!" a young woman in her early twenties with a small chest and flat heels shouted. As Becker passed, she thrust a pencil and paper at him. With nothing pressing, he stopped.

"What about freedom of expression?" he said. The pencil and paper froze in midair.

"What about the exploitation of women?" she shot back.

"Why are you worried? You're safe," he answered and

continued on to his rendezvous with a checkout clerk. He felt something hit his back and looked down. The woman had furiously hurled her pencil at him.

"Dirty old chauvinist!" she yelled. He smiled benignly, pleased he had bested her.

In the supermarket, his good humor lasted until he got to the shelves. No cottage cheese. No flat noodles. "They didn't deliver" the manager explained. Becker contemplated the frustration "they" had caused. He had had a hankering all morning for a dish his mother used to make—buttered noodles with cottage cheese and salt and pepper. It made no demands on his low-level cooking skills He blocked the aisle and ignored "Excuse me's" as he searched the shelves for an alternative. He surrendered with a sigh to a spaghetti, a sauce that a television commercial had insisted couldn't be more Italian, and Parmesan cheese. One had to be flexible if only to keep the blood pressure down. With his spaghetti, sauce, cheese, and a bottle of ginger ale, he lined up at the express checkout. He was invariably "10 items or less." On other lines, carts were piled with groceries. At the thought of homes where people cooked for others, then ate convivially, he sighed again.

Five years before, retirement and solitude had struck almost simultaneously. Two months after Becker stopped going to his classroom, his wife died of the cancer that had been eating at her for two years. Her illness had distracted him from the sudden emptiness in his own life. Her death meant he could no longer occupy idle days at the hospital. At the funeral, his loneliness overwhelmed him. Of the fifteen people at the funeral chapel and the six at the cemetery, the closest person was his sister. His only child, a boy, had died of leukemia at five. When he and his wife buried him, they decided never to risk that heartache again.

Now at the second funeral, Becker cried in bitterness about having no children to turn to. With her penchant for taking over, his sister offered him the spare bedroom in her Miami Beach condominium. But when he thought of sitting through the unchanging passage of time, nothing to mark the seasons except slight dips and rises in the temperature, it seemed to him boredom would drive him into the coffin much faster there than in New York. Boredom notwithstanding, when contemplating his own death, he felt no more anxious to meet it than he had been at twenty. "The next stop after Florida is the cemetery," he told her. Furious, she returned to home and husband and fought off calling him for several weeks.

What was there about life in New York that made him cling to it? The plays, concerts, movies, shops, and museums, he told himself, would fill all the idle moments in his life. And there was his little research project at the public library. It was to be the story of François Villon, who had always intrigued him by being able to write poetry between being a pimp, thief, and murderer. But sustained effort seemed increasingly difficult. With time, fifteenth-century France occupied an ever smaller corner of his mind. He had not been to the library for months. There was not much in the way of research material anyway. Most of Villon's story was in his poetry and he could find it at home anytime he bothered to delve into his bookcase. He had not done that for a long time either.

Increasingly, Becker found himself making excuses for staying in the little studio apartment, creating a desert amid the cultural lushness laid out for him every Sunday in the pages of the arts and leisure section of the *New York Times*. He would make notes on what to see, then decide the prices were high, he was tired, the subway was hot or dirty or dangerous, the wait for the bus cold or wet, the streets menacing. The life of the mind shriveled to neighborhood movies and an occasional paperback. He had tried to read, "or else your mind will atrophy," he warned himself, but his eyes would close after a few pages. He tried afternoon soap operas and fell asleep over them too. The evening screen was full of things that left him indifferent or unnerved—designer jeans, bloody encounters, the predicaments of youth ("Mom, is there really a difference in douches?"). Old people, he noticed resentfully, were objects to be patronized or ridiculed, the implication being that, at their age, they could not be quite all there.

For a time after his wife's death, he would be invited frequently to dinners and evening card games by sympathetic friends who thus far had managed to hold on to their spouses. But his misanthropy, a tendency to mope in silence and look bored, made him a less than charming guest. He could hardly blame them. He gave little inkling of how he enjoyed sitting for a couple of hours with friends over a meal. But when he let the conversation slide by, dropping in muttered monosyllables or sardonic comments, they thought he was being miserable. Invitations became increasingly rare until they virtually stopped. He regretted losing friends and hated to eat alone. Like all other meals, the one he was about to have would be dispatched in less than ten minutes.

Morose, Becker entered the elevator after checking to see who might be coming up from the basement. He found only the harmless bulk of Mrs. Klein, a neighbor two doors away, who seemed almost as round as she was tall and who further encumbered the narrow space with a basket of wash. Mrs. Klein's husband had died two years after Becker's wife, and she lived alone. She was one of the few people in the building Becker did more than nod to. They had found themselves heading down to the laundry room together shortly after his arrival as a tenant, and Mrs. Klein overwhelmed him with her laundering techniques. Since then she often asked him in for coffee, refusing to be discouraged when he accepted one invitation in five and had yet to return the favor, even when he longed for company. Listening to her crabby narrow-mindedness depressed him; it reminded him of his worst self. Sometimes, he wondered whether she had designs on him and imagined her taking charge of him, cracking verbal whips, making him answer for everything he did.

"So how are we today, Mr. Becker?" she asked, peering at him through horn-rimmed glasses that covered half her face. He had barely answered when she was off and running with the latest atrocity from Riverside Park, a young woman losing her purse to a black as she wheeled a baby carriage. By the time the elevator arrived at their floor, Mrs. Klein had denounced the entire black population of New York and the incompetence of the police department. For once, she spared him the sarcasm about her two daughters in Washington, who were nice girls and had good government jobs, mind you, but God forbid they should get married and give her grandchildren! With a bit of a tremble in her voice, she would talk about her funeral with only the daughters in attendance, assuming they took the trouble to come at all.

Once he had made the mistake of provoking her into an argument by asking why the size of the crowd at her funeral mattered. "If you don't care about going to your grave practically alone, that's your business," she snapped back. He let it go at that. The question had been pure bravado on his part, he acknowledged to himself. Of course he cared, like everyone else. Wistfully, he read obituaries where the subjects were cited for their accomplishments, the examples they had set, the admiration they had stirred. In advance, he deplored the low turnout for his own death. For a newspaper to notice it, it would have to be paid.

The elevator arrived at their floor, this time with no provocations on his part. When he got to his door, Becker simply nodded and closed it quickly behind him. Such an ignorant woman! He took pride in his tolerance, his refusal to share the prejudice most Jews of his generation seemed to have against blacks. He had an obligation as an intellectual to know better, he told himself. How could Jews denounce a whole race after what had happened to them in Europe? So why then in the subway did he often catch himself counting whites and blacks, us and them? And why was he annoyed—he a foreign language teacher—when he heard only Spanish around him? At times he thought of himself as a first-world person riding in a third-world subway. Afterward, he would dislike himself for hours for allowing his inner feelings to overcome his sense of what was right and reasonable.

The room was a mess. He always left housekeeping to his wife, except in the last two months when she could no longer do it laying immobile on a hospital bed. When she died, he moved from their two-bedroom East Side apartment into a studio apartment in an old building on Riverside Drive because it would require less cleaning. It was also cheaper, and on a teacher's pension, that counted. He had looked at even cheaper places, but they all faced the backs of other buildings, and he decided he still wanted to look out on the world. For the more affordable rent, Becker got not only less space but a drastic drop in service. The doormen, elevator operators, and handymen he had been accustomed to on the East Side were no longer there, at a time when life in New York had become much more violent than he could remember.

Becker's studio was large, 22 feet by 15, with a dressing room alcove that led to the bathroom. When he moved, he had to get rid of a lot of furniture. A daybed and easy chair near the wide window, at the other end a round teak dining table and four chairs bought when Danish modern was in vogue, in between a bookcase and desk—this was all the room could manage without clutter. The kitchen, little more than an alcove, had no window, but the studio looked out on the park and was light and airy. He took his meals there, covering with a plastic cloth the scratches and stains on the table almost he alone had caused, so rare were visitors.

He made up the daybed and collected clothing, shoes, and yesterday's *Times* from the floor. Then he sat down beside the window and took his binoculars—he had bought them secondhand when he found he had a view—for his prelunch survey of the park. Mothers were beginning to remove children from the sandbox in the playground. Several couples were walking dogs while joggers passed men reading newspapers on benches. "Mrs. Klein, you'll be glad to know things are quiet today," he muttered.

Becker shifted the glasses slowly until they stopped at two men in conversation under a tree. One was short and stocky and wore a broad-brimmed hat. He was white as far as Becker could make out from features obscured by the hat. The other was a tall black. The short one passed something to the other, then began poking him in the ribs. The black did not appear to react, but after a few seconds began walking away. Becker's eyes followed him as he strode athletically up the incline toward the exit in his tan slacks and violet sport shirt.

"Hello, Sam. I see you made your appointment," Becker said to himself as the young black crossed Riverside Drive and disappeared into Ninety-first Street. He walked to the kitchen to put up water for the spaghetti. What kind of business required getting poked? he wondered. And why should he care?

CHAPTER

Two

After lunch came a nap. It often struck Becker that he was much the same at seventy as at two, as though obeying a law of nature that required people in their old age to revert to childhood until at the end they seemed about to reenter the womb. He was ready to believe in a steady descent into the first years of life when he reflected on the routines that governed him then and were increasingly doing so again. For his sister and him, Mommy had an almost unvarying schedule. Lunch at twelve, a little play at twelve-thirty, a nap at one, an afternoon at the playground, a bath at five-thirty, dinner at six, reading at six-thirty, in bed for the night by seven.

He was less strict about the hours now, but there were some added routines that he could have done without. Sleep almost never came right away, his mind dwelling on the petty annoyances of his life for an exasperating time before drowsiness took charge. Paradoxes beset him: time was running out, yet lay leaden and motionless; he was living years of relaxation, yet always felt tired; he had trouble undertaking anything, yet was almost constantly bored. Sleep would obliterate the pestering thoughts for an hour. Then a long afternoon and evening would stretch before him, but he no longer had either mother or wife to tell him how to fill them. At night, when he bothered to recall what he had done, he was depressed at the lack of variation.

It was not as if he had not tried for something better. In the months before retirement, Becker took time for lectures sponsored by the teachers' union on how to spend the golden years. "You are lucky people," he remembered one lecturer saying. "You have intellectual resources. You need never be idle or feel useless. But you do need a plan, and with it, the will to live in the present as much as possible, and even," the young woman lecturer paused with a knowing smile, "to look forward to the future."

"Easy for you to say," Becker had muttered, and the old English teacher beside him put her hand on his arm to hush him. But he had to admit it was not all nonsense, particularly in his case. Looking daily at intimations of death in his wife's shriveling face and body, he knew he would soon be both idle and alone. Filing out of the auditorium after the lecture, the English teacher told Becker she had always wanted to try her hand at short stories. She would give it a whirl; what else did she have to do? "Do you have plans?" she asked.

He shrugged in answer, but had actually done some thinking. He might go for the Ph.D. in French literature he had never gotten. He had been rejected for college posts because of that. At Columbia's graduate school, where he had gone to inquire a month after his wife died, he mingled self-consciously with future classmates. They looked at him curiously as if he had taken a wrong turn and missed the faculty lounge or, worse, the custodian's room. Clutching all the proper forms in one hand while the other clung to a strap in the swaying subway car, he made his way home in an orgy of negative thinking. He was shocked at how high the tuition had gone since he had been a student. A stiff investment with no parents to help, he thought, and really just to fill time and improve his mind a little. With muttering and headshaking that caused the other passengers to eye him warily, he went on to the clincher. If he did not have the drive to get his doctorate when he was young, how could he expect to have it now? By the time he reached his stop at Ninety-sixth street, the plan lay amid the other litter.

It was during the walk from subway station to house that the Villon study occurred to him. It was so simple he wondered how he could have missed it. It would be a considerably cheaper self-help project. Teacher, teach thyself! He dumped the graduate school bulletin and the application forms in a wastebasket and bought himself a chocolate ice-cream cone with sprinkles as a reward for clear thinking.

His enthusiasm for the Villon project died quickly. Becker found it required more self-discipline than he could muster. He worked desultorily, letting weeks go by before returning to the project for a few days until he virtually abandoned it. He was ashamed, but not enough to goad himself into action. "You know what you do really well?" he asked, facing the bathroom mirror one morning. "It's finding reasons not to do anything."

His main consolation lay in having a sense of humor, although of a kind that often alienated people. His bench neighbors mostly grimaced at the world as though everything in it tasted bad. Listening to their laments, he wondered how they stood themselves. Some of them couldn't, and he would hear weepy tales of suicide until he got up and walked away.

Of course, there was an excuse for the grimacing. Old people rarely felt completely well. He counted himself lucky. He was doing better than most, his doctor finding little else wrong during the occasional examination than being overweight from a penchant for sweets and the blocked artery in his left leg, which quickly became exhausted when he went up an incline or hurried across a street to beat traffic. He tried to heed warnings about cigarettes but could do no better than reduce the intake to half a pack a day of "Ultra Lights." He assuaged his conscience with mild exercise.

The nap, for example, was followed, weather permitting, by a walk. Today's took him first through well-populated paths in the park. He despised Mrs. Klein for her racist fears, yet constantly imagined himself being mugged and his heart giving out at the moment some huge black pressed a switchblade against it. So far nobody had put him to such a test, which was remarkable, he thought, with all his walking through the West Side over the years.

Broadway was a rough line of demarcation between two

ways of life. West of it the comfortable middle class lived in the apartment buildings and brownstones. He tried to avoid the streets to the east, where blacks and Hispanics crowded into tenements long gone to pot, and regularly made the papers and the six o'clock news with stories of death and violence brought on by drugs, poverty, and the sheer inability to get out of each other's way.

Teeming Broadway was also a cacophonous linguistic meeting ground where Korean, Vietnamese, and Chinese vied with Spanish and various grades of English. The Upper West Side met Becker's idea of melting-pot America, earlier generations of newcomers looking with disdain from their high-rises and carefully protected brownstones on the as-yet-unmelted, who sought desperately to work their way out of rotting tenements. Mrs. Klein counted herself lucky to be native born, her self-esteem constantly sustained by the knowledge that she had been delivered in a New York hospital two months after her parents arrived from Leipzig. She stayed as much as possible to the west side of Broadway, where most of the better shops and nicer people were, and never sat on the benches in the traffic islands because one never knew whom one might meet.

Becker had to smile when he pictured how she would have reacted to Sam this morning. She might have sought a policeman. Well, he was more intelligent. He, at least, could consider the black problem behind the crime statistics. Blacks were, it seemed to him, native-born immigrants who grew up with almost as many language and economic difficulties as the foreigners. Too many blacks were still as far away from the mainstream as those freshly landed, and were confined, when they got a job at all, to the same dirty work America handed out to newcomers. Unfortunately, blacks seemed to give up on education, the traditional way up the ladder, more readily than earlier candidates for the American dream. From his clothes, Becker judged that Sam was making it some other way. He wondered if the black lived in one of those tenements on the wrong side of Broadway. He imagined Sam emerging from some dank, smelly room, so splendidly turned out he would glitter in the dark hallway.

Becker found himself in front of the playground entrance. On impulse, he walked in and stopped by the empty swings. Across the way, children hung from the jungle bars shouting, "Look!" at their mothers, who glanced up distractedly from their gossip and shouted back, "Be careful!" With nobody paying attention, Becker placed himself gingerly on a swing and began to sway gently, thinking of how his mother used to give him a start, but solicitous as always, would do it gently lest he go flying off.

"Wanna push?"

The familiar but unplaceable voice startled him. He turned to face a grinning Sam. Two encounters in one day Becker thought, and a third by long distance, so to speak, and with a black yet. What was he doing back in the park?

"We've got to stop meeting this way, Sam."

"What way?"

"Just another joke. So did you make your appointment?"

"Yeah, I made it." Sam was not being loquacious. Another of those homemade cigarettes came out of his shirt pocket, and he started to light it.

"Not here, Sam. Not in a playground."

"Best place. Nobody around to check."

"But what about the children?"

"Ain't offerin' them any. I'll wait while they grows a little."

And Sam took another deep drag. "Why do you use that stuff?" Becker asked with mounting annoyance. "Do you want to ruin yourself?"

"Hey, man, this makes me feel good. Makes everybody feel good. This smoke's better than yours, jes' read what's on your label. Here, try this."

For the second time in the day, Becker rejected the offer and sought escape. "I've got to get to the store before it closes," he said, opening the gate to the swing enclosure. "If you won't put that thing out, at least be careful." He walked off, wondering why what happened to Sam mattered to him.

"Okay," Sam called after him. "Ya change your mind, ya tell me, ya hear? Maybe I can swing a coupla smokes for ya." He was no longer looking at Becker, but at the children beyond him and, beyond them, at the adults on the benches.

Becker walked out of the playground, then stopped and looked back from behind a tree. Sam was sitting at a picnic table peeling an orange. The peel was deposited in a small paper bag. He was joined a moment later by a couple of young women pushing small children in strollers. They sat down and each drew what looked like a cookie from a bag. As they ate, Sam appeared to push something into their bags and they responded by putting something in his.

From fifty yards away, Becker tried to figure the scene out until a light flashed in his head. "I'll be a son of a bitch!" he exclaimed in a near whisper. "He's a dope pusher!" It had taken him all this time to catch on. He might have suspected something from the offer Sam made him on the bench and just now at the swings. His slowness showed how little attuned he had become even to his own neighborhood. Shaking his head as much at his own denseness as at Sam's activity, he turned to leave the park, then stopped. Sam was standing beside the picnic table with someone else. It was the same short, stocky figure with the broad-brimmed hat Becker had seen him with under the tree earlier. They were talking, then the short man was reaching out and poking Sam as he had under the tree. Sam towered over him but was meekly accepting the jabs. Then the black reached in his pocket, withdrew something—money?—and gave it to his tormentor. They seemed to have nothing more to say to each other. Unsmiling for once, Sam moved out at close to a lope. On his weightlifter's legs, his companion followed more slowly, casting his eyes around until they stopped to focus on Becker. They were undoubtedly in business together, that much he could figure out. Becker could feel the eyes burning into him. He tried to appear nonchalant, pausing to look up at the buildings across the way, then professing interest in the shrubbery about him, terrified the man would stop and poke him too. But the man moved up and out of the park.

Slowly Becker followed behind, nervously trying to figure out what it all meant. For sure, it meant big business. He looked up at the buildings again. In cozy living rooms along Riverside Drive, West End Avenue, and all the living rooms in between, it was like Tangier every day, maybe with even stronger stuff. He had read about how popular cocaine had become with those who could afford it, and with those who couldn't. "Let's not get dramatic," he admonished himself. Not everybody's experience had been the disaster he had made of his, nor was anybody likely to be nagged by it a half century later.

In spite of himself, Becker had to smile. Sam was almost as casual as the Tangier grocer. Sam, the man who makes you feel good. He watched him catch a cab and head east. What happened to someone like that when he got caught? Becker wondered, not that he was about to turn Sam in. Probably nothing much. The age of dope had blossomed, and the effort to stop it would probably work no better than the Prohibition he dimly remembered. Even his righteous, legalistic father had dealt with a neighborhood bootlegger and kept a few bottles in the house.

Becker took a last look at the children in the playground—Sam had plans for them too—and emerged onto Riverside Drive. Lost in his nervous thoughts, he barely missed a small red sports car that pulled out with an arrogant roar just as he stepped off the curb to cross the street. "Cowboy!" he muttered as he leaned against a building on the other side to let his heart quiet down. Uneasy, he watched the car until it was out of sight. What had he seen behind the windshield? Was it his imagination or was it really the same broad-brimmed hat covering eyes that seemed so menacing a few moments before?

However shaky he felt, he was reluctant to shut himself

in too quickly, as though afraid to be alone. He took a circu-
itous route past rows of brownstones still genteel but worn
and slightly seedy. They had aged as he had, but at least
they could be renovated. The thought brought a sigh. The
middle of one block was dominated by a large graystone
church. It was a distressing neighbor to most of the street's
residents, who regularly voted Democratic and would sign
for any liberal cause but who barricaded their doors and
windows against the kind of homeless and hungry men who
flocked daily to the church's "community services." This
evening's crowd was starting to gather in front of the locked
gate to the basement, where a meal was in preparation.
Becker was tempted to cross the street when he came
abreast of the line, but he walked stonily on until his eye
was caught by a sign on the gate.

"The First Unitarian Church," he read, "is initiating a
program of tutoring for high school students experiencing
difficulties in English, mathematics, and the physical and
social sciences. Qualified persons wishing to volunteer their
services may apply to the Rev. Eliot Greenway."

He read the notice again. From behind came a shout,
"You get in line, Pop, like everybody else!" Becker shot a
furious look at the shouter, a young unshaven man with
torn blue jeans and a stained T-shirt. "I'm not here for a
handout," he said, drawing himself up and walking away
full of outraged dignity. He turned the sign's import over in
his mind. The schools aren't what they used to be, and neither are the students. Looking back a moment, he self-
righteously decided that bums never changed.

The thoughts perversely cheered him as he walked
home. He had a roof over his head, he did not have to look
for handouts, and he had just seen proof there was still a
market, such as it was, for an old teacher. When he was
working, not only had the pay been low, but teachers were
also expected to donate free time. His voluntary work had
been largely confined to the French Club, which never got
over ten members. Free time was all he had now, and all he
could do with it was donate it.

Inside his studio, he lay down. He would think about it, he decided. He was not sure he wanted to deal with the kind of people likely to be taking the courses. What if they gave him a hard time? What if they were downright dangerous? He thought back to the polite, middle-class, white students he used to have. If teaching was not a complete pleasure then, at least it was not the daunting experience it had since become in so many New York schools. The problems he could be getting into! Still, a feeling of excitement was stirring in him. It would be something, no longer having to say, "I used to be a teacher," as if his life were completely behind him.

CHAPTER

Three

Becker had not been the only one watching Sam in the park. Lately Carlo had taken to keeping a closer eye on the black. He shifted the Alfa Romeo down, irritated by all the turns on Riverside Drive that kept him from getting up any decent speed. It did not take much to get him worked up; his uncle was on his back all the time about his temper. He waited until Sam had made his little deals in the playground before moving in on him. The bastard had been getting on his nerves in the last couple of weeks. First, he was talking of getting out, "going legit" was the way he put it. Maybe even going back to school. Probably some stupid broad had gotten to him. It was no time to lose his best pusher when he was going into cocaine in a big way. Grass was chicken-shit stuff. Coke was where the money was. He had started Sam out on some. The jerk was afraid at first, so he had to sweeten things by not asking him for any money until he sold the stuff. He hated to do anybody favors, especially Sam. He would just as soon give him a karate chop as look at him. Besides being black, Sam was late handing in money too often, and this was one of those times. He had given Sam the cocaine packets a week ago, and he must have dealt them by now. Being kept waiting drove Carlo up the wall. The thing was, when Sam did pay up, it was usually more money than Carlo got from any of the others he had working the streets. In the past, he just let out a few remarks, underlined by some jabs in the ribs. Yesterday, he let Sam have some more grass because he had customers waiting, even though the bastard still was not handing over any money. What the hell, business was business, as the uncle said, so often, in fact, he felt like giving him a karate chop too.

When he grabbed Sam just after the deal in the playground, all he could get out of him was a few bucks from the marijuana dealing and a promise to meet tomorrow to settle the cocaine account. Aside from the rib-poking, Carlo once again held his temper. Too many people looking. Who the hell was the old man Sam had talked to? And why was he hanging around? Didn't look like a cop, but he didn't look like a customer either. Carlo laughed. The old guy looked scared shitless when the car passed within an inch of him just as he was stepping off the curb. Maybe he'll think twice about nosing around in other people's business. He was sorry he had not knocked him on his ass. Then he would have really done some thinking, if he was still alive.

Stirring sugar into his coffee the next morning at breakfast, Becker had put the incident with the car out of his mind and was thinking of the sign on the church gate. It really was tempting to start doing something again, particularly something he knew about. His mind went back to an experience that had rankled him for years.

A year after he left his old school, loneliness had driven Becker back to it, as if to test the invitation to "come back anytime," the principal had given him at the retirement party. Early one morning, he was mounting steps he rarely used to notice but which now seemed rather high. The green hallways were dingier than he remembered. Among the students milling between classes, there were also more blacks than he could recall from his time. In the faculty room, four former colleagues stood with coffee cups and looked blankly at him a moment before breaking into smiles. There was a round of "Nice to see you again" and "How are you getting along?" followed by sympathetic clucks when he told them of his wife. He was handed a cup of coffee.

"So what are you up to?" someone asked. That was just it, he was not up to anything. He stammered something about the floundering François Villon project and was saved from further embarrassment when they excused themselves with a "Great to see you" and went off to classes, leaving him to sip his coffee alone. Walking out of the room into the empty hallway, he looked at his watch. The reunion had lasted five minutes. In the principal's office, the secretary was heartbroken. The principal had just rushed off to a meeting of the community school board, she explained. "You must come back another time," she added with a smile. "But call first."

Walking down the steps, he felt one illusion lighter: he was out of the mainstream, the picture; call it what you will, he was certainly out of it. The world was divided, he realized with a tinge of resentment, between those who were busy and those who were not. The first were the only ones who were really alive. He had not gone back again.

So now he had a chance to rejoin them. After all, what had he done for the world lately? Zilch. He was not even a good consumer—two peaches, a can of soup-for-one, six eggs from a carton split down the middle, paperbacks at no more than $4, tax included. In stores he often felt he was being sneered at. On rainy days or when he was depressed for no particular reason, he would think of himself as simply occupying space. There would be no encomiums for that on Judgment Day. Indeed, the way the world's population was going, he would not be surprised if an international treaty someday declared, "Mere occupancy of space is dangerous and unlawful." Then he and millions like him would be rocketed into distant orbit. Good riddance, the workers and consumers of the world would say.

He was having another bout with self-pity. He thought of his sister. At his funeral, she would undoubtedly have a tear for him; indeed it would be de rigueur. But she would take over in the same businesslike way she had tried to take charge of him after his wife's funeral. Older by three years and overweight, she was nonetheless likely to bear out the actuarial tables and outlive him. She would be sure to show distress at his injunction against hiring a rabbi to shower platitudes over the coffin but would secretly be relieved at not having to brief the holy man on the barely honorable life and sparse virtues of the loved one.

Becker swallowed some coffee the wrong way and began to cough violently. He was being unfair, he knew. He had no call to think unkindly of his sister. She had never really been unkind to him although, as the wife of a lawyer, she shared their father's scorn for his refusal to become one too. But she had not dwelt on it, particularly after her daughter, who had taken pre-med at great expense, married a hardware store owner shortly after graduating from Barnard and disappeared into the merchant class in Riverside, California. Despite his sister's disappointments—there had yet to be a birth announcement from Riverside—she often showed her concern for him. Better to love and be loved by his sister; who else was there? The world may not be his oyster, but he shivered at the thought it could be both lonely and loveless.

He was being pretentiously morbid, he told himself. He would go to his grave like 99 percent of humankind, with no crowds, no public tributes, no bugles. But a few people anyway, that was not too much to ask. The ninety-year-old woman who shared the hospital room with his wife died one night, as alone as she had been in life. Nobody knew she was gone until morning, and Becker imagined what kind of funeral she had. You lived as best you could, and when you were dead, the world noted it with barely a pause, in Manhattan maybe even with gratitude for the apartment you were vacating.

He was only having coffee with a buttered roll, but the intolerable sadness he felt was making breakfast indigestible. "I'm still alive; let's start thinking of today," he said aloud. The papers, the magazines, the television news were full of stories of old people lending a hand to schools and social centers, retired teachers like himself or even ordinary people without that experience. So what was the big deal? Well, any break in the routine was a big deal with him now, he acknowledged.

Becker wondered if his trouble deciding to lend his talents to the First Unitarian Church might, after all this time, be some kind of religious inhibition. "You can take the boy out of Judaism, but you can't take Judaism out of the boy." Now there was an original thought! It was worthy of the Broadway bench philosophers or one of Philip Roth's obsessive characters, but maybe there was something to it. In Brooklyn, he had grown up in an apartment building opposite an Episcopal church. Standing atop a hill, the church looked incongruous and alien in a neighborhood where Jews moving up and out of the Lower East Side had displaced Protestants years before. In the winter, he had gone bellywhopping down the hill on his Flexible Flyer. That was as close as he dared come to the church, a small building in the same brownstone as the rest of the block, until one day curiosity bested his fear. He leaned his sled against the side and entered after looking around to see if anyone was watching. The somber interior intimidated him, and he stayed close to the door, one hand on the knob. A statue of a lady in flowing robes with a baby in her arms was unlike anything he had seen in the synagogue. He stared at her, admiring the colors the sun splashed on her through the stained-glass windows, until he heard a door open and he fled. He had said nothing to his parents although, he later thought, they probably would not have made much of it. In Paris, he had visited St.-Julien-le-Pauvre, the oldest church, and Notre Dame, the grandest, and the same feeling of being off limits returned.

Now, making up the daybed, he began to rationalize. Would he serve a church or some kids in need? By the time he had given the room a semblance of order, he reached what seemed the obvious answer. Still, donning yet another of his retirement outfits—sport shirt and shapeless slacks— he continued to feel as if he were about to transgress. When he got to the church, he looked carefully up and down the street before mounting the steps. He was beginning to get impatient with himself. If he were in front of a porno theater, he would act no differently. "Come on," he mumbled, "the race will survive, but you're going to demolish another plan if you don't watch out." He went in and found the Reverend Greenway in his office.

Not yet completely rid of his doubts, Becker was further unsettled by the man of the cloth behind the scarred, mahogany desk. He was in a jogging suit still stained with sweat. A tall, dark-haired, athletic man who, Becker guessed, could not be more than thirty-five, he sat mopping his face with Kleenex. Becker stood at the door until Greenway looked up and smiled. "Can I help you?" he asked briskly. Becker hesitated. Surveying him, Greenway added, "Our meal is at six-thirty."

Becker blinked hard, thought briefly of fleeing but instead sought support against the door frame. I guess you haven't been looking at yourself lately, he thought angrily. It was all right for Greenway to be sloppy; nobody was going to mistake him for one of his freeloaders. He answered more sharply than he meant to. "I didn't come for a free meal." A slight emphasis on the "free," then a pause to let it all sink in. "It's about the tutoring service you've started," and as Greenway looked confused, Becker added, "I thought I might be able to do some."

"Oh, sorry," Greenway said. He smiled again and gestured to a chair. "That's very nice. Please sit down."

"Yes," Becker went on from the edge of his seat, "I used to be a teacher."

Greenway leaned forward, looking interested. "What did you teach?

Becker was afraid he would ask and had prepared for it. "I taught high school French. But there is probably not much call for it. I could help with English, perhaps." He made it sound more like a question than a statement.

Greenway nodded. "You're right. French is not a crying need here." After a pause he said suddenly, *"Comment allez-vous?"* Startled, Becker answered, *"Je vais bien."*

Greenway laughed. "I had three years of French not so long ago, but that's about the limit of my conversation. So you think you could teach a little English?"

Becker squirmed in his chair. "You probably have more-qualified people. I only thought I could help." He felt he should reinforce his credentials. "I minored in English in school," he said. How many years ago!

Greenway held out his hand. "You can help; you can," he said emphatically. "It's just that I was expecting college students, you know, people like that. But college graduates are even better." Becker was afraid he would be asked when he had graduated. But Greenway went on tactfully, "We haven't had that many volunteers. As a matter of fact, we have at least ten students looking for help just in English. Individual tutoring is going to be difficult. We'll have to form a class to take care of them all. Do you think you could take that on, Mr. . . . Mr. . . . ?"

"Becker. David Becker." This was getting to be more of a project than he had bargained for. Greenway broke into his thoughts.

"I hope you realize, Mr. Becker, that this is all volunteer work. We can't afford to pay anything, but we do have a textbook." Greenway picked up a worn volume from a shelf behind him and brandished it.

"Oh, yes," Becker answered. "I wasn't expecting pay. It's just that I wasn't expecting an entire class either. What's the schedule like?"

"Just an hour, twice a week." Greenway grinned. "We're not trying to replace the regular schools, although that might not be a bad idea. Some of these kids belong back in the fourth grade." He paused and looked at Becker quizzically. "You're sure you're up to it?"

Becker felt too far in to back out. "I'm seventy years old, but I feel fine. I'm willing if you're willing," he said.

Greenway jumped up and extended his hand again. "Swell. We start the program Monday. Mondays and Fridays at five o'clock in the basement, okay?"

Becker nodded. The basement seemed to be a busy place, but those seeking learning and those with more basic wants would be separated by about half an hour, he noted. He showed himself out as Greenway waved and turned to pick up the telephone.

The die, such as it was, was cast. He was feeling uncertain, but all the same, good about himself. He walked to Broadway, his step springier than usual. With barely a glance at the congregational benches, he picked up his pace even more and proceeded twelve blocks to Zabar's pastry shop where, tired from all the exertion, he sat down with a napoleon. He delighted at the thought he was undoubtedly the only one in the place who knew it as a mille-feuille. Had Greenway jumped into French as a way of running a subtle identity check? No matter, he was back in business, with lessons to prepare again for his students. His students! Bathing in euphoria, he began to consider the first day of classes.

"Oh, Mr. Becker," came a familiar voice from the next table. Mrs. Klein was sitting with a friend, coffee and croissants in front of them. Becker nodded and smiled. Not even she could annoy him today.

"I'm glad to run into you," she said. "I'm having just a few friends in Monday afternoon for coffee and cake. Please come. Five o'clock."

"That would be nice, Mrs. Klein, thank you, but I'll be busy." He said it with the assured tone of someone who needed an appointment secretary to keep track of his busyness. The old woman looked at him, intrigued.

"Busy?"

"Well, yes. I've volunteered to work with high school students who have trouble with English."

She frowned. "Negoes and Puerto Ricans, maybe?"

"Some of them will be, I guess."

"Who else has trouble with English?" Satisfied with the putdown, she went back to her coffee and croissant. Her friend giggled. They barely looked up when Becker polished off his pastry, wished them a nice day, and left.

Thanks to Mrs. Klein, he had something else to think about. In Greenway's office, he had not remembered to ask what the students would be like. When you peeled off the prejudice, her remark probably contained some truth. Images of the blackboard jungle, something he had escaped

— 32 —

in the predominantly middle-class schools he had known as student and teacher, went through his mind. He began to worry about how he would handle unruliness. But he was determined not to lose the upbeat feeling he had taken away from the church. He went back to yesterday's reflections about what blacks had in common with immigrants. If people didn't do something to improve the status of blacks, and of Hispanics, for that matter, the crime statistics would not really improve either. The most Becker figured he could do was to help educate a few. In the meantime, he hoped nobody would pull a knife on him. He felt his gut. Maybe it would be a good exercise for him to type out his thoughts, the uplifting, constructive ones. He could even slip a copy under Mrs. Klein's door. It would do her good too. She would have something else to chew on besides her fears.

In the afternoon, Becker dropped off an old summer suit and two pairs of slacks, liberally spotted with ice cream and other stains, at the cleaner's, a shop he had not patronized much in recent years. "No later than Monday morning," he specified with an important air. Then he took in the warm sunshine in the park, not with the languor ingrained by five years of drift but keyed up by newfound purpose. He kept looking at his watch, as though determined not to be late for an important appointment. Take it easy, he said silently; this is only Friday. He opened the *Times* and delightedly discovered a grammatical error: "data is," instead of "data are"; the *Times* should know better. His students would find him prepared.

He fidgeted on the bench until he thought of something to do. He remembered the textbook Greenway had displayed and decided he ought to have it now. Proceeding with the pace of a man with a goal in life, he made the distance between park and church in record time for him, only to find the door to Greenway's office closed. He lolled in the hallway until an assistant pastor came by and looked at him with the same curiosity Greenway had shown. Becker impatiently explained his mission. "He's in with some people," the assistant pastor said. "But he should be free soon."

Becker tarried outside the door, while in the street the evening diners began to line up. At six o'clock, Greenway's door opened, and he came bounding out, two blacks closely behind. One was a young woman; the other was Sam.

Becker and the black did double takes as Greenway began introducing them. "Glad you're here, Mr. Becker. These just happen to be two of your students." Looking at a sheet of paper, he designated Sam first. "Carlton White, and this is Carolyn Rogers." Becker nodded stiffly and stared at Carlton White, or Sam, or whatever his name was. He was as determinedly elegant as yesterday, sharply pressed, pearl-gray flannel trousers setting off an orange-and-white sport shirt that hugged his trim frame. The girl's rounded figure was poured into black pants and a red blouse, ruffles half obscuring a long necklace of red-and-white beads, thick lips accented in scarlet. He returned their smiles with a severe look, inhibiting Sam's usual ebullience.

Greenway looked inquiringly at Becker. The old man turned away from the black couple and explained about the book. "Sure, should have thought of it myself," Greenway said, disappearing into his office and emerging a moment later with the volume in hand.

Becker thanked him and, with a curt nod at his future pupils, walked quickly out into the street. Since yesterday, he had met Sam three times and had seen him once through binoculars. By coincidence or otherwise, the black had suddenly become a presence, not without charm, he had to admit, but somehow more threatening than benign, almost a nemesis. He wondered whether Sam was actually following him, but he could see no reason. A thought made him smile in spite of himself. And if Sam thought he was the one being followed?

"Hey, man, what's the rush?" came a voice behind him. Sam caught up. "You look like you ain't glad to see me."

Becker looked at the black with confused feelings, trying to remember that he was dealing, after all, with a cheap little drug dealer. "I was just surprised to see you," he said. "You really want to learn English?"

"Yeah, what's the matter with that? I dropped out of high school two years ago. I need some help for . . . what do they call it? An equilavency . . . I mean an equivalency exam I'm gonna take for my diploma."

Becker stopped walking and tried to look stern. "You don't need a diploma to push dope," he said vehemently.

Sam dropped his grin. "How you know about that? You spyin' on me, man?" Becker did not answer but resumed walking.

"Wait a minute," Sam called. "I'm not gonna do that all my life. I'm gonna be a businessman soon, legit-like. I wanna learn to talk and write good."

"Well."

"Huh?"

"The word is 'well.' Talk and write well."

The grin came back. "Ya see? I'm learnin' already."

A bit mollified, Becker spoke more softly. "What is your name, anyway?"

"It's Carlton to my mother, wherever she is. My friends call me Sam. How about a beer?"

Becker looked about him nervously as if the narcotics squad were about to descend on them, but what passersby there were barely took notice of them. "No thanks," he said. "I have to get home. I'll see you Monday."

"Yeah, that's right. See ya Monday. I'm gonna be one of your best students." With another grin and a wave, Sam turned back toward the church and the waiting girl. Gazing at the couple, Becker felt vague distress, as though the girl was an intruder. "A young guy has a girlfriend, most natural thing in the world," he thought. "What does it matter to you?" The encounter in Tangier flitted through his thoughts once more. It was strange how Sam kept reminding him of the equally young and graceful Beshir, who smiled invitingly only at other men. More confused than ever, he walked home, stopping for an ice-cream cone to soothe the malaise within him.

CHAPTER

Four

The weekend suddenly felt like a weekend again, an interlude between working. For five years, all of Becker's weeks had been filled with Saturdays and Sundays. They had palled after the first month of seeming liberation. Now he felt an anticipatory glow as a working Monday loomed. He thought of all the people with jobs they did not like, the majority, he figured, who would morosely awake to the start of another work week, a blue Monday. Well, his Monday would be rose! Once more he had decisions to make. For example, he decided his first class would be devoted to a composition. He would learn what his students knew of sentence structure and get a notion of their ability to spell and express themselves in standard English. He was not expecting much, what with the horror stories he read of students graduating from high school practically illiterate. Things were going to have to be pretty basic, he thought.

My Day would be the subject. At least they would not have to wrestle with abstract ideas. What they had done the day before would be simple and straightforward. Then he thought of Sam. What Sam would have to say of his day, Becker was afraid to hear, if indeed Sam could be straightforward about anything. The future might be safer. My Ambitions—that was it. If they didn't have hopes at their age, when would they have them? Certainly not at seventy, he thought with a sigh. Even Sam had talked to him of moving up to "legit" life, if he could be believed.

He checked his shelves and found the old dictionary that used to serve mainly for his wife's crossword puzzles. He was not such a good speller himself, and he made a mental note to take it with him. Then he sat down to peruse the textbook, *Basics of Good English*. The title seemed apt; it was probably all the students could absorb. He opened the book at random, and his eye fell upon subjunctives. He saw no great advance for society by talking to a group of semiliterates about subjunctives. They would have to come at the end, after simple declarative sentences had been mastered, if the students ever got that far. He went to Chapter One. "A simple sentence is a group of words having one subject and one verb," he read. "To make sense, it must say something about a person or thing." Nothing could be simpler. There were examples and exercises, but his eyes began to glaze, and he opened them wide several times to keep them from closing into sleep. Boredom was not a good sign when he had barely gotten into the subject. He read a little more but could not concentrate.

He went to his binoculars and began a survey of the park. At first, it looked no different from all the other days. There were joggers, walkers, readers, fussing mothers, and children constantly in motion. Becker's binoculars suddenly stopped at a short, stocky man under a tree who kept looking about. He was in a well-shaped business suit. It was his broad-brimmed hat that intrigued Becker. It was the third time he had seen it. His mind went back to the exchange under the tree two days previously between Sam and a shorter man, whose face was also obscured by a broad brim. Then to yesterday and what he thought he had seen as the car flashed by him. Becker kept the glasses trained on him. Every few moments he would look at his watch, then about him at the passersby. Whomever he was waiting for was taking his time. At the end of fifteen minutes, the time was evidently up. With a last glance at his wrist, the man began walking toward the exit, still searching the scene. Was it Sam who had stood somebody up? Becker decided he would never know because he would never dare ask.

He put the binoculars down, sat back, and began to muse about the first two encounters and now one that, presumably, had not come off. He tried to imagine the kind of relationship Sam and the unknown man might have. From a television documentary he remembered, the chain of drug distribution could get very elaborate and compartmentalized. If Sam was a dope pusher, then the other could be his next link in the chain, the local wholesaler, if that's what they were called. Becker wondered what a little retailer like Sam might earn. It was certainly enough to keep him in gold-flecked tassels. How much of his earnings did he turn back? Enough to keep the wholesaler in more than that. Becker looked down into Riverside Drive and watched the man get into a sleek, red sports car. Damn it, it was the same car that had nearly killed him! On purpose? That also, he did not want to know. It pulled away with the same throaty roar, as if sharing its driver's indignation at all the wasted time.

Becker felt excited and nervous. The documentary had come to life through his binoculars, but he felt uneasy about his increasing involvement with one character, particularly after his brush with the other. He decided the less he knew about Sam's private life, the better off he would be. Seventy was no age to become his brother's keeper, as if there could be brotherhood anyway with a black one-fourth his age. Nor could he be like some eighteenth-century tutor helping a youth prepare for life. He would not emulate the French family that tried to keep such close tabs on him in his Paris days. Better to stick to Sam's grammar and let him, and maybe his girlfriend, worry about his morals.

Which led him to practical matters. He rummaged through drawers and came up with three pencils and four ballpoint pens, only two of which still had ink. He would have to make an investment in writing materials if he was going to spring a composition on his students. If all the Reverend Greenway could produce was one old textbook, he was certain to plead a lack of funds for anything more. "Maybe Sam ought to treat the whole class," he said aloud. Devoting ill-gotten gains to education, that would be justice for you, but it sounded like another television script. He resigned himself to putting out a little money of his own, as little as possible.

The 72-degree sunshine continued Sunday. Tired of being cooped up in the apartment, Becker walked to Broadway. The benches were starting to fill. He sat down with a perfunctory greeting to his neighbors and bathed himself in warmth. After three months of little rain, the city officials had begun to warn of a water shortage, but for people like him the sun was a balm. Who needs Florida? He thought of his sister, who at this very moment was probably doing the same thing he was, but amid palm trees and the distant roar of the sea. The place had its attractions, and he began to imagine what it would be like for him. He would not at all mind the scenery, but he also saw himself surrounded most of the day by old, unoccupied gossips. The thought depressed him. On Broadway, you never knew whom you would see or meet, as Mrs. Klein would say. Was not Sam living proof? His head began to nod.

Tangier, too, had palm trees and the sea, but he did not remember it as an old-age colony. *Au contraire*, the café terrace had been thronged with a young-looking crowd. The few women were Europeans; Moslem women stayed home, or if they did go out, it was to do the marketing. Several men stared at him, and one or two smiled. Being an object of interest made him feel ill at ease. He turned his head away and was thinking of leaving when the Canadian and his boyfriend entered his life. In Fez, he wandered through the souks and found himself staring every few minutes into the smiling faces of young Arab boys with the looks and grace of Beshir. He stood it for two days and then hurried to Casablanca and caught a ship to New York.

A car backfired, and Becker came fully awake. Across the way, a heavyset man in a dark suit was going down the line of bench sitters, showing each something. Each in turn looked at it and shook his head. A few moments later, the man crossed to where Becker and three other elderly men were sitting. Close up, he looked like a former football player who had not kept in shape.

"Excuse me," the man said, showing a police badge with one hand and a small photograph with the other. It showed a young man with dark hair and an aquiline nose on a broad face. The neck was thick. "Have you ever seen this man around here?" the detective asked. Becker and the others studied it and shook their heads too.

"What do you want him for?" one of Becker's neighbors asked. The detective smiled but was not disposed to give anything away.

"We just have some questions for him." He put the picture in his pocket and after turning to leave, paused to add a word. "If you do spot him," he said, "I'd appreciate it if you'd call precinct headquarters. Ask for Sergeant Mulvaney." He handed out cards: "Robert P. Mulvaney, Detective Squad, 24th Precinct, 151 W. 100th Street, 678–1811." The name was written in as if its owner were merely in transit.

Becker and the others silently watched Mulvaney cross Broadway. When the detective disappeared into the crowd, a shabby man with a couple of days' gray stubble on his creased face spoke up. "Who do you think the guy in the picture is?"

"Looks like a Mafia type to me," his most immediate neighbor answered, with the assurance of one with insider's knowledge. He looked at Becker as if for confirmation. But Becker stared straight ahead, lost in his own thoughts. He could have said something to Mulvaney but had stopped himself. He had never gotten a good look at the face below the broad-brimmed hat, but the one in the photo fitted the short, stocky body. That would not have given the detective much to go on, he reasoned. But still, he felt a twinge of guilt. Talking would have involved Becker in other people's business. He thought of the incident with the car. Involvement could be dangerous. He also remembered how indignant he had felt at a story in the *Times* years ago of a woman in Queens who was murdered in front of a railroad station in the small hours of the morning while people in surrounding buildings listened to her screams and did nothing, not even call the police. Nothing so dramatic now, but his passiveness still bothered him. He looked at the others on the bench. The Mafia expert was back to reading a newspaper while the others gazed at the passing traffic. Why did he have qualms when they apparently did not? He got up and began to pace parallel to the bench, to the annoyance of his neighbors. Because, he said silently, Jews were supposed to be good and do good whether they went to a synagogue or not. It was curious how he could torture himself with Jewish ethics and be so detached from religion.

Becker took the quickest way to soothe his distress. He went to an ice-cream store a block away and treated himself to a cup of chocolate ice cream with sprinkles. He reseated himself on the bench, the others looking at him and his cup of ice cream as if it confirmed his strangeness. He glanced at them. I did do something really strange once, he said silently, his lips moving slightly, but I won't tell any of you because it was a little embarrassing and you wouldn't understand. Did he understand all of it himself? Tangier was not a tale easily told about oneself, even in this indulgent age. Besides, having fled almost in panic the one moment he could really call an adventure, he could hardly cast himself as its hero.

That was really the story of his life, he reflected between licks of ice cream. Life had mostly just happened without much propulsion on his part. Try as he might, he could not remember ever taking a strong stand on anything, aside from standing up to his father a couple of times. He was merely argumentative. He thought he would have made a good lawyer if he had taken the trouble.

He began to doze again until the man next to him gave him a poke. Chocolate was dripping over Becker's pants. He finished the ice cream, now almost liquid, and walked home. He thought about the detective and what he had not done to help him, then looked at his pants and sourly estimated the cleaning bill.

Sleep came fitfully that night. The vague sense of menace that passed through him when he learned Sam was joining his class, thus entering more deeply into his life, was now taking on immediacy and shape. He felt he was brushing up against an underworld web, if that was what the man in the picture represented, and the contact, however slight, was upsetting. It was all so fortuitous and innocent. Everything had come about through chance meetings, chance observations, chance initiatives, like his decision to become a teacher again. The worst thing was his inability to back away. How could he go to Greenway, for example, and explain that it was all a mistake, that he should look for someone else? He felt trapped, with no way out. It was like trying to escape the sun in the middle of an empty parking lot. He kept shaking his head until he fell asleep again. When he awoke, it was almost nine o'clock of a rainy Monday morning.

The city's warnings had been heeded just in time to complicate Becker's shopping, such as picking up the dry cleaning and getting a supply of paper at the stationer's. Fate was certainly not making life easier for him, he sighed. He put water up for coffee and popped an onion roll into the toaster oven, as he had done at the start of so many idle mornings. But this will be a different day, he told himself; it will turn out all right. He did not want to live with the kind of forebodings that visited him during the night, just when he was feeling good about himself for the first time in years.

The phone rang as he was washing the breakfast dishes. The brisk, urgent-sounding voice of Greenway barely gave him a chance to get his "hello" out.

"Mr. Becker? I just wanted to make sure everything was set for tonight." Becker said yes and Greenway continued, "We have someone else, a graduate student from Columbia, to share the burden, Mr. Becker. So you'll only have six to manage. I think you'll find that easier, right?"

Becker said yes, he would find it easier, and promised to be at the church a little before five. With that, Greenway was gone, reassured that Becker's memory was still functioning. Becker thought about the six he might get. With luck, Sam would not be among them. Did he really mean that, or would he, in fact, miss him? He had no ready answer, or rather, he had answers that made him uneasy. Attraction and repulsion seemed to be working with equal force. The repulsion he could explain easily enough by Sam's chosen vocation. The attraction he did not want to think about too much. Why, Becker asked himself, was he reminded of Beshir when he thought of Sam?

By two o'clock, the rain had stopped, and Becker recovered his clothes at the cleaner's. At the stationery store, he chose a few cheap ballpoint pens and a large pad of yellow lined paper, the kind that presidents, and half-literates, scribbled on. The lines would help to keep the compositions readable and—who knows?—perhaps even introduce some order into his students' thoughts. As to his own, they were still in a jumble about Sam.

At five o'clock, there he was all right, seated on a metal folding chair, his girlfriend next to him, and four other young men were strung out around an oval oak table in a little room off the main basement hall. An old, badly scratched mahogany breakfront filled with hymnals stood in the corner. Becker nodded to the students as he closed the door against the noise of crockery in the nearby kitchen.

"Hiya, Mr. Becker." Sam was being ebullient as ever. Becker nodded again. He had devised a scenario in which he would introduce himself and ask for names in an impersonal, businesslike way. Sam's familiarity was throwing him off stride. The others looked at him and the black curiously.

"I, uh, I am Mr. Becker," he said, determined to proceed as planned. "I am here to try to help you with whatever problems you have in English. I'd like to know your names." He looked up inquiringly. A swarthy boy said he was Julio Rivera. Becker noted it. Another was Cesar Lopez. A black at the end of the table said, "Thomas Baskins." A fair-skinned youth with blond hair identified himself as Robert O'Shea. Becker looked at him. A race of poets and storytellers had evidently produced a defective specimen. Carlton White and Carolyn Rogers answered with knowing smiles.

"Thank you," Becker said, putting aside the list. How many were carrying knives, he wondered. "Now I'd like to find out just where you stand in English, so I thought it would be a good idea to spend the first session writing a little composition. I'm going to hand out sheets of paper and some pens and pencils, and I'd like you to write about a page and a half, or longer if you want, on what you hope to do later in life. You can call it 'My Ambitions.' "

Becker looked around in the cold silence that followed his good idea. The prospect of having to apply thought to paper, to put in some effort, had produced six glum faces followed by some restless shuffling of feet. He had seen those expressions before, when, for example, he had sprung a test on his unsuspecting students of French. "I'm sure you all have some ideas," Becker said encouragingly. "Take your time; we have a whole hour."

He distributed his supplies, and for the rest of the session the silence was broken only by more shuffling of feet, twistings and turnings in chairs, and the tapping of pens and pencils. Had any of them written anything more than a phone number lately? It was visibly tough work. Only Sam seemed to be getting any enjoyment out of the exercise. Becker watched him, fascinated. Long pauses would be suddenly broken by furious bouts of writing accompanied by an occasional chuckle as an evidently happy idea occurred to him. Becker began to feel better about having Sam in his class; at least he was showing some enthusiasm. His girlfriend seemed less inspired, staring at the paper more often than she wrote on it.

At six o'clock, Becker called a halt and collected the papers. Nobody protested, although he had interrupted one or two in a last flurry of creation. He ended the session reluctantly, tempted to let them go on, so pleasant did he find the classroom atmosphere again. He bade them good-bye with a promise to have the papers back Friday. When the last one was gone, Becker glanced at the pages and winced. Deciphering some of the writing would take some doing. By the same token, at least for the next day or so, he would get a break from the deadly routines of his life. That was something.

CHAPTER

Five

Im gonna be a bizness man. on my own you dont get nowere in this world depending on uthers speshuly wen your black. So Im gonna wurk for myself, me and my girl frend. My girl frend she bin to byutishons school and noes how to fix hair good. the way we got it figgered out, were gonna opun up a byuty salon wich i will manage and shell be the byutishon. I gotta little mony saved up from doin a little wurk for uthers. then wen we make sum more mony from the salon well opun up anuther won and pritty soon well have a chane of salons all over wich ill be the manager. Shell be kinduv a manager too only ill handel the mony and shell tell the girls how to fix hair good makin the rounds every day me collecting the mony and her givin orders on how to fix hair. thats the way to makout you dont depend on nobody but yorself and you dont have to take crap from sumbody who maybe is out to getya becuz you havnt plaid by his rules. thats the way the world is. you got respect wen youv made it on yore own and youve erned it yorself. educashon is usful like wen your riting a letter orderin suplys ya shud now how to spell and rite sentences well.

Becker read over Sam's declaration of independence several times. He had finished supper quickly, treating himself to a Japanese concoction of meat and vegetables, one of the new deluxe frozen dinners—gourmet style, it said on the box. He had picked it up at more than usual expense at the supermarket as a way of observing his first contribution to society in years.

Now he sat beside the window, reading by fading daylight the painful literary efforts of his students. He had been in a hurry to get to them, particularly Sam's. When he finished it, he was thrilled. Amid the dismal English, he saw an opportunity to help someone who wanted to climb out of the animal pit he was in. He smiled at the ending. In some obscure corner of his brain, the author had tucked away the impromptu street lesson on the use of "well" and had brought it out at the last second, in a tribute to education, no less. Thank you, Sam.

The language of the others was about on a par with Sam's, without his thoughtful considerations on the virtues of determination and self-reliance in a dog-eat-dog world. All expressed hopes for modest business and civil service careers in stores, garages, offices, and the police force, except for the Irishman, who had visions of making it big as a pool shark and used words like "precizion" and "acurasy" to describe his talents with a cue.

Sam's reference to someone who may be out to get him did not make Becker smile, but launched another train of thought. He sped back to yesterday's scenes, first that of the short, stocky figure waiting in the park until his patience gave out, then the detective's visit to the bench with a picture of someone who fitted the park denizen's description. Was he the one who was giving Sam "crap"? Would Becker have helped the black by telling the detective what he knew or thought he knew? Why should he help Sam anyway? Becker had no sure answers to these questions, only a resurgence of his uneasiness over possible dangers to come. He wondered if he was growing fond of the young man despite his present occupation and the memories it helped dredge up of the one encounter Becker had had with drugs. There was something likable in the composition, along with a toughness Becker could only envy. He would have to guard against intimate involvement with Sam and whatever predicament he might be in. Old people had all they could do to take care of themselves; where would he get off playing cops and robbers with people less than a third his age and three times as strong? Teacher and student, that was his speed. Perhaps even that was too much, but it was too late to change it.

Becker put the papers away for another day and turned

on the television set. A scene of mountains and thick forests with large clearings here and there appeared. A small single-propeller plane was landing on a dirt strip. The announcer was describing how strips like it all over Bolivia served to bring out the tons of coca leaf that, processed into cocaine, would eventually inundate the United States and bring its producers and distributors uncountable billions. With an infinitesimal part of those billions, a string of beauty parlors was soon to be launched. What a great little item for the script, Becker thought. He nodded off, his dozing occasionally interrupted by the sound of gunshots as law enforcement officers caught up from time to time with a small link in the dense chain of distribution. He missed the interview with the head of Bolivia's armed forces, a stout man with heavy features and a pencil mustache, who sternly deplored the drug traffic and swore to stamp it out, once and for all, at the source. The camera had then swept to the general's mansion on the outskirts of La Paz, and Becker came awake long enough to hear the commentator estimate the cost of the house, with its marble and gold fixtures, as well over $1 million. Becker wondered where Sam lived and in what conditions. He certainly dressed well, or at least expensively, but perhaps that was where his money went, aside from the savings he said he had for his future business venture.

The documentary over, he treated himself to chocolate fudge ice cream, picked up with the Japanese delicacy. He had heard that people who took drugs had no weight problem because they usually had little appetite for food. Well, he was not going to repeat his drug experience just to keep his waist from expanding. Shaking his head, he turned off the television set in the midst of another hospital emergency room that seemed to be getting a constant flow of drug addicts suffering from overdoses or knife wounds, and went to bed.

He restudied the compositions the next morning over breakfast. They presented few problems he had not anticipated. Some of the scrawls were childlike. Nobody had any clear idea of sentence structure, spelling was approximate, grammar almost nil, the organization of ideas chaotic. He marveled that those who had not yet dropped out of school had been able to get so far without someone blowing the whistle. Nobody seemed to care anymore. Well, he would care starting Friday, if anybody showed up to care about. He half expected some to be turned off by the composition they had been made to do. Over the next few days, he tried not to think about the possibility he might have torpedoed another experiment in education.

Five of the six were in their places, Becker gratefully noted, when he arrived at the church a bit late because he had stopped for some emergency shopping. Clinging to the hope he would have some students left, he had asked for and gotten a small blackboard, a donation the Reverend Greenway had in turn persuaded a parishioner to make in that urgent way he had cultivated so effectively. Announcing the good news on the telephone barely an hour before the class, the minister made it clear that the chalk would have to be on Becker.

Sam's girlfriend was absent, and Sam himself was looking unusually subdued. "Her sister's sick," he explained. "She gotta stay with her." Becker said he was sorry and proceeded with a lesson on sentences he felt more appropriate to a class of second or third graders. But none of the teenagers gave any sign their intelligence was being insulted. Becker hoped he was getting through to them and told himself he would probably have to spring a test sometime to find out. A shifting in their seats, an occasional glance at a watch, one or two yawns, indicated they would rather be somewhere else. But for the sake of what?—their parents? their futures? their self-esteem?—they were making an effort. For the moment, nothing was more important than subjects and predicates. Becker avoided lecturing all the time. He introduced movement and participation by having each student go to the blackboard to write an exercise. At six he called a halt. Nobody lingered except Sam.

He hung back with a preoccupied expression as the

others filed out. Becker looked at him while he gathered his materials.

"Mr. Becker, ya gotta minute?" The old man nodded.

Sam hesitated. "It's this way." Another pause. "Carolyn ain't got no sister, sick or healthy. She and me, we had an argument. She say she ain't goin' with me no more, not for a while anyway."

"Oh?" Becker wondered what to say that would not lead him more deeply into the unsavory parts of Sam's life.

"Yeah," Sam continued, ignoring Becker's hesitations. "She not comin' here 'cause she don't wanna be with me."

"I see." Again Becker could think of nothing that did not sound stupid or overly interested. Why was Sam telling him this? he asked himself silently. He could have stayed with the story of the sick sister.

Sam seemed determined to press on, although it was visibly costing him. His face was sullen, and his eyes looked everywhere but at Becker. "Yeah, she don't wanna be with me," he repeated. "She say she come back when I get out of the business."

"So?"

"I say I get out in a few weeks, but I got a coupla things to finish first, but she don't buy that. She scared."

Becker blinked. He did not want to ask questions, but one seemed inevitable.

"Why is she scared?"

"That's the way she is, no special reason." For the first time, Sam smiled and tried to look reassuring. "Mr. Becker, ya do me a favor, I be grateful."

"What's that?"

"You keep this for me for a few days, please?" He pulled out of his pocket a thick manila envelope sealed and folded with a heavy rubber band. He extended it to Becker, who looked at it as if it might explode and made no move to take it.

"What's in it?" Becker asked in a slightly quavering voice.

"Just some private things I need to keep safe for a few days. I'd be much obliged."

Sam's vagueness, his effort to be polite, did not make Becker feel better. "You have nowhere else to put this? Why me?"

"I trust you, Mr. Becker. You don' wanna help?" This last in a plaintive, almost hurt tone.

Becker hated being put on the spot. Sam was making him look as if he were turning his back on a friend. Damn it, Sam, he said to himself again, we are not friends. He tried to speak calmly.

"Sam, you know I don't mind helping you if I can. But I really don't want to get mixed up in your private affairs, if you know what I mean?"

"Yeah, I know. It's not like that. It's just that I need a place to store this for a few days."

The old man stared at him and said nothing. After a moment of silence, Sam put the envelope back in his pocket, evidently deciding this was one stone wall he could not surmount. He grinned, a little weakly, Becker thought, and slapped him on the shoulder. "Hey, that's cool, man. Don't you worry, I'll figger somethin' out." Without another word, he was gone, leaving Becker stunned at how quickly he had dropped his pleading. Becker wanted to shout, "Wait, let me think!" but he held back.

Becker picked up his papers again and followed Sam out. In the street, the black was already out of sight. What was that whole scene about? he wondered. The envelope probably contained money, he reasoned, a lot of money, judging by the thickness. Why would Sam entrust him with it? They hardly knew each other. The young man must be desperate to put it in a place not obvious to whoever might be looking for it. The man Mulvaney was after, was he looking in turn for Sam and his money? His mind buzzed with more questions than answers, and a headache accompanied him all the way home.

Waiting for some chicken soup to heat up, Becker began

to rue the decision to go back to a little teaching. What would Greenway say if he told him he was backing out of the class? The minister would ask why, and Becker would be unable to come up with any avowable reason. Because he wanted to be rid of Sam? That was what he could tell himself, not Greenway, who would have more questions he would find difficult to answer. The chicken soup was giving him heartburn after barely two spoonfuls. Who says it can't hurt? He picked up the *Times*, which had lain on the kitchen table unread since morning. In Lebanon, they were still killing each other. On the Lower East Side, the police had driven dozens of dope pushers off the streets, and the crime rate had dropped precipitately. How about the Upper West Side? Becker asked. What would happen to people like Sam? Here we go again. The young black was not yet an intimate part of his life, but, like Tangier, he seemed to be invading his thoughts with depressing regularity.

Becker went into the studio and sat down with the lesson book. Lesson two was on making sense with sentences by avoiding fragmentation of thought, like Sam's wanting to be a businessman. On his own. This wasn't helping either. He turned to the record player and from his meager collection pulled out *My Fair Lady*. The lilting account of one person's transformation into a well-spoken grande dame entertained him only for a while. After a few minutes, he stopped listening and thought of his own modest effort to improve the language capabilities of six New York versions of the London cockney. After six months of intensive drill, would they be able to hold their own in a roomful of Harvard and Princeton accents at, say, a meeting of the Council on Foreign Relations? He was really letting his imagination go wild. Becker wouldn't be able to hold his own either.

He turned the record off after Liza's triumph at the ball and turned on the television. There was skulduggery in Dallas followed by skulduggery in a California winery all by well-heeled, well-educated, and well-spoken people. Sam has more excuses, he said drowsily and went to bed.

Two hours later, a buzzer wrenched him out of deep

sleep. He struggled back into full wakefulness, disoriented by a sound he rarely heard. It was the bell for the downstairs door. Someone was at the downstairs door, he repeated, still logy. He had few visitors at any time, but this was two in the morning, according to the little clock radio beside the daybed. The buzzer sounded again, now repeated in short bursts. Becker rose slowly, switched on a lamp, and stumbled toward the intercom beside his door.

"Who is it?"

The voice was distorted but unmistakable. "It's me, Sam, Mr. Becker. Let me in, please."

"For God's sake, you know what time it is? What do you want? How did you know where I lived?" All this Becker shouted in one breathless, panicky tumble of words.

Sam's pleading sounded more desperate. "Please, Mr. Becker, let me in. I'll explain all that."

Becker placed his finger over the buzzer and hesitated. He could not think clearly, and all the time someone who seemed in trouble was waiting. He pressed the button with the feeling he was opening a dam whose turbulent waters would soon engulf him. He put on a bathrobe and slippers and returned to the door to wait for the sound of the elevator and of approaching footsteps. When he opened it, Sam looked as if he had been through a strenuous workout. He was drenched in sweat and breathing heavily. Becker let him in quickly, looking nervously up and down the hall, half afraid Mrs. Klein or some other neighbor might be peering at the strange scene. Almost the only blacks ever seen in the building were delivery boys and repairmen.

Catching his breath, Sam gazed about him, seemingly full of curiosity at the artifacts of Becker's private life that he was seeing for the first time. Becker impatiently broke off the inspection.

"Now what's this all about?"

Sam approached the window without answering. "Please Mr. Becker, will ya turn the light out." The voice was more pleading than commanding.

The old man's alarm was turning to panic. He started to

say something but gave up and did as he was asked. In the darkened room, Sam carefully turned back an edge of the shade and peered down into the street. He looked up and down for a full minute. Evidently satisfied, he sat down in an easy chair. "Ya can turn the light back on, if ya like."

If he liked! Becker stood over him. "Why are you here?" he demanded.

"A guy's lookin' for me. I been runnin'."

"Why is he looking for you?"

"We had a sorta argument. I owe him money. I met him near the park but I didn't have it all. He got mad, so I took off. I run faster than him. He's a heavy dude and don' run so good." Sam displayed his first grin of the evening at the thought of being the better athlete.

Against his good judgment, Becker yielded to curiosity. "Why do you owe somebody money?" he asked.

Sam looked up surprised, as though not expecting such a direct inquiry into his private affairs. The grin disappeared, and a look of fear returned. Becker thought of the classroom conversation. Sam's girlfriend was not the only one scared. He rose, walked over to the bookcase, and studied the contents a moment.

"You read all those books?" he asked. At Becker's nod, the smile returned. "You one smart man, Mr. Becker." Sam took out a volume and studied the title. "Who's Francoy Villon?" He pronounced it like "villain," and Becker made a face. He was not going to start French lessons when English lessons were hard enough.

"A French poet. Sam, I asked you why you owe money."

The youth put the book back and looked down at the floor. "Mr. Becker," he said suddenly, "can I stay here tonight?"

It was Becker's turn for fright. He sat down on the rumpled daybed. "Absolutely not!" he said more loudly than he would have liked. "Don't you have a home?"

"Yeah," Sam answered glumly. "But it ain't healthy to be there right now. They know where it is."

"Who's 'they'?"

"They's the people who's after me. Please, I'll just curl up in a corner, and ya won't even know I'm here."

"There's just no room here, Sam. You still haven't told me what's going on. Why do you owe money? Who's after you?"

Sam leaned forward and for the first time seemed resigned to telling all.

"For two years now, I buy from this guy, see? I always deal in pot, but lately he's after me to push a little coke." A fleeting grin. "That ain't somethin' ya drink, ya know. Anyway, I say 'No way, I don't have no money for that. I mean, that's heavy stuff.' But he say, 'Ya can make more bread with the white stuff.' That I dig. He say, 'I tell ya what, ya take a few packs, and ya pay me later.' I figger he jivin' me, I mean 'cause he never trusted me like that before. I don't say nothin'. Then he say, 'Don't worry, we know where to find ya.' I say, 'okay,' and he give me twenty packs and say, 'I'll be back on the fourteenth to collect $1,000.' That don't bother me 'cause I figger I can unload the stuff easy like; I got customers who ask me sometime, have I got any coke? That's what happen. I sell out in a coupla days at one hundred bucks a pack and I got me two thousand big ones. Man, that starting to be real money, 'cept only half is mine, ya see what I mean? Then, my girl, she see a store for rent near Morningside Park jus' perfect for a beauty salon. The owner he not askin' too much, but he want a deposit down front and a month's rent when we move in. The place need paintin' and some furnishin's. Some of it I can rent, I already ask about that, an' I got me a friend who makes signs good. So right away it means about four thousand bucks. I got some of it. Like I tol' ya, I saved some, but I need some of the coke money too. So I don't show on the fourteenth the way I supposed to" (Becker nodded on hearing the confirmation of his hypothesis). "I figger with a little more time, I can make up what I owe 'cause I still got some pot to sell, but this mother, he catch up with me tonight, an' he don' wanta know about that. He want his bread right away, and he really get pissed off when I tell him I don' have it. Like man, he was out for blood."

The words flooded over Becker until he felt he was drowning. What was he supposed to do? The kid was way over his head and was drowning too. He had gotten in the way of forces as unstoppable as the waves of the ocean and sooner or later they would obliterate him. Becker was grateful the youth did not break down and cry; he might have been tempted to take him in his arms and comfort him as one does a lover. Becker put his hand over his eyes. The wrong image. He must never think things like that. He could console him as one would a grandson. That's much better, Becker thought. Except that now a pang of longing shot through him for what might have been. The grandson would have had a sheltered existence, and if he had walked into trouble, it would have been almost blindly. How did someone as streetwise as Sam walk into trouble so naively? Well, he is a kid after all, he reasoned.

Stirring in his chair, Sam broke the long silence. "So ya let me stay jus' for tonight, Mr. Becker?"

Again Becker tried to put off an answer. "What was in that envelope you wanted to give me this afternoon?"

"Money." Becker started another question but Sam cut him off. "It was the rent and deposit money. I figger, if I don' have it on me, that mother, he can't beat it out of me." Again an inquiring look. "So can I stay?"

"You'd have to sleep on the floor."

"That's cool. I done that already."

Becker had more questions, but he surrendered to exhaustion. "Okay," he said. "But you have to get out early tomorrow morning."

The black nodded. Becker took some of the daybed cushions and laid them out in the dressing alcove near the bathroom door. He found an extra blanket and handed it to Sam. "Good night," the old man said, turning out the light and climbing back into bed.

In the dark, a forgotten question came back to him. "Sam, how did you know where I lived?"

"I followed ya home after class this afternoon."

Becker let out a low groan, then lay silent. Through the dark came the quiet, regular breathing of one who seemed to have dumped his problems on another and could now sleep in peace. Sam, he thought, why are you after me like this? I really don't owe you anything, nor am I responsible for your troubles. Don't throw the centuries of slavery and oppression at me either. At my age, I owe nothing to no one. On the contrary, it is the world that owes people like me something. Including you, Sam. You probably don't even contribute a cent in taxes to my social security check, not the way you make your money. Becker sighed. All right, he was being testy. But things really were closing in on him. He let his mind go blank until he too was engulfed in sleep.

CHAPTER

With age had come a weak bladder. At four o'clock, Becker awoke with a need to empty it. The little night-light next to his bed illuminated the room softly, revealing part of the slumbering form of Sam stretched out in the dressing alcove and blocking the entrance to the bathroom door. Becker stepped over him carefully and closed the door as noiselessly as he could. He did not use the flush, which was loud, like the rest of the old building's plumbing. He stepped out and gazed at Sam. He had piled his shirt, trousers, and shoes neatly beside him and lay curled in the blanket, as innocent in sleep as a child. Even covered, the outline of the long body again reminded him of Beshir. The resemblance was more than physical. Both had an uninhibited quality that, at vastly different periods of Becker's life, had shocked his conventional sense of right and wrong. His sense of morality had certainly shifted little over the years, and maybe that was the right way. There was such a thing as lasting values. He smiled weakly when he recalled his fumbling attempts to look like a man who adjusted to changing mores. Already at twenty, he had had to be more than tipsy to look calmly at, even appear to be interested in Beshir's portrayal of a sex act not sanctioned by right-thinking people. Any other explanation but the drinking he had done he found almost unbearable. In any case, it was clear he had encouraged Beshir. Later, after they had eaten and drunk some more, the Moroccan had put his arm around him as they sat on the cushions sipping brandy and listening to music. He did not reject the advance, it seemed to him now, but rather reveled in the warm embrace of comradeship and good feeling. Beshir, joined by the Canadian, had tested him further with those insistent, caressing hands.

He again looked uneasily at the outstretched youth. It was as if Sam in his sleep was seducing him, drawing the dark, unavowed and unavowable side of his nature to the surface. "Homosexuality" had always been a word he could not even bring himself to pronounce. He would resort to circumlocutions—"unconventional behavior," "peculiar attitudes," "confirmed bachelor" (which he picked up from the magazines), and the like—in speaking of others. As far as he could remember, Tangier had proved little, one way or the other, about himself, except his deep fear of what normal, conventionally decent people would say. His feeling for Sam bothered him in another way. Sam was leading him toward danger, and he could not think of a way of halting the process. The thought was dizzying when he considered how uneventfully banal most of his life had been up to now. Seventy was hardly an age to start flying blindly toward unknown dangers and ambiguous feelings. But here he was, harboring, however reluctantly, a fugitive from what looked like mob justice, and everyone knew how pitiless that could be. He sighed deeply as he snuggled back into bed, puzzled at how to deal with a situation Sam had created and he had so ineffectually resisted.

Becker was wide awake at seven o'clock but feeling almost exhausted, as though he had slept only a few minutes. He had to get Sam out early before the rest of the building could spot him. The black was sleeping soundly. Nothing bothered him! Becker shook him, and he aroused himself slowly, looking blankly at Becker and his surroundings. Then he grinned as he came fully awake. He sat up and stretched his long arms, and Becker watched the play of muscles in his back.

"Hiya, Mr. Becker. What time is it?"

"Early. I'm going to make a little breakfast; then you've got to get out of here."

A worried look crossed Sam's face. He rose and went to

the window, where he carefully pulled aside the shade and made the same inspection of the street as a few hours earlier. He turned back to Becker and nodded. "Okay, I guess there won't be no trouble."

Becker went into the kitchen, put on water for coffee, and placed two frozen waffles in the toaster oven. Looking at Sam, who leaned against the kitchen door and yawned from interrupted sleep, he added two more waffles.

Despite Becker's hurry to send Sam away unnoticed, questions continued to gnaw at him.

"Sam, what did you do with the envelope when I wouldn't take it?"

"I went back home and left it with an uncle, he got a plumbin' shop on my street."

Becker waved his fork in Sam's face. "Why the hell didn't you do that in the first place instead of trying to involve me?"

Sam interrupted his industrious eating and looked contrite. " 'Cause those mothers, like I said, they knows where I live and they knows who my uncle is. When you wouldn't take it, I had to stash it someplace. So I took a chance."

Becker had more questions he wanted to ask. Where had the confrontation with the mobster taken place? How and why did Sam work his way back to this neighborhood? And further afield, how could Sam, a minor, sign a lease? Or was his girlfriend, who looked a little older than he, the signer? Becker looked at the kitchen clock and held off. Besides, each question he asked drew him ever more deeply into Sam's life.

Sam finished, and Becker went to the door and peered out nervously. None of his neighbors seemed to be stirring, but it would be only a little while before Mrs. Klein or someone else would be carting laundry to the basement or going down for the mail. He motioned Sam out and pointed to the elevator.

"Thanks, Mr. Becker," Sam said in a whisper. He laid a hand on Becker's shoulder and added, "See ya Friday."

Becker thought of something else. "Listen to your friend Carolyn," he whispered back. "Get out of this business fast." Sam patted Becker's shoulder again and nodded.

Shutting his door softly, Becker shook his head. He was getting emotionally involved, if nothing else. For his own peace, it would be better if Sam were to pursue his educational ambitions with someone else. But Becker could no longer bring himself to suggest it, he realized. Sam was putting a certain amount of faith in him. And in the process of—what could he call it?—redemption? rehabilitation? he, Becker, had assumed a role that he could not, in good conscience, shuck off completely. Sam thought his pursuer had not yet spotted him at the church. Becker hoped to God he was right but, to be realistic, it could only be a matter of time before that place was spotted too. He had not read Mafia novels for nothing. Mobsters were implacable. He was using the word "Mafia" loosely. He assumed that to move narcotics from producer to consumer, some elaborate organization was necessary, and what was more elaborate than the Mafia? Somewhere he had read that an older generation of Sicilian dons had eschewed drug trafficking, but more modern ones could not resist the money it brought in.

For a nice Jewish boy, it was all too much. Tired and nervous from one of the most agitated nights of his life, he stretched out on his bed and tried to get a little more sleep.

On West 120th Street, Sam paused at the entrance to his block and peered down the street of decayed brownstones and tenements. Only a few people were stirring. Here and there, garbage spilled out of piles of black plastic bags. The dogs and cats had had a busy night. He looked at the silent rows of parked cars and saw nothing suspicious. He could associate an owner with almost every one, and the few he could not identify were too old and beat-up to belong to anyone but a resident. He moved quickly to a graffiti-ridden four-story house in the middle of the block, bounded up the steps, and let himself in.

A ground-floor door opened just as he began mounting

the stairs to the second floor. An old woman stuck her gray head out and looked at him sternly. "You up early," she said.

"Yeah," he said. "How are ya, Mrs. Parsons?"

"Where was you las' night, Sam? You had a visitor."

"Las' night?"

"More like this mornin'. This man he come in, it must have been three o'clock. He make an awful racket apoundin' and abangin' on the front door. I go to it, but I don' open it. I ask him what he want this time of night, and he say he lookin' for you. I tell him if you don' answer your bell that mean you ain't there, and if he don't stop makin' that racket I call the cops. Well, he look at me through the glass kind of mean-like, and he go away. What kinda friends you got anyway that come wakin' up decent folks in the middle of the night?"

"That wasn' no friend, Mrs. Parsons. I'm sorry you got woke up."

She let out a "humph" and closed her door. Sam went up one flight and unlocked his door. He had to move fast and get out. The tiny room was filled by a small bed, a chest of drawers on casters, a sink, a chair, and a shallow closet. He moved aside the chest, went down on his hands and knees, and pulled up two floorboards. Sam's remaining supply of marijuana lay neatly spread out in little plastic packets. He took off his shirt, then a money belt from around his waist and filled it with the dope. From the closet, he selected a fresh shirt, took out a canvas duffel bag, and carefully stowed two pairs of slacks and a few more shirts in it. From the chest, once it had been moved back into place over the floorboards, he took socks and underwear. A razor, shaving cream, a hairbrush, and bottle of cologne from the shelf over the washbasin were almost too much for the bag, and he had to struggle to get the zipper closed.

Downstairs, he looked cautiously in both directions before descending the steps. He quickly walked two blocks to a coffee shop, where he sat in the back and tried to figure out what to do next. One thing he knew. He had to get back to Becker's apartment somehow because a book by that French poet Villain and one next to it contained some real poetry: $4,000 in hundreds, fifties, and twenties. The money had been on him during his meeting, his confrontation rather, with the man he knew only as Carlo.

Sam had an uncle, but he had no plumbing shop on his street. James Benson was a school janitor who had raised him, with four children of his own, after his mother, Benson's sister, had abandoned him at the age of six to follow a jazz musician, first to Chicago, then to places brother and son had never learned of. Of his father, he had no inkling, not even a mention by his mother. Sam was grateful to his uncle, but soon after dropping out of high school at sixteen, he had left the crowded apartment on 126th Street and taken the little room six blocks south. There he could avoid further lecturing from Uncle James about the advantages of education, entertain his girlfriends, and shelter his supply of grass from prying eyes and hands.

Having sampled the dope himself starting at thirteen, he had begun dealing it out to classmates, then to the neighborhood. It was a small market, as dope markets go, the money available for such pleasures being limited by the chronic depression that seemed to grip Harlem's customers.

There was also strong competition. Six months before Becker leaned on him on the bench, Sam had transferred his operations to the bars, benches, and walkways of the Upper West Side. Winning ways—in a politician it would have been called charisma—plus a steady supply of good quality Acapulco and Colombia Gold quickly overcame the color barrier, especially with young professional couples seeking to ease the strain and fatigue of upward mobility. The distributors he dealt with, particularly Carlo, had reservations about a young black moving into a white, middle-class neighborhood but forgot them when Sam proved as good a pusher as anyone they had. He was better than most, in fact, considering he had managed to avoid arrest so far despite an offhand, even brazen, way of displaying and using his wares. He built up a lot of confidence, despite his casualness about making his payments, so Carlo had been willing to extend credit on the cocaine in the interest of opening up new sources of revenue. Sam's delay in paying enraged Carlo to a large extent because he had to pay people higher up. The burly Italian had unfeeling ways of dealing with welshers. Through the grapevine, Sam had heard he was being sought by the police after a Puerto Rican pusher was found with two broken kneecaps on a street in Washington Heights a few weeks ago.

Sam examined his knees, then his situation, over a second cup of coffee. He had a little trouble keeping straight the stories he had recounted to the various people in his life over the past few days. All he was sure of was that he had told the truth to his girl, and it had done him no good. He was starting to get a hard-on thinking about her. He could have reassured her that he was quitting the business right away, avoided a bad scene with her, and been getting it on with her right now at her place before she went to work in a beauty parlor on Lenox Avenue. Anyway, he thought, he had to get in touch with her quickly or the deal for the empty store would fall through, and they would have to start all over again. He also had to stow his duffel bag someplace. There were a lot of reasons to make up with her. While she was busy fixing the shop up, any little business he conducted on the side, she wouldn't have to know about. He would not be really jiving her. He did want to get out. It wasn't healthy. If the fuzz don't get you, motherfuckers like Carlo will wipe you out and then you're nobody before you can be somebody. He might keep a little grass in the back, but he wouldn't be dealing, just helping out friends once in a while.

The trade had taken unexpected turns. He tried, for example, to sell some grass to Greenway one morning in Riverside Park while the churchman, disguised in a sweat suit, was sitting on a bench recovering from a jog. Sam struck up a conversation; Greenway seemed friendly and open, and the black thought he had a customer, one who looked like all the other youngish, middle-class people he was supplying. But Sam was stopped in his tracks. Greenway took over and was soon delivering his own sales pitch, avoiding outright condemnation of Sam's trade but delving into Sam's formal education, his ambitions, his thoughts about the kind of future he would have if he kept doing what he was doing. Then the tutoring service Greenway was organizing was broached. For once, Sam was letting someone else do most of the talking. He had been caught at a receptive moment, only a few weeks after he and Carolyn had hit upon their business plan. He was conscious of his educational limitations, had even inquired about overcoming them and getting his high school diploma. The offer of tutoring in English appealed to him as one of the best things he could do, especially when white people offered to do it for free. He could not get over the coincidence of finding Becker as his teacher, an old man he assumed was just hanging around waiting to kick off.

Sam decided he really liked Becker, although he wondered about the looks he sometimes got from the old man. Maybe they were the looks a grandfather gave a grandson. Whites had families; he even did business with the parents while the kids waited in strollers. None of this shit about mothers who take a powder after being knocked up by some dude who don't want to know nothing about being a father. When he was ten, alone and without a dime on him, he watched with envy and resentment some white kids being bought ice cream by their parents in Central Park. He was going to live "just as good" as they did, he told himself. Why were all the blacks so poor except for a few who made it as athletes or performers? Whitey kept them down, he had heard. Well, not him. He would use Whitey to make money, even learn from him. He was serious about it; he really did want to show people he was not stupid, especially the honkies with their college degrees to whom he sold dope.

He needed the money he had stashed away at Becker's. The old man sure had been jumpy last night. He had to be handled carefully, and besides, Sam didn't want to mess up

Becker's life, at least what he had left of it. He was sure he would find Becker sometime during the day on a bench on Broadway or else in the park. He would say he was sorry, he couldn't help it, he wouldn't bother him again, and could Mr. Becker please get the money out of the books, put it in an envelope and bring it to him. He felt sure the old man would cooperate if only to get rid of the stuff. Where he would sleep tonight he would worry about later. Staying with Carolyn might be dangerous; Carlo could have staked the place out. But it would sure be nice having her a whole night. Yes, it would, it certainly would. He went into the washroom and masturbated.

On Ninety-second Street, Becker's nap had not lasted long. He straightened up his room, gathering the blanket and cushions from the floor. He wondered where Sam had gone and if he was avoiding trouble. Smoothing out the daybed, he shook his head in wonderment. If someone had told him two weeks ago that he would be concerned almost obsessively with a young, half-literate black dope pusher, he would have thought him crazy. It just goes to show how unpredictable life could get. His life had been so quiet, almost predestined, but then Sam had moved in almost before he realized what was happening.

Becker sat down, lit his first cigarette of the day, and made himself a little shopping list. Such as it was, he still had his own life to lead. The little routines, like house-cleaning, shopping, and reading the paper, gave him special comfort at this moment, when he needed a respite from stress. The list in his pocket, he opened his door. Mrs. Klein was waiting for the elevator, a basket of soiled clothes at her feet. Becker wondered whether she invented laundry to give herself an extra routine. For everybody old and alone, getting through the day took some doing.

"Good morning, Mr. Becker," she said, a little coolly, it seemed to him. The elevator arrived, and they got in. Mrs. Klein was never one to let silence alone, even if she was miffed about something.

"So how's the teaching?" she asked.

Becker realized that for such a close neighbor, he had not seen her since announcing his new class and excusing himself from her little coffee-klatsch.

"I was sorry to miss your party," he answered. Then defensively, "The students really need help."

"Who are they? Negroes and Puerto Ricans?"

"Well, we have an Irish boy," he said, trying not to confirm her prejudices.

The old woman looked smug. "No Jewish boys, I'll bet."

"There's another class. Who knows?"

Becker was reprieved by the elevator door, which opened at the ground floor. "See you soon," he said. He headed out as the elevator closed behind him. "But not too soon," he murmured.

It was another sunny day. The city was back to issuing water warnings, and Becker was in no hurry to buy the few things he needed. He headed for the Broadway benches and chose one not yet filled up. He nodded to an elderly couple at one end and took a seat after removing a small, empty bottle in a brown paper bag and stowing it under the seat with other trash. The benches had a diverse clientele, Becker reflected, from old Jews who did their imbibing, if any, at home, to white and black derelicts trying to acquire a cheap buzz. Looking at the broken slats on this particular bench, Becker included at least one young pot smoker. This was where he had met Sam for the first time. He was not likely to meet Sam here today, not with someone on his tail.

"So what have you got to lose?" The old woman at the end of the bench was addressing her companion with a note of exasperation while pointing to the newspaper spread out between them. "A call won't kill you."

"I don't know. It sounds too cheap to be any good. Has to be a catch somewhere."

Becker looked at them, a mistake he realized the moment he did it. The woman appealed to him.

"All winter we stayed in the house." (A shrug from the old man at the exaggeration.) "Who needs it? He couldn't even get out for his pinochle game. But will he do something about it? Here's some ads for places in . . ." (she consulted the page) "Hollywood, Florida, a nice price for two bedrooms, and he won't even call the number; it's toll free. What are you worried about," she went on, turning to her husband, "you won't find pinochle players? There'll be plenty, believe me."

"So all right already," said the man in surrender. "I'll call when we get home." He stole an embarrassed glance at Becker, who tried to look unconcerned. He had always resisted his sister's badgering, but he had to admit that Florida had its points, particularly lately. He watched the couple rise painfully from the bench, she leaning on him, he leaning on a cane, and go off in the slow shuffle of the old. Well, he was not like them, yet. But in the past few days, New York's excitement had gotten to be more than he had bargained for. The game of hide-and-seek he was caught in was decidedly less recreational than any he ever played as a kid.

He looked about at the crowded, noisy street scene and wished he could hide himself. Maybe he would give his sister a call. A few weeks on the beach and in the Collins Avenue delis wouldn't hurt. A small red sports car flashed by him heading west toward Riverside Park. Becker's eyes followed it until it disappeared down Ninety-first Street. There might be more than one red sports car in New York, but it stood out in this neighborhood, he thought. Was it the same one that had almost run him over? Becker recalled its owner's vain wait in the park. If this was Sam's nemesis, wherever you are, Sam, stay away for your own sake, and for mine. With this Sabbath prayer, Becker rose and went to the supermarket.

The day would not be a total loss. There was cottage cheese and flat noodles on the shelves, also black pepper, an indispensable ingredient of the dish he had wanted to prepare for days. If everything else could turn out so well! Walking home, he reminded himself that his own life had become decidedly nerve-racking in recent days. The image of the red car flashed in his head, and he hurried his pace.

Inside the apartment, he laid his package down on a kitchen counter and went to the drawer for his binoculars. Today's exercise in voyeurism would be less casual. He scanned the street, then the park slowly in every direction. Nothing, no car, no driver. Sam's pursuer—Becker had decided it had to be he—was not in sight. Nor, to Becker's relief, was Sam. He checked again with the same result and returned to the kitchen to fix lunch.

Sam had a delivery to make near the Seventy-ninth Street boat basin. It had been arranged days before, and he was determined to keep his date because, as he kept telling himself, he needed the bread. A few more scores like this one, and he could face Carlo. In the meantime, he had to keep out of Carlo's way. He also had to get to Becker sometime during the afternoon. He had to have the dough that he stashed in the old man's bookcase by tomorrow evening at the latest. Sam had taken a chance and made an appointment with the real estate company for Monday morning. Leaning back in the cab, his long legs touching the front seat, he reflected on how messy life had become and how short it might be if he didn't watch out. He started to take out a joint but put it back after looking first at the gray-haired black driving him, then at a sign hanging from the dashboard. "The Lord is my shepherd but smoking still hurts my lungs," it said.

Becker lit a cigarette after lunch, his sixth of the day. He stubbed it out halfway through and lay down for his nap. But sleep was longer in coming than ever and, propping up his pillow, he opened the so-far-unread newspaper. The police commissioner hailed the success of the drive to get the pushers out of the Lower East Side, although remarkably few of them were getting heavy jail sentences. Citizens groups were worried the activity would merely be transferred elsewhere. Maybe not just citizens groups, Becker thought. If I were you, Sam, I'd worry too. Another reason for choosing a more tranquil profession. His eyes closed and the paper dropped from his hands.

The nap lasted an unprecedented two hours. Becker felt

good about it but had to acknowledge unusual circumstances. When had he last entertained company in the middle of the night? He washed the sleep out of his eyes with cold water but still felt tired. He did not even feel like going out. He would read, a much neglected pastime lately. François Villon beckoned, the volume sticking out slightly from the neat line of other books on the shelf. It seemed to him unusually heavy and thick as he sat down with it in his easy chair and prepared to tackle some of the ballads.

Money tumbled into his lap, slithered past him into nooks of the chair, and rustled onto the floor, some of it even catching neatly in a trouser cuff. He stared at the bills, his mouth agape. He vacantly picked some up, crinkled them, and stared some more. He shook his head as if to arouse himself from a dream. It took almost a full minute before he could think clearly. Sam, you goddamn lying son of a bitch. Your uncle, the plumber? Your adopted grandfather, the jerk, you mean. When had he done this? Undoubtedly when he found the old man sound asleep.

Becker began to sweat as he gazed at the green mass covering him. He did not even want to count it. There were hundreds, fifties, and twenties in abundance, so there had to be a couple of thousand at least. He collected the bills, found a large manila envelope in a drawer, and stowed it all under his mattress. It wasn't safe, but he could think of no place where it would be more out of sight until he got rid of it. Now to look for Sam.

He took his binoculars and surveyed the park. The lawns, walks, and benches were crowded with people taking in the sun, but there was nobody who looked like Sam. He had better go out and look some more. If he did not find him, he assumed that sooner or later Sam would get in touch with him. The youth had not made him his heir.

Becker went to the elevator as Mrs. Klein stood in front of her door, testing the lock. He would have to find a way to unsynchronize their movements. At least, she had a shopping cart this time instead of the laundry basket. She looked at him agitatedly as the elevator arrived.

"I tell you, Mr. Becker, I'm almost afraid to go out," she said as the door closed behind them.

"What's the matter?"

"I had the news on. That park is getting impossible. They found a Negro boy with I can't remember how many stab wounds near the boat basin. I wish there was a way of keeping those people out."

Becker leaned against the side of the elevator, his heart pounding.

"Was he dead?"

"As I remember, they said he was in Roosevelt Hospital, the one on Fifty-eighth Street and Ninth Avenue. I know because my sister died there, may she rest in peace. Critical condition, the young man, I mean. Mr. Becker, are you all right?"

He was clutching the worn railing at the back of the elevator car, his head pointed down to restore blood to it. He managed a short nod.

"Did they give his name?"

Mrs. Klein thought a moment. "I don't think so. Maybe they couldn't identify him. Why? It couldn't be somebody you know, could it?"

Becker didn't answer but was out of the elevator first when the door opened. He plumped himself into a lobby chair and thrust his head between his legs.

"Mr. Becker, is there something I can do for you?"

"Thanks. I just feel a little faint. I'll be all right."

She looked at him dubiously, hesitated, then headed for the door, pushing her shopping cart. Funny the way he was reacting about some black man. Why should he be so shocked? Those people were always getting into fights. She looked carefully about her as she stepped out the door. They were little better than animals. She thought everybody knew that.

CHAPTER

Seven

Becker could remember passing out once, not a glorious moment, but how many had he had of those? He had come upon an automobile accident minutes after it happened, and a woman was being pulled from the driver's seat, her face covered with blood. He hurried on, unable to look further, but the picture stubbornly stayed with him, and a block away, he fainted. When he came to, he was looking up at a dozen people grouped around him, and a man was raising his body so that his head hung down. The man turned out to be a doctor, and the lesson of this experience stuck.

Now, as he attempted to draw blood back to his brain, he kept trying to dismiss another image—blood oozing from stab wounds in Sam's well-groomed body. The youth in the hospital could be anybody, he told himself. He had always had a disposition to fear the worst, but in this case it was the worst that seemed to him the most likely. And if it was Sam, what was he to do about it?

He could go to the hospital, find out for sure if it was Sam, and be more mixed up with him than ever. Or he could stay home as if nothing had happened and at least wait until Monday's class. But he *knew* Sam would not, could not, show up. It would not be such a bad thing. He would be well away from Sam's troubles, and Sam would be out of his life. And then he could go back to the normal pulse rate of the unfrightened, bored man. What was he doing anyway in this jungle Sam evidently inhabited? He had been sickened by the news as if he had actually seen the blood. He was in a cold sweat, and his stomach felt on the verge of giving back whatever was in it. He made it upstairs, wiped his face, neck, and hands, and stretched out on the daybed.

Provoked by Mrs. Klein, he had not long ago laid out the reasons why he should have a responsibility for some-one like Sam. He even tried to get it down on paper with the little Hermes typewriter he fished out of the closet and dusted off. And he would have too if the ribbon was not so dried out he could barely read the letters on the page. But that was an exercise, not even original, in reason and his-tory. He had been talking about blacks in the aggregate, not one black who might now be dying in a hospital. It is not very involving to talk of misfortune in the mass. You cluck your tongue and maybe send a contribution to the NAACP. Getting close to people with faces and names, that was something else. Sam, he thought, there is something be-tween you and me, and it's not just the money you so de-viously stuck me with. What else it might be, Becker was afraid to analyze too closely. The same fear had kept his feelings about Tangier obscured in the darker regions of his being, in the hope perhaps that they would dry up, like the typewriter ribbon, and leave traces too faint for anyone to discern.

The nausea passed, and his hands stopped trembling. He looked at his watch. It was only four-thirty, still plenty of time to get to the hospital and inquire. He rose, drank some water to help settle his stomach, and changed his soaked shirt. He went into the street a little unsteadily but stronger than he had been a half hour before. He caught a cab on West End Avenue going south. Bouncing on the worn seat, he wondered if he would get sick again looking at the wounded Sam. When he was drafted into the army in 1942, he lived in constant fear not so much of the battles to come but of the blood he would see. But basic training was the only time he saw guns fired. Assigned to French transla-tion and interpretation in an intelligence unit, he followed the fighting in Europe at a considerable distance. When he got to Paris, it had been a month into its liberation, and after nostalgic visits to cafés and streets he had known, he was sent back to Normandy to help Texans and Oklahomans deal with the natives. His relief at not having to face combat, he kept to himself, but when the warrior came home, he could tell little about the war. His father was not surprised.

"Hey, buddy, you wanted Roosevelt Hospital, right?" Becker was startled back to the present to find the driver staring at him. He paid him off and climbed wearily out of the cab.

The waiting room in Roosevelt's emergency section was crowded, and Becker looked about him with distaste. It was his first time in a hospital since his wife died. He had been in a different, quieter part where pain and death usually work their ways more gradually and the victims are mostly older. The room he was in handled the sudden catastrophes that belong to all ages. A mother rocked her crying baby, a young man held a handkerchief against a bloody head wound, a middle-aged woman sat moaning, her hand against a swollen cheek. She had a black eye.

At the reception desk, a nurse was busily writing. It took three timid throat clearings before she emitted an inquiring "Yes?" without looking up.

"I'd like to find out about a man named Carlton White," Becker said. "I think he was brought in here a few hours ago."

She finally looked at him, then at a register, and shook her head. "Don't see anybody by that name. You a relative?"

Becker hesitated. "This is a young man, a black they found with stab wounds in Riverside Park. The radio said he was brought here."

The nurse pondered this information, then turned to a colleague across the room.

"Rosie, that kid they brought in from Riverside Park, he ever identified?"

The other nurse shook her head, and the first turned back to Becker.

"How do you know his name?" She looked almost accusingly at him.

"I don't. I just thought it might be him. Is he all right?"

"He's been unconscious, but maybe he's come around. Wait here."

She left her desk and disappeared into a corridor. She was gone a good five minutes, and when she came back there was a policeman with her. She pointed out Becker to him.

A meeting with the police was not what he had in mind. In panic he looked toward the exit door but knew he was not going anywhere. He began to feel shaky again and hurried to the closest seat he could find. The cop came around and planted himself in front of him.

"What did you say this man's name was?"

Becker hung on to the edge of his chair as if this would keep him from sliding deeper into complications. "I was just wondering whether somebody I heard about on the radio was a young man I know."

"Come with me," the officer said briskly. He turned and began walking off, and Becker rose a little weakly and tried to follow. The policeman stopped and waited impatiently for the old man to catch up at the entrance to another room. It was full of beds, some with curtains partly drawn around them. Most of them were occupied with people in various stages of undress. Doctors and nurses were bent over them. In a corner, the policeman drew back a curtain. Becker thought of a chocolate sundae, the image popping into his mind in spite of himself, as he gazed down on the dark-brown head against the white pillow. Again it was a quietly sleeping Sam as he had appeared to him only a few hours before, but this time with tubes running into his nose and one arm.

Becker looked at the policeman and nodded. "This man's name is Carlton White," he said. Anticipating a question, he added, "He's a student of mine."

The officer took out a notebook and began jotting. "You know where he lives?" he asked.

The no was hardly out of Becker's mouth before the next questions were upon him.

"What made you think it was him? He in some kind of trouble or something?"

Becker imagined himself navigating among reefs. One

wrong word, he thought, and he would be crashing into God-knows-what-trouble too.

"I really don't know," he said. "He told me that sometimes when there is a class he spends a little time in Riverside Park before or after. I just took a guess."

There he was, in so deep that he was tossing out wholesale lies. He turned away from the policeman and looked at Sam, who began to stir slightly. A nurse came up, and Becker, grateful for the diversion, addressed her.

"How is he?"

"He's lost a lot of blood," she answered. "A lung was punctured. He just got out of surgery a few minutes ago. They tell me he was lucky; the knife missed his heart and stomach by less than a quarter of an inch." She looked at the policeman. "He won't come to for a while."

"Okay," he said. "Somebody'll be back to try to get a statement." He turned to Becker. "Can I have your name and address, please?"

The first statement of his life to the New York City Police Department had not been in his plans either. He started to ask why, thought better of it, and in a quavery voice gave the information. The policeman did not seem to notice the nervousness and walked off, leaving Becker wondering what to do.

The nurse looked at him curiously. "You know the patient?"

Becker explained again about the school. "When do you think he'll be conscious?"

"Hard to say. Anyway, he'll probably be too weak to talk much."

Becker nodded and walked slowly out. The nurse called after him. "He'll probably be in another ward tomorrow." Becker nodded again.

He hated places like this, he told himself again. But he would be back in the morning. At some moment, he had gone past the time when he could ignore Sam and his problems. What was the expression, "In for a nickel, in for a dollar"? Something like that. He was not thinking very straight. At least he had not compromised himself too much, he thought. Still, he felt uneasy about his entry into police records after all these years.

Outside, he suddenly remembered his other recent encounter with the police. The scene with the detective making the rounds of the benches with a picture flooded back. He had been much less a part of Sam's life then, yet even in such less compromising circumstances, he had avoided telling the plainclothesman the little he knew. The detective's card was in a drawer. Should he now call what's-his-name and tell him what were after all only his suspicions? Heavy-set men were not that uncommon. But what Sam had said fitted what Becker had seen from a distance through binoculars and what the picture showed.

Becker walked down the hospital ramp and headed toward the Columbus Circle subway station, trying to figure his way out of what seemed a tangled web indeed. He was amazed how in a few days his life had become so complicated. It was its simplicity that had always been his principal problem, at least in the last few years. He was becoming nostalgic for what now seemed like a better time when his heart did not beat so fast and he did not feel himself constantly being dogged.

In a coffee shop across the street from the emergency entrance, a short, stocky young man, a broad-brimmed fedora half hiding his face, sat puzzling over what to do about a bungled attempt at murder and what he was going to tell his uncle Anthony. The uncle was constantly warning Carlo about his temper, the complications he was causing the business by his brutal rages over penny-ante welshers. First of all, you're careful about who you give credit to. Then you just don't start chopping people up when they don't come up with the bread right away. You give them a little time, but you let them know that you're on their backs. They'll come around after a while, and if they don't, then you start with the threats, and if that don't work, maybe work them over a little. Patience. That's what it takes to run a network of street punks. You have to expect a little leakage. The important thing is to keep the police off your back. All these things Carlo had been told time after time, but he didn't listen, shouted the uncle the day he discovered the cops were after Carlo for the trouble in Washington Heights. This on top of the arrest eighteen months ago when Carlo got caught in a police raid on an Upper East Side playground that had become a hangout for dealers and buyers. He had been booked, mugged, and fingerprinted, but he had sold all he had minutes before the arrest, and the case was dropped. But he was on file, the uncle pointed out, so he had better watch his step.

Several times, he wanted to get rid of the nephew, but he would never hear the end of it from his sister. Christ knows, she had nagged him enough into helping her kid after he had been thrown out of school for regularly beating up other kids just for fun. What could she expect after all the beating-up she had done on him when he was little and she had a little too much wine? Things had gone sour for her, and she had taken it out on her son, after her husband took a knife in the heart for trying to muscle in on somebody else's numbers territory. So now he was stuck with Carlo. He had to admit, though, that Carlo was a tough little son of a bitch who knew how to push the stuff. He just had to learn to control himself.

Earlier in the day, Carlo had nothing more pressing to do than to wander around Broadway, then Riverside Park, looking for Sam. It was not so much the money—that was chicken-shit stuff—as Sam's weaseling that infuriated him. A headache and a sour stomach had kept him up part of the night, and the softly rustling trees along the walks, the people reading quietly on benches or sunbathing on the grass had not calmed him. When he spied Sam coming up from the boat basin, he felt a moment of triumph, but then the nigger's shit-eating grin and cocky walk had driven him up the wall. The bastard had run away from him only the night before, and now he was smiling? He pulled Sam by the arm into a dark underpass, where his powerful arms kept the black pinned against the rough stones of the archway.

"You fucker, how come you took off like that last night?" Carlo demanded.

Held as tight as he was, Sam decided not to try to break away again for a while. He covered his fright with a smile.

"Hey, man, why ya gettin' your balls in an uproar?" he said, the cajoling voice unable to overcome a tremor. "Have I ever tried to cross ya? I give ya what I can, like I always done. I got $200 for ya now, on account like. You get the rest in a little while."

Sam started to reach into his pocket, but unmollified, Carlo stopped him.

"I just about had it up to here with your cheap shit," the Italian said. "You think I don't know you got more than $200 on you." He removed one arm from Sam and began himself to reach into Sam's pockets. This is the time, Sam thought. With a sudden wrench, he broke free and started to run. Carlo stuck a foot out, caught Sam's right leg, and sent him sprawling. Sam tried to get up, but Carlo pulled him down with one hand. The other reached into a back pocket and drew out a pearl-handled knife, one he had had specially made because it went so nicely with all his clothes. He pushed a button, and five inches of blade snapped out. His face an inch from the pavement and Carlo's thick knee on his back, Sam's eyes bulged when he heard the click. He suddenly wrenched himself away from the knee, turned to face the knife, and started to rise.

Carlo was always a little hazy when he tried to recall the frenzy that seized him when someone tried to resist him. He stuck the knife in, three or four times maybe, he wasn't sure. The black collapsed, moaning at first, then still. Licking spittle from his lips, Carlo leaned down to go through Sam's pockets. But he heard approaching voices and steps. He closed the bloodied knife quickly, stuck it back in his pocket, and took off with what he could grab. He was able to count the wad of bills only when, puffing hard, he finally reached his car on Columbus Avenue: $350—$150 better than if he had been nice to the bastard. Carlo, who knew something about loan-sharking too, stuffed the money away in the inside pocket of his jacket. "That's only interest," he thought. "You still owe me a grand." He peeked at his back pants pocket. It was stained with blood. The son of a bitch owed him for a cleaning bill too.

Now, taking another sip of coffee, a few hours and one suit change later, Carlo tried to figure things out. His car radio alerted him that Sam was still alive, if not exactly well. He was itching to finish the son of a bitch off before he opened his mouth, maybe even get the rest of the dough out of him. But he was afraid even to enter the building; it was probably crawling with cops.

Carlo left the coffee shop and walked east two blocks behind Becker, still wondering what to do, particularly how to handle the scene with his uncle. He was starting to have it up to here with the old son of a bitch, who screamed when he had a little trouble with the pushers, but just let him be a little short in the accounts and the uncle really went ape. So what was he to do? Either way, he couldn't win. If the old fart didn't get off his back, he would stick a knife into him someday, uncle or no uncle. Close to where he had parked the Alfa Romeo, he stopped to buy an Italian ice at a little stand and sat in his car sucking on it. He looked down at himself and frowned. A bulge was starting around his middle. He would have to cut down on the beer and the sweet stuff like the quart of strawberry ice cream he had downed the night before while going through accounts. Then he remembered something that made him smile for the first time that day. He had always kept close tabs on his people, and now it might pay off. After seeing Sam several times with the same girl, even being introduced to her once, as if he gave a shit who the nigger was balling, he had her checked out by some of his black dealers. He didn't like to go into those neighborhoods himself, but he knew where she worked and where she lived. He was slightly more cheerful until dripping some ices on his trousers made him curse again.

Carolyn turned on the television a minute after she got home from work. It was six o'clock, and Sam had not yet shown up or called. She looked at the corner of the room where he had set down his duffel bag in the morning just as she was getting ready to leave for work. It had been hard for her to tell him she couldn't stay, but one of her best-tipping customers had made an early appointment. It would be good tonight, she thought. Then she frowned. He was on the lam, he had told her that much this morning, and whoever was after him might know where she lived too. Sam was here often enough, practically lived here, when he was not at his place stashing away dope or changing clothes.

She had some confused feelings about Sam at the moment. She thought she loved him; Lord knows she loved their times in bed. And if things worked out, he would be her meal ticket, the chance to be somebody. She had made it out of high school because nobody was paying much attention to grades, and when her mother pushed her to get a job, she found there was not much she knew how to do. She worked awhile as a waitress in a bar until she let one of the customers take her home one night and knock her up. God, her momma was mad, what with the abortion and everything! She was pulled out of the bar in a hurry and sent to a beauty school, with help from her father, who didn't see his wife much but had a soft spot for his daughter. She liked the work well enough, even had an aptitude for it, so customers would ask for her. But here was Sam giving her a chance to be boss and make more money than she ever thought she'd see.

When she had met Sam for the first time at school, she was a little dazzled even though he was just a kid, three years younger. He sure knew how to dress and turn on the charm with presents and good times, and in sex he turned out to be no kid. He was smart too. Not the kind of smarts that would keep him in school until graduation but the cleverness that kept him out of trouble and made him imagine in bed one night, when they were winding down from their frenzy, how they might start a business on their own. His imagery had fascinated her: they could work together as well as they made love together, cock fitted to cunt like precision parts, their thrusting so well coordinated, their climaxing so synchronized it was as if they were using a timer. From there he had gone on to a business partnership, she furnishing the expertise of the beautician, he the money and management. Running a beauty parlor shouldn't be that complicated, he insisted, and when they had learned something from the first one and had made it successful, they could start others until there was a chain. Again she was dazzled by him if not entirely convinced of his abilities in this kind of business, indeed of her own capacities to handle it. But the *idea* of running a shop made her fall quickly in with his enthusiasm.

The one thing that bothered her about Sam was the way he was making his money now. She knew about drugs. Everybody in her class, including herself, had taken something or other, but selling it was something else, and if the business he was talking up was the way to make him stop, then it sounded like a real bonus to her. She had no qualms about using the money he had already made to get things started. But he had to quit after that because sooner or later he would be in big trouble, maybe dead, and the dreams he had to make it big, without the hassles he was having now, would have to be buried too. To her surprise, Sam agreed. She had been half afraid he was intending to use the shop as a front for pushing dope. Other things he said also gave her hope. He had the idea of trying to get his diploma, he told her, because you have to know something to make it in business and had arranged for the tutoring at the church. She laughed when Sam explained how he already knew the teacher. Mr. Becker seemed okay, after that first meeting when he had looked at her, she thought, unfriendly like. But he knew things, that was for sure, that could help them both. She hoped Sam hadn't tried to push dope on him. That's the kind of classy person she wanted Sam to be, talking like businessmen are supposed to talk, not cursing every other word but sounding educated. All of that too could be out the window if Sam carried on business as usual.

She was taking a Coke out of the refrigerator when the news announcer started to talk about a young man found unconscious with stab wounds in Riverside Park. She returned to the set and stared blankly at the screen as the youth was described in critical condition after an emergency operation in Roosevelt Hospital. In the same brisk tone, the announcer went on to the inauguration of a new school building, but she was only half listening now. She began to whimper. "What's his name? Tell me his name, you fucker." She banged her hand on the set, then turned it off and ran to the closet for the phone book. Frantically she shuffled pages until she got to the hospital address, then grabbed her purse and rushed out. An off-duty cab driver's first instinct was to ignore her frantic waving, but he decided he liked what he saw. Maybe afterward, he thought, you never know. But when they got to the hospital, she thrust five dollars into his hand and rushed away without giving him a chance to ask what she was doing later on.

Sam was still unconscious, and at the information desk the nurse tried to fend off the almost hysterical woman. Carolyn finally was admitted into the room where Sam lay since the emergency operation. She confirmed his name and added his address to the hospital's knowledge but would say nothing about how he might have gotten in such a mess. The nurse gave up and left her sitting in a chair watching her lover and business partner silently battle for his life. Half an hour later, a detective came by, hoping to catch Sam awake. He settled for Carolyn.

"What's he to you?" he asked.

"We's friends."

The detective allowed himself a smile. "If you're friends, maybe you know what he does for a living?"

She hesitated, then came up with the only thing she could think of. "He go to school and help his uncle; he's a school janitor."

The detective wrote in a little notebook as she continued to answer questions. Uncle's name, uncle's address, uncle's school. The kind of schooling the guy was getting didn't sound like much, but he let it go. Carolyn made a mental note. She would have to remember to call Uncle James when she got home to keep the stories straight.

"You sure he's not pushing a little dope on the side?"

Carolyn said she didn't know anything about that. She tried to keep from fidgeting.

"We found a couple of marijuana cigarettes in his shirt pocket," the detective informed her.

She clenched her fists. "This man's maybe gonna die, and you worried about a little grass?"

"Take it easy. It's only a misdemeanor anyway. Who do you think knifed him?"

Carolyn didn't know anything about that either. "Maybe a mugger," she said.

"Yeah, maybe." He decided he was not getting anywhere and left.

A nurse came in. "He gonna be all right?" Carolyn asked.

"He's stable. We'll know better in the morning. You'd better go now. He's going to be asleep for a while."

Carolyn made her way back uptown by subway, dabbing her eyes and feeling a little guilty. She had thought some terrible things only an hour before and now almost the worst had happened. She looked so mournful that a young black next to her, after a tentative smile, dropped the whole idea of making a little conversation just to see what might turn out. When she got home, she was still so dazed by the sudden turn of events that she noticed nothing around her, not even the red sports car ablaze in the light of the dying sun a few feet down from the house.

While a frozen chicken dinner heated in the oven, Becker took stock and had another jolt. In the excitement over Sam, he had forgotten about Sam's money. He lifted the mattress, removed the envelope and counted the money: $2,150. Not bad for an eighteen-year-old. What should he do with it? Every minute it stayed in the house, he felt in danger. He could wait until morning, hope Sam had regained consciousness and ask him, gently, for he would not have the heart to berate him. But what if Sam never woke up?

He remembered the girlfriend and went to the sheet of class names he had kept. "Carolyn Rogers," he read. He hoped that was her real name. According to Sam's plans, she was to become his partner. Perhaps she could take the money. Anything was better than holding it here. He went to the phone book, then paused to allow a pang of conscience to pass. He was being awfully calculating about his own safety while a kid he was mixed up with, though he hoped for the better, might be dying in the hospital.

Becker, he thought, you are still no hero; that's for sure. Shaking his head, he went back to his research and found three listings for Carolyn Rogers in the book, one on Christopher Street in the Village, one on East 61st Street, and one on West 130th. He decided on the last as the most likely.

A low female voice answered. "Is this Carolyn Rogers? I'm Mr. Becker, David Becker."

"Yeah, Mr. Becker. You know about Sam?"

"I was at the hospital this afternoon. They say he has a good chance of pulling through."

Carolyn sounded surprised. "You went to the hospital?"

"Well, yes. I was concerned. I wasn't sure it was him they were talking about on the radio." He felt uncomfortable trying to explain his interest in Sam. He had not fully explained it to himself.

"Carolyn," he went on, "I've got something here that belongs to him."

"Yeah?" she answered tentatively.

"It's some money, Carolyn, and I don't know what to do with it." Becker's voice had dropped to a whisper as if he were trying to thwart a bugging device.

From the other end came silence. This morning, a century ago, Sam had told her about stashing away the rent money for the store somewhere. Not only had she forgotten about it but was having trouble understanding how the old man had gotten connected with it.

"You still there?"

"Yeah, Mr. Becker. I still here. How come you got it?"

"Sam left it here last night without telling me. Carolyn, maybe you'd better take it."

So he had holed up in Becker's place. She was having trouble handling that one also.

"Mr. Becker, I's scared."

"That makes two of us. Somebody's after Sam for some money he owes, and I think he caught up with him. Sam left a lot of money here, and I don't want any part of it. Could you meet me?"

I wouldn't go out now if the building was on fire, Carolyn thought. "I'm going back to the hospital tomorrow morning," she said into the receiver.

Becker considered this. Much as the money made him nervous, he had no more desire to face the streets at night than he supposed Carolyn had. Besides, he did not want her coming to the apartment at this hour. "Okay, I'll be there myself," he answered. "We'll talk about it some more then. I'm sure Sam will be awake. About ten o'clock?"

The only answer was a click. He put the envelope back under the mattress and walked resignedly to the kitchen. The chicken was ready. It was rubbery, and he threw most of it away. What he ate, he washed down with an Alka Seltzer.

CHAPTER

Eight

Later, Becker was hungry again. He sat down by the window with a dish of peach ice cream. He tried to think of nothing in particular, but the picture of Sam lying in bed full of holes kept coming back. For one of the few times in his life, he was being roused by anger. Sam was no innocent bystander. He seemed childishly casual about his conduct, and $1,000 was still a lot to owe, even with inflation. But to be stabbed repeatedly and left to a bloody death! A person who did that had to be deranged or have the temperament of Genghis Khan. Becker began to tremble, but it was not really surprising. The drug business, it seemed to him, fostered this kind of implacable cruelty. The papers were full of it. One good thing had come out of his encounter with hashish. He had been put off drugs for life and did not have to deal with knifers. At least not up to now.

The ice cream was starting to pall. He stopped eating, went to the drawer of his night table, and found Mulvaney's card. He dialed the number, and a desk sergeant came on.

"I'd like to speak to Mr. Mulvaney, Mr. Mulvaney the detective."

"That's the only Mulvaney we have. He's gone for the day. Can I help?"

Becker was a little ashamed at feeling relief. Outrage had not stripped him of all his hesitations. "Will Mr. Mulvaney be in tomorrow?" he asked.

"No, not until Monday. Call about nine. You wanna leave your name?"

Not really, Becker thought. With a "No, thank you," he hung up. The first time he had met Mulvaney had been a

Sunday. The detective must have been on overtime, really anxious to get his man. He seemed to have relaxed since.

Becker would have a whole day to think about getting in touch with the law again. In the meantime, he felt exhausted. It had been a day of physical and emotional drain, and he was not in shape, if he ever had been. Channel 13 had a nature program on, and in no time at all, he was fast asleep. He awoke in his chair at two o'clock, undressed, and went to bed.

While Becker slept, Sam's eighteen-year-old body was bouncing back nicely. He awoke just before dawn, and an hour later was moved from the emergency room to another ward. At eight o'clock, a detective was at his bedside. Sam was not surprised, and with his mind clearing, he had tried rehearsing a bit.

"You're a lucky guy," the detective said. "Your name Carlton White?"

"That's me. How you know my name?"

"Couple of friends of yours came by yesterday. They told us who you were. Tell me what happened."

"Who was the friends?"

The detective consulted a notebook. "David Becker, who says he's your teacher, and Carolyn Rogers."

Sam managed a grin. Mr. Becker, he thought, he come by to see me, hot dog! He really nice to do that. And Carolyn, she stickin' by me too. That's cool. Now I gotta get rid of The Man.

"You wanna tell me what happened?" the detective asked again.

"I don't like really know. I was walkin' in the park, and the next thing I know, this dude come up and he starts hasslin' me for money."

"Do you know who he is?"

"Never seen him before."

"What did he look like?"

"He white and big and mean."

"You sure you don't know him?"

Sam shook his head. The detective kept pressing.

"You know, we found some marijuana on you. That's an offense."

Sam tried to look ingratiating. "Hell, ya start lockin' up folks that's got a little grass on 'em, pretty soon there won't be nobody on the streets."

"That's all you got to tell me?"

Sam nodded. The detective leaned down and looked at him sternly. "Okay for now," he said, "but we'll be back to talk to you. Maybe you'll remember better."

Visitor number two was Becker, redirected from other sections of the hospital. It was past ten o'clock and he looked around for Carolyn. But Sam was alone and wide awake.

"Hiya, Mr. Becker, what's happenin'?"

"That's what I came to find out. How are you?"

"I'm not ready for steppin' out, but I'm doin' okay, considerin'."

"You gave us quite a scare, Sam. Who did this to you?"

Sam hesitated, then motioned Becker to lean over.

"A cop ask me that a while ago. I didn't say nothin' to him 'cause that could be a lotta hassle, ya dig? But I don' min' tellin' you. It was the same mother that was after me the other night. I deal with him, but I don' know him, ya know what I mean? He calls hisself Carlo. That's all I know about the bastard; he don' talk much."

After raising himself up slightly, Sam sank back exhausted. Becker sat down and looked at him in silence for several minutes before broaching the next subject.

"Sam, you listening?" When the youth nodded, Becker went on.

"I've got something of yours I didn't expect to see. I don't know what to do with it. You know what I'm talking about?"

Sam nodded. "I'se sorry Mr. Becker. I didn' mean to do that to ya. I couldn' think of what else to do." Again he motioned to Becker to approach. "You get that money to Carolyn; she know what to do."

Becker suddenly remembered somebody was missing

from the little reunion. "Have you seen Carolyn this morning?" he asked.

Sam shook his head. "I called her last night," Becker went on. "She was supposed to meet me here at ten o'clock. She's almost half an hour late already."

Sam's eyes widened. "Mr. Becker, I be afraid; maybe she in trouble too. That Carlo, he know about her."

Becker was beginning to feel a little sick again. He sat down and considered his situation. A lunatic was running around loose, responsible for one near-homicide and maybe willing to make another try. And thanks to Sam, he, David Becker, seventy and trying to live out his life with as little strain as possible, was in line for a possible third. How could he get off this merry-go-round?

The black broke into his thoughts. "Mr. Becker, you hang around a little while? Maybe she show up."

But an hour later, there was still no Carolyn. Becker found a pay phone in the hall, looked up the girl's number again, and dialed. He listened to it ringing for a full minute before hanging up. He returned to the ward and told Sam.

"There only one thing to do, Mr. Becker, if you willin'?"

"What's that?" Becker answered a little suspiciously.

"You go to Carolyn's place and see what's up."

"I don't know, Sam. Where does she live?"

Sam gave him the address. It was in the middle of Harlem, a point obvious even to Becker with his imperfect knowledge of New York. There were some places he had never visited and would never think of going to. He looked at the black silently.

Sam seemed to read his mind. "Ain't nobody gonna hassle ya, Mr. Becker. Them's nice folks on that street. And ya can unload what ya got in them books," he added encouragingly.

Becker tried to remain noncommittal. "When I get home, I'll try her phone again. Then I'll see."

Sam nodded. The old man took him by the hand. "You take care of yourself, Sam. I'll be back to see you." With that, he was off, Sam's eyes continuing to follow the round, slightly slumped figure as though Becker had become, however frayed and frail, a tether to life.

A half hour later, Carolyn was still not answering the phone. The thought of going to her house had become no easier. To carry more than $2,000, in addition, made him shudder. That he had to do something he could no longer question, despite the vagueness of his promise to Sam. But there were limits to the risks he could take. Already he was stretching his willingness to take them far beyond what he had ever known before. He would leave the money behind and arrange for its delivery when he saw the girl.

He heated up some tomato soup and followed it with yoghurt. Then he stretched out on the daybed, unwilling to abandon the comfort of his rituals completely. But he was up fifteen minutes later, too nervous to sleep. He decided he would ride a taxi rather than the subway into Harlem. Damn it, if only she would answer her phone! He tried again but gave up after ten rings.

He went to Broadway to find a cab, one eye on the passing traffic, the other on the casual, seemingly worry-free bench sitters in between. He felt almost nostalgic for the days when he had nothing more on his mind than passing a few hours with them.

The first cab to stop was driven by a black. When the driver got the address, he looked at Becker as though he had been asked to proceed to California. Becker pretended not to notice, but the driver's expression made him feel more on edge than ever. The ride uptown was a twenty-minute descent into a decay he had only heard about and spent most of his life ignoring. The Broadway of his neighborhood was seamy enough, but he had only to walk a little to escape it. He could find no relief here as the taxi honked its way through dirty, desolate streets full of boarded-up stores and houses.

Carolyn lived in an old brick tenement complete with graffiti and rusting fire escapes. Becker paid off the driver, who gave him another quizzical look and left. Five steps led up to the front door, and like ascending notes on a scale, they were occupied by three young boys who inspected him silently and, Becker thought, as uncomprehendingly as the cabbie had.

He looked up at the boys almost timidly and addressed the one who seemed the oldest. "Is this where Carolyn Rogers lives?"

"You a cop?"

He smiled weakly at the unexpected question. "Just a friend," he said. But the stony expressions told him this information had not been accepted at face value. He put himself in their place. What would Carolyn be doing with a rumpled, old white fart like him? Becker was searching for a convincing answer when inspiration came. "Sam asked me to go see her," he said.

From the steps came an immediate stirring. "You know Sam?" asked another boy, who looked more curious than hostile.

"Well, yes," Becker answered. "We ... we do some business together."

The boys did not look surprised. Becker thought the lie had gotten him somewhere. None of the three could have been more than thirteen, but all seemed to know Sam's kind of business. The first boy looked at him and allowed himself a smile. "Carolyn, she on the secon' floor, 2E," he said. "I ain't seen her this mornin' so maybe she home."

Becker thanked them and walked up. There was a set of buzzers in the vestibule, but when Becker sought to find the right one, a boy called out, "They don' work no more. You jes' go in; the door's open."

He climbed to the second floor, his leg aching a little, and found 2E at the end of a dark, noisome hallway whose dirty green walls matched the cracked linoleum. He knocked gently. There was no answer. The smell of greasy cooking was making him vaguely nauseated. He knocked again and heard slow steps. The door opened slightly. Carolyn, her hair disheveled and her face half covered by a huge set of sunglasses, cocked an eye at him.

"Mr. Becker, what you doin' here?"

"Sam and I were worried when you didn't show up at the hospital this morning. Are you all right, Carolyn?"

She undid a chain and opened the door. Becker walked into a room obscured by dark shades, but he could see the devastation clearly enough. A mattress, sheet, and pillow lay half on, half off a small bed in the corner; a sofa was tilted on its side with ripped cushions surrounding it; clothes strewed the floor or hung from half-open dresser drawers; broken crockery and boxes of food covered the sink and tiles of a kitchenette, together with a telephone trailing a loose wire. Becker found a still upright chair and sat down, feeling a bit faint again. Carolyn stood in front of him.

"I couldn' go to the hospital like this," she said with a tremble. She had removed her glasses. Her right eye was half shut, and that side of her face was puffy. Her upper lip was split.

Becker looked at her a full half minute before finding his voice. "My God," he said. "What happened?"

"That Carlo, the one who's after Sam, he come here last night. I don' wanna let him in, but he reach through the door and grab my wrist like he gonna break it. So when he inside he don' waste no time. 'Sam, he leave any money here?' he say. I tell him no, but he don' believe me and starts hittin' me. Then he tear up the room lookin' for the bread, but he don' find nothin' 'cause there's nothin' to find. Then he takes off 'cause he makin' a lot of noise, and the people down the hall, they come bangin' on the door wantin' to know if I'm okay, and he points a knife at me and makes me say, 'Yeah,' but I guess maybe he a little scared too, so, as I say, he takes off."

Becker felt he was hallucinating. It was like a recording, female version, of his session with Sam two nights before, only Carolyn had not gotten away. Nor had Sam, finally.

"Are you feeling all right? Maybe you should go to a hospital and get looked at," he said.

"I'm okay," she said. But she touched her eye and grimaced, then looked around the room and began to sob. "God, look at this place!"

Becker took her hand but could think of nothing consoling to say. The only comfort he could offer himself was his foresight in leaving the money home. He went over to the bed and put the mattress back on.

"Don' you bother, Mr. Becker," she said. "I fix things later."

"What should I tell Sam?"

She thought a while before answering. "Tell him I had to stay with my momma; she not feelin' well. I come see him tomorrow. I think the swellin' be down by then."

Becker stood up and surveyed the room once more. "What can I do to help?" he asked.

"Don' you fret none. I'll be okay." She hesitated, then went on. "Mr. Becker, you got somethin' that belongs to Sam?"

The reminder startled him. "It was what Carlo was looking for," he said. "I'm not happy having it."

She nodded. "Sam and me, we had this appointment for tomorrow with the renting agent for the store. I figger the quicker he get the money, the safer we is. You too, Mr. Becker. You be home tomorrow? I come by around ten o'clock; that okay?"

It was okay. It had to be okay. The hell with Mrs. Klein and the other neighbors. They could gossip all they liked. He could not stand the thought of the money being in the house one more day, particularly with that maniac on the loose.

He left her after a last look around the room. It would take her hours to clean up. As for the damage to her features, that would probably take weeks. He walked down the dim staircase and out into the street. The boys were still there. "I guess she was home," one said.

"It would have been better if she wasn't," Becker said.

"What you mean, man?"

"You boys see a white man come here last night, kind of short and heavy, maybe with a big hat?"

They consulted, then shook their heads. "What he do?" one asked.

"He beat Carolyn up. Maybe you ought to get that outside door fixed so you don't have people walking in you don't want."

The boys listened in silence, then stood up. "You tell that to the landlord, man. You see how far you git," the eldest said. "He don't wanna know nothin'; that's what my momma say. Carolyn okay?"

"Yes, but maybe you can help her with the mess she's got. Where's the nearest subway station?"

They told him and filed inside without another word. Becker turned and walked down to Lenox Avenue, so intent on his worries that he forgot to feel uncomfortable at being the only white man on the street. He found the station at 135th Street and, aware again of his surroundings, thankfully discovered that he could get a number 2 or 3 train to his stop at 96th. He had spent enough money on taxis in the last two days.

He found a seat on a platform bench and thought, now what? Carolyn would relieve him of the money but not of his role in what had become—his heart skipped a beat—a murderous affair. What was his role exactly? He felt an obligation to help Sam; as much as he might like, there was nothing he could do now to bow out. All his life he had fled drama, content to live each day as unexcitingly as possible. But he did have a conscientious streak. Had he not always tried to help students when he could? How about the time he had caught those two boys in the washroom? He had done nothing to ruin their lives. So they were gay. Live and let live. Except that someone didn't practice that philosophy and had to be stopped. Of this much he was sure.

The train roared in, and at the half-open door he distractedly blocked a large black woman from getting out. "Hey, ain't you got no manners!" she barked at him. "Sorry," he muttered, stepping aside. The other passengers, almost all black or Hispanic, glanced at him with little sympathy. Hey, he wanted to tell them, you won't believe me, but I've got a black friend I'm trying to protect. But that was just it. They wouldn't believe him. He went back to his problem. How was the maniac to be stopped? Neither by age, temperament, nor training could he see himself as a dragon slayer. He smiled at the thought he could be a knight rescuing two innocent, well, not so innocent, babes. It was a job for the cops. But how was he to explain things to them? If he identified Carlo as Sam's attacker, they would ask him how he knew. Then he would have to explain the connection between the two, and that would finger Sam as a dope pusher. True enough, but why expose Sam to a possible jail sentence when he was trying to make a clean break with his past? Becker nervously asked himself another question. Why expose himself as well? What, the police would ask, is his connection with Sam and Carlo? Becker was simply doing his duty as a citizen, he could answer. And besides, Sam was a student, and teachers have their students' welfare at heart. He could see the detectives looking at him a little strangely. This Sam, he means something else to you? You like young, good-looking blacks? Becker would dismiss the suggestion indignantly. The thought made him turn red, and he looked around the car to see if anyone was reading his thoughts. But after the first unfriendly look, the other passengers were ignoring him. For once, he was grateful for their lack of interest.

An idea struck him. What if he talked to the Reverend Greenway before talking to anyone else? He needed allies, and Greenway was young and energetic and seemed to know his way around, all the things he was not. He would at least be a sympathetic listener and might know what to do. Even with Greenway he would have to leave certain things out, like the money Sam had left him. The more Becker thought about the idea of bringing Greenway into the affair, the better he liked it. He was so pleased that he almost missed his stop and lost a button on his shirt when he had to squeeze through the closing doors.

CHAPTER

Nine

The church was locked tight. Becker had assumed that the Sabbath would be Greenway's biggest day for "the worship of God and the service of man." He had looked up the Unitarian creed in the one-volume encyclopedia he had gotten as a retirement present from his fellow teachers. But the doors of the church refused to yield, and the bell summoned no one. He turned to a plaque beside the door: "Morning service at 11, Evening prayers at 6." It was four o'clock. It would not surprise him if Greenway was out jogging or playing tennis. Or maybe he was having a long lunch with a dry white wine at one of those yuppie places on Columbus Avenue.

The yuppie life was not for Becker. He thought of himself as an increasingly tired old man for whom the world had become too much. He walked slowly down the church steps and headed for home. If he had the energy, he would try to catch the pastor after the evening service. At any rate, he would have time to nap and change his shirt or at least put a button back on the one he was wearing. Aside from threading a needle, which required an interminable number of passes before he made it, he had become quite proficient at sewing. In the past five solitary years, he had to learn several little skills, none of which he cared for much. The best he could say for cooking, cleaning, washing, repairing, and shopping was they met his basic needs and occupied time.

A block from his house it occurred to him that the refrigerator contained nothing he could call dinner. He had been doing even less housekeeping than usual lately. Half a barbecued chicken, already prepared in one of those Broadway shops, perhaps with a little salad he could pick up at the supermarket, would do fine, and there probably would be something left for tomorrow. He reversed direction and walked to Broadway, where he was delayed on the traffic island by a red light. On the bench he so frequently warmed, the one where he had met Sam, sat a thin young man with stringy blond hair, whispy beard, and ragged blue jeans, staring forlornly down at an empty beer can propped between his soiled sneakers. He looked up at Becker.

"Hey, man, you got any change?"

"Sorry, all out," Becker mumbled, looking hopefully at the light.

"Any grass?"

"All out of that too." It seemed the light would never change. He felt a hand on his shoulder. The young man was standing behind him.

"Look, man, I ain't askin' for much. I need a quarter."

The words came out blurred and halting. He stood close to Becker but gave off no smell of liquor. He's stoned, Becker thought, maybe as stoned as I was fifty years ago. Only this was probably not his first time.

"What can you do with a quarter?" Becker asked.

The young man tried a grin, but it came out crooked. "A quarter from you, a quarter from someone else, pretty soon I got enough for Burger King."

"You sure it's to eat something?"

The dull expression tightened into a grimace. "Hey, man!" he suddenly shouted. "What are you, my father? You don't wanna help, fuck off!"

Still at the edge of the curb, Becker felt himself being pitched forward. He landed on all fours in the roadway. A horn blasted and brakes screeched. A taxi skidded, swerved ninety degrees, and halted a few inches from a parked car. Becker looked up at the glaring face of the cabbie.

"Ya can't stand up, buddy, try drinkin' at home. Ya oughta be ashamed, at your age."

Becker was too dazed to be indignant. A few people across the way had stopped to look as the taxi screeched to a stop and now stood gazing at him, but nobody moved to help. He picked himself up and half stumbled to the bench as the driver righted his cab and drove off with a last glare and imprecation. He looked around him, afraid the blond was still there. But he was already on the other side of Broadway, accosting shoppers. Becker felt his arms, hands, and knees, but nothing seemed broken. His trousers were filthy. Now he would have to make a complete change of clothing. But first he would sit for a while until his heart and his breathing slowed down. Several people looked at him as they passed, and he realized he was doing the one thing he prided himself in not doing. He was talking aloud to himself. He was having a lot of unusual days lately. He tried to wipe the grime off his hands with a handkerchief, but all he achieved was a dirty handkerchief. He shook his head at the new addition to his laundry.

An elderly man sat down next to him, and Becker recognized him as one of the regulars, a little friendlier than the others, not so upset that he would no longer talk to him after Becker had shown a lack of interest in the synagogue. They nodded to each other.

"So what's new?" the man asked.

Becker gave him a description of the blond's stoned behavior and his own brush with death, and was rewarded with sympathetic frowns and clucks. When Becker paused, the other immediately took the floor.

"I tell you, I'm not surprised. These young people nowadays with their drugs, it's a wonder they're not all crazy in the head. Why, even my grandson, a nice boy, he works hard in school and gets good marks. My son the doctor found him in his room with some friends, and do you know what they were smoking?" Becker was about to guess, but the other did not wait. "Pot!" he exclaimed as if he had just invented the word. "Pot! Good Jewish boys and they're smoking pot, and in a beautiful home in Scarsdale. My son has a nice practice and gives him every advantage, can you imagine?"

Becker could easily imagine. If the grandson lived in the

neighborhood, he would probably be one of Sam's customers along with all the other nice people regardless of sex, color, or creed, who lived in nice buildings and lived nice lives. Becker too had been a nice boy, and if the hashish had agreed with him a little more, he figured, he too might still be indulging. Becker was too tired to continue the discussion. Besides, the subject had shifted from himself, and he was getting annoyed. He remembered he still had something to do, excused himself, and once more headed in search of his dinner.

The Reverend Greenway was not trying to be in vogue on Columbus Avenue. In a white tennis outfit, a racket and a can of balls in one hand, he was waiting his turn in the crowded barbecue shop when Becker entered and spotted him. Well, he had not been completely wrong. The old man sidled up to the pastor and spoke his name, a little too loudly perhaps, judging by all the heads that turned in his direction. Greenway's greeting was friendly, and Becker had a sudden inspiration. He tried to sound offhanded.

"If you're buying something for dinner," Becker said, "could I invite you for a bite at my place tonight?"

Greenway looked surprised. "Why, I don't know," he said after a pause. "I wouldn't want you to go to a lot of trouble."

Becker assured him he would have only to heat up an extra piece of chicken. He explained he wanted to have a talk and told of the locked church. Greenway said he was sorry about that, took the address, and promised to be there at seven o'clock. "As a matter of fact," he said, looking around at the other customers, "I was starting to get tired of waiting. And I don't like to eat alone. Thank you very much."

He left in his usual brisk way. Becker was delighted. Once home, he would not have to go out again. He remembered there was a bottle of Bordeaux that had been lying for almost a year in the cabinet under the kitchen sink. It was twenty minutes before he was served, but some peace of mind had returned as he waited patiently. Feeling extravagant, he recrossed Broadway to a pastry shop, where he picked up a small cheesecake at a price that would normally make him shudder. At the corner where he turned off Broadway, there was a bookstore, and he stopped to inspect the display in an outside bin.

"Hey, Mac, got some change?"

The voice behind was unmistakable. He turned to face the blond youth, who looked at him as vacantly as before. Becker began to reach in his pocket as if in surrender, then stopped. His face flushed and turned grim. He set his packages on top of the books and reached back into the bin. He grasped a large volume on French impressionists by both hands and brought it down with all his strength on the young man's head. He staggered back. Becker raised the book and struck again, this time against the side of the face. The youth crumpled to the ground. He lay there silently, looking up openmouthed at his attacker, blood trickling from a welt on his cheek. Becker put the book back in the bin, picked up his packages, and walked away as the store owner rushed out and stared down at the fallen man.

Becker did not look back until he was halfway down the block. Nobody was following him. He was almost awed at what he had done. What had gotten into him? He had drawn blood for the first time in his life, more or less on purpose. What would his mother have said? he wondered. Sorry, Mom, but it really felt good. He was exhilarated, and when had he last felt like that? Somehow, with the spontaneity of the gesture, all the more amazing at his age, he had the feeling he had struck a blow against the whole crazy drug scene, against those who dealt, like Carlo and his death-threatening mayhem, and those who were dealt to. Who knows? It could have been Carlo who had supplied the blond zombie with his pot. It also could have been Sam. Becker grimaced at the thought.

By the time he reached his building, he had calmed down. All he had done was to assert himself for a change, boosted his ego a bit, against a drug-addled schlemiel who did not know what he was doing half the time. The sad point was that Carlo was still out there, untouched, as were all the problems connected with him. "Becker," he said, once more talking aloud but with no one to catch him at it in the empty lobby, "all you did was attack a junkie. The kid will be back buying more just as soon as he gets a little money together."

He washed his hands with scouring powder. In a closet, he found a white tablecloth badly creased by years of lying folded. He set the table with dishes, glasses, and flatware his wife used to reserve for company and now so dusty they had to be wiped. He uncorked the wine to let it "breathe" after searching several minutes through drawers for a corkscrew, put the chicken in the oven to heat, and opened a can of peas. He changed his shirt and pants, surveyed himself in the full-length mirror in the dressing alcove, and sat down to await the guest of his first dinner party since becoming a widower.

The telephone rang. It was Greenway, with a note of agitation in his voice. "I'm sorry, Mr. Becker, something's come up. I'll be a little late."

"Don't worry about that, Reverend." (Remember to take the chicken out of the oven, Becker said to himself.) "What happened?"

"There's been a break-in at the church. I'm waiting for the police."

Becker passed his hand over his face, trying to wipe away his anguish as though it were sweat. A perfect end to the day, a promising start to the week, he thought. There was a bright side. What had happened would simplify things. At least Greenway would have an idea of what he was talking about when he described the violence of recent days.

"Mr. Becker, you still there?"

"Yes, Reverend, I'm sorry. What did they take? Is there much damage?"

"Nothing in the church itself. But you know that room where you hold classes? The breakfront is a mess. All the drawers pulled out and on the floor, the psalmbooks too. Some cabinets in the dining hall have been gone through, and there's some smashed crockery, but I don't know what they took. I can't figure out what they were looking for. You didn't see anybody hanging around the side, when you went by this afternoon, did you? That's where they came in."

Becker had seen nobody. And probably just as well. Whoever it was would have seen him too, and what would he have done? Run for the police or run for his life? He had no answer.

Greenway was talking again. He had thought about it some more and was not sure he could make it for dinner, and would Mr. Becker excuse him? "I don't know how long I'll be with the police," he said.

Becker was feeling desperate. Now more than ever, he needed allies, and Greenway maybe had become one. "Reverend, please," he said, "I have to talk to you about something. I'm not sure, but it may have a connection with your break-in."

Greenway sounded intrigued. "How's that?"

"Come, please, when you can, and I'll explain. I'll keep the chicken warm."

"I think I hear the police now. Okay." Greenway was gone.

Becker leaned back in his chair, his heart beating almost as fast as it had after his near encounter with the taxi. Was it a casual break-in, or was Carlo still on the trail of his money? If it was really he, he had to be given points for persistence and thoroughness, a real one-track mind, as if he had nothing else to do but recover his lousy $1,000. How would he know about the English class, and why would he think Sam would stash bills in such a place? Becker was bewildered and frightened by all the unanswered, perhaps unanswerable, questions. He put a Mantovani record on the turntable and let the syrupy music lull him into a half-doze.

The downstairs buzzer startled him. It was Greenway,

arriving two hours later than planned. Becker let him in, turned on the oven, checked the table, and ushered in his guest.

The dinner did not go badly, Becker thought. He had eaten worse chicken, and so apparently had Greenway, who seemed to relax as the meal progressed. The wine, the last of a half-dozen bottles Becker had splurged on three years before at a sale, was all right. At least Greenway seemed to think so, for he drank at twice Becker's rate. Neither had seemed willing to get to the point right away and, mellowed by the wine, they had kept the table conversation to small talk about the neighborhood, the church, the classes. Becker thought the classes were going well, but he would know better after a few more sessions, he said. By then they had finished the cheesecake and, taking the rest of the wine with them, had moved to the other end of the studio where Greenway made an easy transition from the classes to what had happened in the classroom.

"The police checked for fingerprints," he said, "but I don't think they found any. And I can't find anything missing." He paused and looked so depressed that Becker was afraid he was about to cry. "All those hymnbooks torn and scattered around," he continued. "Do you know what they are about? They are hymns for the celebration of life. Life!" he exclaimed, "not violence." Becker was starting to be sorry he had served wine, but Greenway suddenly became quiet and looked quizzically at his host. "You had something you wanted to tell me?" he asked.

Becker nodded and drew a breath. "You remember two of the students you assigned me, Carlton White and Carolyn Rogers?" It was Greenway's turn to nod and Becker was off, pouring out the story of their troubles and his involvement, getting so caught up in the tale that he omitted nothing except his personal feelings for Sam. He had not intended to talk about the money for fear that Greenway might be shocked at his becoming Sam's bagman, so to speak. But there he was, showing the churchman the enve-

lope stuffed with bills and explaining what they were supposed to be for and how they had gotten to him.

"I don't know," Becker said, concluding his tale at last,
"but this fellow who is after Sam, this Carlo, he may have
been looking for the money in the classroom."

Greenway had been looking at Becker with increasing
amazement, and at the end of the tale, he sat openmouthed.
Becker noted the expression, and a little thrill of satisfaction
ran through him. For once he was fascinating someone. It
made all the troubles seem almost worthwhile.

When Greenway got his speech back, it was he who
sounded stuffy. "You know, Mr. Becker," he said, "you
must go to the police as quickly as possible."

Expecting that, Becker nodded silently, and Greenway
went on. "I feel a little responsible. After all, I put those two
in your class. I'll find someone else to take over the teaching. You lie low and let the police worry about Carlton and
Carolyn and Carlo. The three C's; it sounds like an act."
Greenway smiled at his little joke, then got serious again.

"What are you going to do with the money?" he asked.

"It's not mine," Becker replied. He was starting to feel a
little let down by Greenway. "What am I supposed to do
with it?"

"Take it with you to the police as evidence," Greenway
said. "If you want, I'll go with you. And another thing. We'll
have to tell Carlton and Carolyn to go somewhere else for
lessons."

Yes, Becker thought, Greenway is giving me an easy
way out. I let the police take over and wash my hands of the
three C's. But will they wash their hands of me? And had he
not, maybe in spite of himself, contracted some moral com-
mitments?

Greenway could have been reading his thoughts.
"You're not a young man anymore, Mr. Becker. You
shouldn't have to expose yourself to this kind of trouble.
You're entitled to a little peace of mind. Besides, this fight
over money has put the church in danger, and maybe it will
put you in danger too."

Greenway was being temptingly reasonable. When the idea of talking to the pastor had occurred to him, had he not been looking precisely for this kind of advice? Why then was he not satisfied with it? Something has changed, Becker thought. The role reversal was continuing. He was a rash old man being restrained by a young sage. Maybe it was the wine. He looked at Greenway, who was waiting for him to say something.

"I suppose you're right about going to the police," Becker said. "Carlo has to be stopped. But the money is important to Sam's future and Carolyn's. Can't it be kept out of the police's hands? I don't like the way it was earned any more than you do, but who are the rightful owners now? If it can be used to help some young people get a fresh start in life, isn't that worthwhile? How did the Crusaders come by their money?"

Becker the Crusader! He continued to surprise himself, preaching sanctimoniously to a man of the church, who, from his expression, didn't seem to be enjoying it. There was an edge to Greenway's voice when he spoke up.

"Let's not get carried away. What kind of Crusade is this? Do you really believe this story about the beauty parlor?"

"Why not?" Becker answered. "You of all people should believe in redemption."

"Come on!" Greenway exclaimed, becoming annoyed. "What do you know about redemption? You're going to save him from sin? When a dope pusher can make the money Sam does, why would he give it up?"

Maybe it was the wine, but Becker was feeling increasingly bold. "Then why did you let him join the class if you thought he was hopeless?"

Greenway jerked his head up and flushed. Why had he, in fact? He let his mind go back to the scene on the park bench when he was catching his wind after jogging and the personable young black had struck up a conversation that quickly got around to "smoke." Greenway had looked at him calculatingly. The church had launched the schooling program, and he was under pressure from the liberal do-gooders in the congregation to make a big place for blacks. In the chow line, they had systematically been elbowed aside by whites until they no longer bothered to come around. He had watched it happen passively. Now, with Sam, he took over the conversation, fascinating himself, in fact, with the sound of his preaching as he offered Sam an opportunity for free education. It would look good in his next report to the church board.

He looked resentfully at the old Jew, who was presuming to give him lessons in Christianity. Becker seemed transformed. What had happened to the meek, scruffy old man he had admitted to his office for the first time after directing him to the chow line outside? Becker had him on points, he had to admit. He still had his doubts about the redemption of Sam, but he no longer wanted to argue. It was time to go. He rose and held out his hand. Becker made no protest. The jousting had gone on long enough. Even without it, it would have been a rough day, and he was exhausted.

But Greenway suddenly thought of something else. "Do you believe in God?"

God yet! Becker clasped his hand to his forehead as if in pain and searched for an answer. "I don't not believe in Him," he finally said.

"What?"

"I mean, I won't argue for or against Him. If you want to believe, it's all right with me."

Greenway looked incredulous. "You seek redemption for Sam and you cop out on God?"

"I've always thought that human beings could do things for others and even redeem themselves without getting their inspiration from some supreme being."

Would Greenway please leave? Becker looked at the minister almost pleadingly. The latter seemed to take the hint. "You're on shaky ground, Mr. Becker," he said. "But we'll continue the discussion another time. Anyway, you will go to the police?"

"Yes," Becker said. "But, Reverend, please don't talk to the police about the money, at least not yet. I'll think of something and let you know. And I really believe Sam wants to get out of the business. Especially after what has happened to him. You won't throw him out of the class, will you?"

"I can't endanger the church," Greenway answered. But the old man looked so distressed that he added, "We'll see." He thanked Becker for a nice evening and headed for the door. With his hand on the knob, he suddenly turned.

"Tell me, how do you feel about Sam personally?"

Becker had feared the question all evening. He cleared his throat a couple of times before getting out an answer. "Why, I don't know. He has a nice personality and a lot of charm and enthusiasm. And he can be very persuasive."

"He's good-looking, too," Greenway interjected.

Becker reddened. "I guess so. I hadn't thought about that much."

Greenway grinned and put his hand on Becker's shoulder. "We in the Unitarian Church are very tolerant," he said, and walked out.

Becker was still a little unsteady and red in the face. What was "tolerant" supposed to mean? "Tolerant" about what? The questions were rhetorical; he knew damn well what Greenway had in mind. In the last seconds of their evening together, the minister had cut open Becker's soul, and now it lay bare and bleeding. He sat down heavily on the bed and held his head between his hands. No, actually the first incision had been made fifty years ago in Tangier, he thought, and the wound had festered ever since. He had tried to ignore it as one would a particularly loathsome birthmark, hiding it from himself and others, but now Greenway had simply opened it wider.

Greenway had been a great help all around, he thought bitterly. As if he needed to be told to go to the police! And then the sexual innuendo! He hadn't needed that either. There would be more than innuendo from the police, he was afraid. Everybody had sex on the brain, as if that had

— 108 —

anything to do with a situation like this. All right, suppose it did, for the sake of argument. Self-control was what mattered. Greenway could keep his "tolerance" to himself. He, Becker, had no need of it. All his life, after that one episode in Tangier, he had stood guard over himself, his sense of what was right and moral a shield against the possible onslaughts of wayward urges. He had nothing to be ashamed of.

On the daybed, the envelope with the money lay waiting to be disposed of. Becker suddenly remembered that Carolyn was coming by for it in the morning. He would give it to her, and Greenway could go to hell. For all the moral support he had gotten from him, he needn't have bothered with the good dishes. He took the empty wine bottle into the kitchen and put it next to the garbage can. He was too tired to do any more cleaning up.

CHAPTER

Ten

Becker woke with what he thought was a hangover. Never having had one that he could recall, he could only suppose the slight headache, the dry mouth, and the woozy feeling were from the wine. He raised the shade and blinked almost in pain as sunlight flooded into the room. He hastily covered the window again. Last night's conversation remained clear. He marveled at how bold and firm he had been with Greenway until the last moment when he had been punctured by the question he feared more than any other. Had the minister simply taken a stab, reaching a conclusion only when he saw Becker's embarrassment?

Becker had to go to the bathroom before answering questions or doing anything else. Despite all he had drunk, he passed the night without once getting up, and now his bladder was hurting him. In old age, emptying it was one of life's great pleasures. Were he to write a guide to the golden years, that's what he would say, a fetching bit of candor, he thought, about on a par with running a cockroach farm he had announced when someone asked him at a dinner party about his retirement plans.

What other pleasures? Sexual desire lasted until very late in life even though prowess diminished. He had read this but could hardly furnish proof. There was the business with the blocked artery just below his waist that made it difficult for him to get hard. In the last years of his marriage, he would let weeks go by before making love to his wife, and when he did, it had not been easy. She had been tactful about it, and he was grateful. Greenway had been less than tactful. He intimated that Becker still had a sex drive and that it was directed toward Sam. A few days ago, when he looked down at the black boy's sleeping form, had anything stirred in him? A little tenderness maybe, but was it anything more than what one might feel for a grandson? Except that in looking at Sam, he had let his mind travel back fifty years to Beshir.

Anyway, he had been twenty then. The sort of attraction he might have had for the Moroccan had not been respectable then, and it was even less so now that he was seventy. If only he could put such things out of his mind! He looked at the wall clock in the kitchen. It was nine-thirty, and Carolyn would be coming soon. He put coffee up and found a slightly stale roll, which he popped into the toaster oven. He hurriedly shaved and dressed. For the aggressive go-getter he was supposed to be, Greenway had offered safe advice, he thought, the kind that some old-time brokerage firm might have given on an investment. Ordinarily, he would have embraced it wholeheartedly, but something had come over him. When he learned Sam had been knifed, he should have been terrified and had, in fact, come close to fainting. But he had also become determined to help the youth even if it meant some risk to himself. He was still amazed by this. When had he been willing to take risks even for himself? "The heart has its reasons that reason knows nothing of," wrote Pascal long ago. That would have to do for an answer.

The downstairs buzzer suddenly broke into Becker's thoughts. Carolyn answered the intercom, and he let her in. He opened his door and waited impatiently, one eye on the elevator door, the other on Mrs. Klein's. The old busybody, on a shopping or laundry expedition, was sure to appear at the same time Carolyn did, and then he would have to endure snide remarks, accusing looks, persistent fishing for information for God knew how long. Today he was in luck. Carolyn stepped off the elevator and was ushered into the apartment unobserved.

She wore the same huge sunglasses that covered most of

the upper part of her face. As far as Becker could tell, it was about as swollen as it had been yesterday. He was surprised by the rest of her outfit. A severely cut gray suit, an almost prim white blouse, white low-heeled shoes, and a battered black plastic briefcase made her appear like someone with executive ambitions who had stopped off on the way to the office. Becker looked at her admiringly. Several times, not the least last night, he had thought about his initial feeling that she had somehow come between him and Sam. It was the kind of shameful gut reaction that had to be banished in the name of self-control. If he wanted Sam to lead a normal life, she had to be part of it. Any other thoughts about her, he told himself several times, were unworthy.

Last night, she had finally gotten to sleep after the boys helped her to straighten up the room. This morning she woke with more serenity than expected but still frightened and needing more reassurance than the old man had been able to give her. If she and Sam allowed a creep like Carlo to wreck their hopes along with the furniture, they would never get back on track, never see the good life they had promised each other. She wanted to hear this from Sam, longed to feel the bounce of his optimism. She made herself a cup of coffee and tried out her voice. It sounded calm and steady to her, and she reached for the phone before remembering how brutally it had been disconnected from the world. She slammed the receiver down, put on a bathrobe, and walked up one flight. Soft but insistent knocks on a door brought a sleepy "Who's there?" from the woman inside, an out-of-work substitute teacher with whom she had a nodding acquaintance. Then Carolyn had to endure wide-eyed exclamations and questions before she could get to use the phone. She called the hospital and felt a rush of exhilaration when Sam came on after a while. She was intently matter-of-fact, and in return Sam gave her the cheery message she wanted to hear, making her almost eager to go ahead with the plans. They talked about Becker, and Sam told her some things she had not known. She called her boss and excused herself from work, at least for the morning. Then a sudden thought: she turned to the woman and asked if she could borrow something to wear. Her collection of blouses and slacks didn't strike her as serious enough for the business ahead.

Becker offered Carolyn coffee and cleared away a part of the dining table, still encumbered with the remains of last night's dinner.

"I talked to Sam this morning," she said. "I didn't say nothin' about what happened to me, only that I was comin' to your house." She hesitated, and Becker tried an encouraging smile.

"Sam," she resumed, "he wants me to ask you if you'd come with me to the landlord's office. He expectin' me to sign the lease." She became silent again and looked at Becker as if to say, "Don't fail us now."

I know what you want, Sam, you little bastard, Becker thought. Will I be a guard for $2,000? He drank some coffee to avoid an immediate answer.

"Sam must be feeling better to talk on the telephone," he said finally.

"Yeah," Carolyn answered. "He sittin' up now, he tol' me, and they give him his own phone."

Becker took a bite of his roll and offered one to his guest. She declined and continued looking at him for the answer she wanted.

What the hell, he thought. He was committed. "Where's the real estate office?" he asked cautiously.

"It's downtown, Sixth Avenue and Forty-sixth Street," she said eagerly. "It's an okay neighborhood," she added with a broad smile.

Becker was relieved. It wouldn't be so bad. He had imagined some address in Harlem but now realized that the area probably had lots of absentee landlords. "Okay," he said and finished his coffee. At least he would finally be rid of the money. He went over to the still unmade daybed, drew the envelope from beneath the mattress, and handed it to Carolyn. "There is about $2,000 in it," he said.

Carolyn put the envelope in her briefcase, then turned to Becker.

"Mr. Becker," she said, "there's somethin' else."

He wasn't feeling much better now than when he awoke. Why couldn't things at least be simple? "What else?" he asked.

Carolyn pretended to ignore the edge in Becker's voice. "Sam, he tol' me he put money in a couple books, some in a French poetry book, he say you know which, and some in a book next to it."

Becker stared at her. Sam had turned his house into a regular Fort Knox, except that the son of a bitch should have realized this one had particularly weak defenses. His good feelings for the kid were starting to evaporate in the steamy irritation rising up in him. He went over to the bookcase and took out a large and bulging French grammar next to the Villon volume. He took it back to the table, held it by its spine, and watched as bills tumbled and fluttered onto the tablecloth. Carolyn drew in her breath.

They looked at each other, then wordlessly began gathering the twenties, fifties, and hundreds into piles. Ten minutes later, they had counted $2,150. Becker lit a cigarette with shaking hands, his eyes glued to the money.

"What's supposed to happen with this money?" he asked.

"Sam say we need it for fixing up the store, rentin' stuff until we can buy it," Carolyn explained. "But I reckon he gonna need a lot for the hospital bill."

"How's he going to explain to the police where he got the money to pay the bill?"

Carolyn hesitated. "We thought of that. He can say you lent it."

Becker sighed. Sam thought of everything except how to stay out of trouble. When he asked his next question, he was already resigned to the answer.

"Where is this money supposed to go?"

"Sam, he wonderin' if you'd keep it a little while until we need it. Mr. Becker, you all right?" The old man had suddenly broken out into a sweat and was bending over with his head between his knees.

"Yes," he answered weakly. "Just a little faint. Carolyn, are you sure you weren't followed here?"

It was the girl's turn to look frightened. "I don't think so. I didn't look, but I don't think so."

Becker was not reassured. "How long am I supposed to keep it?" he asked.

"I don't rightly know. Sam didn't say." Carolyn smiled encouragingly. "Probably not long. The way Sam's goin', he should be out in no time."

Becker tried to look at the matter calmly. "You know, Carolyn," he said, giving her a solemn look, "if you and Sam want to be businesspeople, sooner or later you're going to have to open bank accounts. Businesses don't put their money under mattresses," a pause and then, "or hide it in books."

Becker supposed he was talking sense, never having run a business. At any rate, his sententious advice seemed to be having an effect on the girl. She was nodding at him with the respect one reserves for investment counselors.

"I know what you're sayin', Mr. Becker," she answered after a pause to take it all in. "We're certainly goin' to do that. But this money we're talkin' about right now, it's a kinda special business money, if you know what I mean."

Becker knew only too well. It was time to resign himself and drop the discussion. He could only hope that the extra $2,300 would not bring further trouble.

"Okay, Carolyn," he said, trying to sound as unenthusiastic as possible, "I'll hold on to it if it's not for too long."

He gathered up the bills, found another large manila envelope, and stowed everything under his mattress. He was starting to feel like those French peasants who slept with their gold. He looked inquiringly at Carolyn. "You ready?"

At the door, Becker looked out and found the hallway empty. But his luck held only until the lobby. Mrs. Klein was back from early shopping, waiting as the elevator glided open. She began to smile at Mr. Becker, then her expression froze as her eyes took in the girl.

"Mr. Becker, how nice!" she exclaimed with what struck Becker as forced friendliness. "How are you feeling now? You didn't look so good the last time I saw you."

Becker suddenly realized that he had not run into the old lady since the afternoon she had told him of the stabbing. It seemed so long ago. Other things had happened for the worse.

"Better, Mrs. Klein, much better," he answered and tried to move briskly past her, Carolyn close behind. But Mrs. Klein stood rooted and staring, and had to be almost circled before they could get out of the elevator. She looked at Carolyn, then at Becker as if expecting an explanation. You can stew in your own racist juice, Becker thought; you're getting none from me.

"It was nice seeing you, Mrs. Klein," he said. "Have a nice day." He took Carolyn by the arm and piloted her out of the building, leaving his neighbor to stare after them. She was having friends in for coffee in the afternoon. She could hardly wait.

Becker and Carolyn turned toward West End Avenue to look for a cab. Across the street, one foot propped against a building, a young black tried to overcome his boredom by ogling the women joggers along Riverside Drive. Becker and Carolyn were halfway down the block before he realized what was happening. The black man dashed for his car, double-parked on Riverside Drive, and brought it slowly into position twenty feet behind the couple, who were now waiting on the corner. His heart was pumping fast. There would be real trouble if he had to tell Carlo he lost the woman. Already he nearly let her taxi get away in the traffic when he had followed her down from her house. Who the old guy was he did not know, and Carlo would be pissed off enough that he didn't.

An empty taxi deigned to stop. Carolyn gave the driver directions and settled back in silence. But Becker had another question.

"Carolyn, when Carlo came to uh . . . see you, did you tell him about the English classes at the church?"

Carolyn frowned at the need to recall the scene. She thought at length before answering.

"Carlo, he say he seen Sam come out of the church the other evenin', and he try to catch up with him but couldn'. He want to know when Sam got so religious, or maybe he doin' somethin' else there. So I tol' him about the class in the basement." She put her hand on Becker's arm. "But I didn' say who the teacher was."

Thank heaven for small favors, Becker thought. So it was Carlo, after all, who had ransacked the church. Carolyn looked at him.

"Why you wanna know that?"

Becker explained what had happened at the church. Carolyn looked contrite and stared moodily out the window. She thought of something else. "I tol' Carlo we goin' into business. No more dealin'."

"What did Carlo say?"

Nothin' at first. He jes laughed. Then he say he heard that one before, and we full of shit, and anyway we ain't goin' into business on his money, and he starts tearin' up the place some more."

Behind them, the black man weaved his car in and out of traffic in his effort to keep them in sight. When the taxi pulled up in front of a large office building on Sixth Avenue, he watched helplessly as they entered, cursed the honking cars behind him, and moved out reluctantly for the return uptown.

Moses S. Tompkins, in white shirt, small-figured tie, and gray pinstripe suit, was the agent in charge of Harlem for the realty firm of Rosenberg Associates, which owned or managed large parts of northern Manhattan. Tompkins was well paid for handling sometimes difficult tenants in an area his employers seldom saw or bothered much about as long as the rents were paid and the maintenance costs kept to a minimum. His position was often made uncomfortable by disgruntled "brothers" who threw the Oreo cookie joke at him as if he were any whiter inside than some black realty firms he knew. It was true that he housed his family in a comfortable white section of Queens, but how many other middle-class blacks who made such a profession of their blackness had not also abandoned Harlem to the welfare families, the junkies, and the winos? He refused to bother his conscience further than that.

To Carolyn and Becker, at whom he first shot a quizzical glance, Tompkins could not have been nicer. The firm had been having difficulty getting occupants for stores, particularly the one Sam and Carolyn had liked. Arsonists had visited adjoining properties, and the street consequently had as bad a reputation as any in Harlem. But the location near Morningside Park at the western edge of Harlem was in an area likely to make a comeback if gentrification continued its northward push with help from prospering blacks anxious to return to their roots. Tompkins himself was thinking of buying one of several abandoned brownstones facing the park that were cheap enough to be worth refurbishing either for himself or as an investment.

The papers were neatly stacked for signing, but Carolyn was anxious to show she was no child when it came to business. She leaned intently over the desk and began reading them, Becker leaning in turn over her shoulder. He knew little more about it than she did, having signed a few leases in his day but never bothering to read them all the way through. The rent seemed low to him, $800 a month, with the first month free, as in the old days when landlords would regularly offer "a month's concession." On the other hand, the lease was for only a year, as if the landlord was contemplating some quick revisions. Some of the same thoughts were occurring to Carolyn; her boss paid much more than that for only slightly more space.

They looked at Tompkins, who seemed to be reading their thoughts. "I'll be frank with you," he said, an earnest look suddenly replacing what had seemed a permanent smile. He adjusted his perfectly straight gold tie clasp

(Becker, who had decided he did not like Tompkins, thought it was probably fake) and went on. "I know I'm dealing with people who've been around. There's been trouble in that neighborhood, I don't mind telling you. We're anxious to get things going again, so if it looks like we're giving you a break, you're right. We're giving you the first month free to get things fixed up before starting business. How's that?"

Becker thought it was important to avoid enthusiasm. "What kind of trouble?" he asked.

Tompkins was starting to get annoyed with the old guy. How did he get involved in a deal among blacks? But the real estate dealer had a big supply of patience.

"A few of the stores were fronts for drug operations and the numbers," he explained. "From what we hear, some other groups wanted to muscle in, there was a bit of disagreement, and the stores got burned down." Becker and Carolyn looked at each other, and Tompkins knew he had said too much. "That was last year," he added quickly. "I'm sure a legitimate business would have no trouble, and there's plenty of people in the neighborhood who need services and want to see things nice and quiet. And the police have their eye on the street."

Carolyn, who knew little about how people lived outside Harlem, was not surprised at what Tompkins was saying, although she was not sure the police were that helpful. Almost any street they could have picked had the same trouble. Besides, they had explored the neighborhood a little; there was not another beauty parlor within a six-block radius. She looked inquiringly at Becker as if he could offer expert advice on Harlem's safe spots. He shrugged. She picked up Tompkins' proffered pen, hesitated a moment, and signed. She then had to produce $1,600 to cover the second month's rent and a month's deposit. From the envelope, she extracted a wad of bills and counted out the amount carefully. Tompkins watched in silent amazement, but cash was cash, there was no arguing with that. He too signed;

there were handshakes all around, and the deal was consummated. Becker and Carolyn walked across town to report to Sam.

In his overpriced, one-bedroom condominium on Seventy-third Street off Lexington, Carlo already had his report and was even grumpier than usual. The girl he had picked up in a bar on Third Avenue had been a lousy lay, practically going into hysterics when he tried to tie her up, finally freezing into a block of ice when he backed her against the bathroom sink and screwed her before throwing her out. Now this. He wanted to blame the kid but had to admit it would have been hard to double-park on Sixth Avenue and follow Carolyn and the old man into the building. But still, all his elaborate plans had not produced much, and he had had to give the kid fifty bucks and some grass for waiting outside her house from early morning and following her cab down to the building on Riverside Drive. And who the fuck was the old man?

He was starting to get worked up again. Furiously stirring his coffee until it sloshed over, he turned the puzzle around in his mind. Was it the same guy he caught spying on him and Sam in the park? Was he the teacher Sam was trying to learn English from? Why was he the first person Carolyn visited? Why him rather than Sam? He was getting heartburn. Then it came to him.

Because the old bastard had the money, that's why. The answer seemed so obvious that he became even angrier at his slow thinking. Son of a bitch! So that was where Sam had stashed his dough. Carolyn had stopped off to get it, or maybe only some of it. What she had done with the money—he was sure she had it in the briefcase the kid had mentioned—was a mystery he would have to solve. There might be some left in the old man's apartment. That too he would have to find out. He could forget about Sam, at least as far as getting his money was concerned. It was now between him and the old man. Why the fuck hadn't he knocked him off with his car the other day when he had the chance? He wouldn't have this complication now.

He finished his coffee and heavily buttered croissant in a better mood, convinced he had it all figured out, except for some small details, such as breaking into the apartment or catching the old guy on the street and threatening him unless he cooperated. There were a few other problems. Sam might be singing to the cops, and there was the still-to-come scene with his uncle when he got wind of the trouble his temper had once again created. It will be even worse, he figured, if he is short on what he owed. The uncle was a strict bookkeeper. He went to take a shower. With soap and water might come ideas.

Becker and Carolyn found Sam sitting up and smiling. The old man tried to imagine how he himself would be looking at this point and gave it up because the only image that came to him was that of a lifeless body in a satin-lined coffin. Quick recuperative powers were reserved for the young. Sam excitedly slapped the sides of his bed as the just completed deal was recounted. "Oh, man!" he exlaimed. "We're on our way now, I jes know it." He looked at Carolyn and Becker for confirmation, and they nodded vigorously as if afraid any note of discouragement might bring on a relapse. Then Sam took a closer look at Carolyn. The smile disappeared, and his voice dropped to a whisper.

"What happened to you?" he asked.

The answer came in great uncontrollable sobs that caused heads to rise painfully from the adjoining beds and brought a nurse running in alarm. Carolyn calmed down and was coherent enough to give Sam a clear idea of Carlo's fury. He looked at Becker as if he would find in him the strength that would protect them all. But the old man could only manage a consoling hand on Carolyn's shoulder and a weak smile for Sam.

"Sam, we have to go to the police," he said. "Something worse is going to happen unless this man is put away."

Sam wilted and lay back meekly under his covers. He had no answer to Becker's reasonableness, only reflexes built up in his years in the street that made him shrink from any contact with the law. Becker looked at him as if reading his mind, but what else was there to do, short of organizing a wild-West posse? Some posse they would make! A seventy-year-old man who could not run 50 feet without feeling exhausted, an eighteen-year-old recovering from near death, a young woman beaten up and full of fear, and a young minister with the gumption of an old English vicar.

It was clear that Sam could no longer take his chances alone with Carlo. However embarrassing they might prove, the police had to be brought in as soon as possible. Becker decided he would try to call Mulvaney when he got home.

"What we gonna tell the police?" Sam asked in a small-boy's voice.

Well, there's the rub, Becker thought silently. He had tried to devise the least compromising story but could not think of anything that would get Sam completely off the hook. He was not yet sure how to explain his own involvement without causing embarrassment to himself and becoming a witness, even an accomplice, to Sam's illegal activities. But lives were at stake. That, Mulvaney was likely to say, was the bottom line. He turned to Sam, who was still waiting for an answer.

"Sam," Becker finally said, "I know you don't like the cops, but what else can we do? Maybe there's a deal you can make for being a witness for the state. I know the cops have been looking for the guy. The district attorney may be so happy for your help he won't prosecute you for anything." Becker smiled encouragingly at Sam as though he meant every word.

Sam looked so glum he seemed on the verge of crying. His whole body had collapsed into exhaustion, whether from all the thinking he was being called on to do, Becker could not tell. A nurse came to the rescue.

"He needs to get his dressings changed," she announced, drawing a curtain around the bed. It was a good occasion to leave. "I'll be back tomorrow," Becker promised. "We'll talk some more." Sam nodded weakly. Carolyn followed him to the door.

"Mr. Becker," she said, "I don't think Sam's ready for what you tellin' him. Besides, he done tol' the police he don' know who knifed him."

"That's okay," Becker answered. "He wasn't under oath. He can change his story; the police would probably be grateful." He looked at her in silence for several seconds. "As I said, what else should we do?"

"I don' rightly know," she answered. "I'm as scared as you are, scareder maybe. I'll talk to Sam some more, okay? Can you wait until tomorrow?"

Becker nodded and walked out more hunched over than usual. It was only one o'clock, but he felt he had already put in a full day in "the service of man." The Unitarian slogan made him suddenly remember it was Monday, and he was expected to teach this evening. He did not really feel up to it. Two of his pupils, one of them in the hospital, were now unwelcome, and the classroom had become part of the battlefront. He was not sure he wanted to deal with Greenway after last night. So many reasons for not showing up himself. But he knew he would. In forty years in the public school system, his only absences had been due to illness, and those were rare. The record was proof enough of his conscientiousness, something he had always taken pride in. He had not lost this trait, never would, he thought, straightening up as he walked toward the subway station. So he would be there tonight. There were four students depending on him. At least he liked to think they were. Speeding home in the roar and rattle of the graffiti-ridden car, he made a mental note to look up the next lesson. The noun, if he remembered correctly. The noun it would be, even if it killed him.

CHAPTER

Eleven

"The table is in the center of the room," intoned Becker as he wrote the sentence on the blackboard. He looked at the Irish boy. "Robert, tell me all the nouns in that sentence."

Robert studied the blackboard at length and looked at his three companions as if for encouragement before finally speaking up. " 'Table' and 'room,' " he said. Becker waited for more, but the youth had settled back, satisfied with his effort. "Anything else?" Becker asked, looking this time at Cesar, the swarthy Puerto Rican. " 'Center'?" Cesar asked tentatively.

Becker congratulated him and went on to the difference between common and proper nouns. The four students around the table tried to look interested, but twenty minutes into the lesson they were already shifting in their chairs and stifling yawns. Their teacher was in much the same mood; six o'clock would come none too soon for any of them.

When Becker had gotten home in the afternoon, he looked restively around his studio, checking nervously on the manila envelope under the mattress, and putting his hand several times on the telephone receiver. Despite Carolyn's pleading to hold off calling the police, he was tempted to call and make an appointment with Detective Mulvaney. If he did not call, Greenway would, spilling their whole conversation and bringing an angry cop to his doorstep to accuse him of withholding information and virtually make him an accessory to crime. He was probably exaggerating, but what did he know of the police mind except from the murder mysteries he used to devour until he lost patience and from the cops-and-robbers series that cluttered evening television?

He put the call off another day, justifying his inertia by the desire to give Sam a chance to resign himself to the inevitable. If Sam was to get Carlo off his back and safely into prison, there would be a price to pay. He would have to make a clean break with his past. The connection with Carlo would inevitably bring out what he did for a living. What Becker had told Sam in the hospital had been an inspiration of the moment, but the more he thought about it, the more he was overwhelmed by its logic. If Sam did not make up his mind by tomorrow, he, Becker, would force his hand. In the meantime, there was the class to prepare for. He hoped he would not run into Greenway; one confrontation was already too much. He sighed and reached for the grammar book. "A noun is the name of a person, a place, or a thing," he read. He wondered who would show up tonight to find that out. "Don't get smart," he said aloud. "This is important. This is what you know how to do. So do it." First, he lay down.

When he awoke, he had five minutes to get to the church. He could remember being late only once for a class and that had been toward the end of his career. He had been about to leave home for the school. Washing the breakfast dishes, his wife suddenly let out a series of terrifying rasps. He thought she had reached her end. But she quieted down and insisted he leave. The lesson in irregular French verbs began only ten minutes after the bell had rung. It included a dogged run-through of one of the most irregular of all, *mourir*, "to die," in the face of surly students who had been hoping for a free hour. In a way, it was one of the milestones of his life. The next day, his wife entered the hospital and came out only for her funeral.

He was five minutes late to class this time, but he thought his leg would collapse from the forced march. He looked about quickly, but Greenway was not in sight, and he took the basement steps at a fast limp. Four students, the maximum he could have counted on, were still in the little classroom, inspecting the breakfront now bereft of its windows. Here and there, a jagged edge of glass indicated a less than thorough cleanup. The psalmbooks were back in place, looking a bit ragged. The break-in had been in the newspapers and mentioned on a couple of local TV news programs, the students informed Becker. Then they fell silent as if waiting for more, but he had been as close to an item in the news as he wanted to be. He talked only about nouns.

Six o'clock finally came. Becker was out the door a minute after he delivered a cursory "See you Friday" and watched the students file out. He got away from the church without running into Greenway and went to Broadway to shop for dinner. He would have ham and eggs, maybe with a little peach ice cream for dessert. As a danger, cholesterol couldn't compare to Carlo. He could still make bad jokes, so maybe he had not yet gone to pieces. Still, as soon as he closed his door behind him and double-locked it, he went to the daybed and felt for the envelope. Reassured, he put butter in a saucepan, poured two well-beaten eggs into it, and patiently stirred the mixture over a low flame, removing it while it was still moist. The year in Paris had been good for something. A few cooking tips had stayed with him, though he had only a dim memory of the foster family that imparted them along with all the warnings about the pitfalls of the city after dark. He wondered what they would have thought of New York. The eggs tasted as good, he was sure, as those he had first been served by his temporary guardians.

Tomorrow, there would be another talk with Sam and, whatever the outcome of that, a meeting with the police. Sleep would be useful. Except that as he walked into the studio, the insistent bass beat of disco music suddenly thudded through the wall from the apartment next door, one that separated his from Mrs. Klein's. It had been empty for a month after a quiet-living accountant and his pregnant wife, whom he had known only on nodding terms, moved out to the suburbs, to accommodate an expanding family.

Now the painters had finished, and someone had unmistakably replaced them. He had been used to calm, indeed felt it was coming to him at his age, but what was he to do about this?

The doorbell rang. Mrs. Klein was smiling sweetly in a flowered dress that emphasized her bulk. "Isn't it awful?" she said, pointing next door. "Anyway, I had a talk with them, a nice young Jewish couple, lawyers. They won't play their stereo after nine o'clock except maybe once in a while for a party, and then they'll warn us." She paused for breath and plunged on.

"That's not really what I wanted to see you about, Mr. Becker. I know this is the last minute, but I was supposed to go to a Mostly Mozart concert tonight with a friend. We bought the tickets weeks ago, and now she calls and says she's not feeling well, and here it is almost seven o'clock and the concert's at eight. I was wondering maybe if you weren't doing anything special ..." She trailed off and waited for an answer.

An evening of Mozart and Klein. Who could ask for anything more? On the other hand, he was being offered an alternative to the drum whacks assaulting his already fragile nerves. It could be worse, like an evening of Wagner and Klein. Mozart he could handle. He even had a record of serenades, bought on sale, that he put on every couple of years. He found himself smiling back at Mrs. Klein and accepting. "I'll come by your door after I've changed," he said.

She glanced at her watch. "It's very informal," she said. "I don't think you have to bother."

"I'll only be a minute," he said and closed the door on her. He had long ago acknowledged that he was a philistine when it came to classical music, but he would not go into a concert hall or theater except in a suit. At his infrequent evenings in either, he would look askance at people in blue jeans and T-shirts. He replaced the flowered sport shirt he had worn to the class with the white business shirt and blue tie he had put on in the morning when he saw Carolyn's getup, then donned his only summer sport jacket, a beige affair that went more or less with his baggy blue slacks. He was heading for the door when a thought struck him. He returned to the daybed and removed the thick envelope from under the mattress.

Mrs. Klein had purse in hand when he rang and was about to shut her door when she saw the envelope. "What's that?" she asked.

"It's some valuables. Maybe you could put them in your safe until we get back?"

She looked a little startled. He had not been in her apartment for months. Yet it had suddenly come back to him how odd the old office safe looked in the corner of her bedroom when he peeked in on the way to the bathroom. A memento saved from her husband's business life? He had not inquired, but the image had stuck in a corner of his mind.

She glanced at her watch again and shrugged. So he had seen the safe. She supposed a lot of people had. After all, she had not been exactly hiding it. But she was not a bank either. She took the envelope and walked back to her bedroom, trailing words behind her.

"You should get a safety deposit box, Mr. Becker. They're not expensive."

"I have one. I just haven't gotten around yet to putting this in," he said to her back. He allowed himself a smile. What would she say if she knew whose valuables she was now protecting!

A minute later, he heard a metal door slam shut, and she was back after checking her hair in the bathroom mirror.

The evening went better than he had expected. The bus to Lincoln Center came quickly, and there was only the most passing allusion to the morning meeting at the elevator. Amazingly, there were no questions about Carolyn to fend off. Becker was gracious, treating her to an ice-cream cone from a little stand in the plaza before the concert. The program included the Serenata Notturna, which he had on his record, he remarked to her just before the lights dimmed. "Such a coincidence," she said agreeably. She

hummed only once, being shushed into sullen silence by
the neighbor on her left, who had already spoiled things
a little by being black. Outside in the lobby at intermis-
sion, she started to remark to Becker about the rarity of
blacks at Lincoln Center, but caught herself and shifted to
the pianist of the evening, Murray Perahia, a nice Jewish
boy who played like an angel, but he should eat more, he
was too thin. She chattered on about other soloists she had
heard.

Mrs. Klein thought she had to be careful about how she
handled the evening. The coffee-klatsch had ended in in-
conclusive speculation about Becker's black companion this
morning. When the women left, she thought some more
about her neighbor. For one thing, she had the impression
he was particularly sensitive on the subject of blacks. Why,
she could not figure out. But had he not almost collapsed on
her when she told him of the one knifed in the park? And
now, the girl. How did he get mixed up with her? She decided he was in trouble or, if he was not, soon would be, a
foolish old man who needed caring for.

Her thoughts took wing. Who better to care for him and
his possessions than someone who lived practically next
door and had nothing better to do. God knows, nobody else
needed her, least of all her daughters whom, two times out
of three, she had to call. As for pets, cats were destructive
and dogs had to be walked. It had taken some doing to per-
suade Doris, her concert companion for years, to give up
her seat tonight. She had taken a chance, drawing on her
observations of how Becker led his life to bet that he would
probably be doing nothing special this evening. Gazing at
Becker's round, slightly stooped back as he unaggressively,
even meekly, worked his way to the bar for ginger ales, she
tried to imagine what kind of double life he was leading.
You never know, she thought; perhaps there was a devil in
him unknown to her except in tantalizing moments like this
morning's. Obviously, she told herself, he needed protection but would have to be approached carefully. He was a
big bear who fled when someone looked as if she might

have designs on him. Mutual friends had told her of their vain efforts to get him together with other women.

The Jupiter Symphony, Becker could have done without, a sentiment he kept to himself. Still, it was only ten o'clock when they entered their building. Their floor was blessedly quiet. The disco concert had ended too. "Some coffee and cake, Mr. Becker, or a little schnapps maybe?" she offered as she walked back to her bedroom to fetch his envelope.

"Thank you, Mrs. Klein, but another time. I'm a little tired. And thanks for a nice evening; I enjoyed it." She handed him the envelope, looking at it with seeming fascination. "Of course," she said. "You're welcome. We'll do it again." She made no further effort to keep him. One should not push too hard, she decided, otherwise the quarry flees. She had gauged correctly. Becker was grateful. He was even having warm feelings about her, but enough was enough.

He put his key in the lock. Strangely, it turned only once. Entering or leaving, he always double-locked. Perhaps he had forgotten this time in his hurry not to keep the impatient Mrs. Klein waiting. He opened the door, turned on the light, and froze.

He should not have been shocked. He had anticipated just such a thing when, without thinking about it too much, almost as a reflex, he had moved the envelope next door. Still, from the precaution against disaster to the disaster itself, there was a horrifying jump. Every book he owned was on the floor. The drawers of the desk were out and overturned, their contents jumbled with the books. The daybed was undone and the mattress upended and ripped. The hall closet and the one in the dressing alcove spewed piles of clothing and opened boxes. The kitchen floor was a salad bowl of smashed crockery, groceries from eviscerated boxes, garbage from the overturned can, eggs, butter, cheese, and fruit from the refrigerator along with its two bins and ice trays. The bathroom sink was full of broken bottles from the medicine chest.

He double-locked the door. His mind was almost as

disordered as the apartment, but it occurred to him that there had been artistry involved in entering without breaking, even with the simple lock he had. As far as he could see, there was not even a scratch on the door. He restored the miraculously intact seat and back cushions of his easy chair and sat down, dazedly contemplating the havoc. Gradually his head cleared. He had asked for it, practically invited Carlo to exercise his decorator talents. First you become your brother's keeper, then the keeper of your brother's money. How did Carlo know? Never mind, he knew. So now you are as much in his line of fire as Sam or Carolyn. Getting a stronger lock would no longer do. He looked for the telephone. It was on the floor near the overturned night table, but its wire still seemed connected. He lifted the receiver and heard a dial tone. Carlo, you're getting careless.

Enough with the humor. He should call the police immediately. Now he had a personal reason. He reached again for the phone, then paused and thought of the scene that would ensue. A couple of cops would show up eventually, let out a whistle, open their pads, and start asking questions. Anything missing? No, not as far as I can see, officer. Any ideas about who it was and if there's nothing missing, what do you think they were here for? Officer, it's a long story. It's okay; we got time. Well, there's this kid who owes a hood dough from a drug deal, and he asked me to keep it for a while because I'm teaching him English. Who, the kid or the hood? The kid, you see, he don't . . . (careful, you're an English teacher) doesn't want to pay off the hood right away; he needs the money because he wants to mend his ways; he's going straight and wants to start a beauty parlor with his girlfriend. I can sympathize with that because I know about drugs. There was the time in Tangier . . . but that's another story. To get back to this one, the hood is not the kind who likes to wait; he thinks the kid is holding out on him, and he doesn't like that. As a matter of fact, he gets so mad about the kid jiving him that he knifes him in the park, then goes after the girlfriend, but she doesn't have the money either. Then he thinks I have it, and the rest you can see for yourself. You see, it is really a case of evil standing in the way of redemption. If you don't believe me, you can ask the Reverend Greenway. (The cops have stopped writing long ago and stare at him as he babbles on.) You'd better come with us to the station house, they say; we've seen drug cases, but this is a beaut.

Becker put the phone down and began to sob. What had he gotten into when a meeting with the police would turn into a Marx Brothers movie, every word true but sounding so weird that the cops would look knowingly at each other and dial the number of the Bellevue psychiatric ward? He collapsed into the cushions, wet and quivering, feeling so soft and diminished it was as if his bones had dissolved. Gradually the sobbing turned to quiet weeping; then the tears stopped, and he was seized by an overwhelming desire to sleep. He put the mattress back on the bed, pushing back a spring that had popped through one of the rents in the side. He would have to buy a new mattress, taking the money out of his savings account because the next pension check was not due for a week. He was lucky. Coming back from class, he had passed a bedding store on Broadway that was having a sale. Some luck! He put back the sheets, the light summer blanket, and the pillow, which had been spared the knife.

He picked his way through the room to the kitchen, found a plate still intact on the floor, and went to the refrigerator freezer. His hand groped for the ice cream. It was not there. He looked around the floor. The open container lay on its side in a corner amid the cornflakes. It was empty. He flung the plate against the wall and watched hopelessly as the pieces showered the tiles. Tears would no longer come. He undressed, dropping his clothes where he stood. He fell into bed and turned off the light, obliterating the horror around him.

On Hester Street in Little Italy, the restaurants were still crowded with late diners. Anthony Rossi, squat and powerful like his Calabrian forebears, was having dinner later than he liked, fuming at his nephew for keeping him waiting. He drank some wine to calm his nerves. The doctors had warned him about getting upset and sending the blood pressure up higher than it already was, but they didn't know about the crazy nephew who was always giving him fits. There was no tradition anymore. In his day, kids had respect for the older generation and listened when they were told something. When Carlo had not shown up at nine, he had gone ahead and ordered. He was in the middle of his spaghetti when the kid finally arrived, looking a little breathless. He glared at him.

"Where you been, you keep your uncle waiting like this?"

"Sorry, had a little last-minute business. Just a plate of spaghetti bolognese," Carlo said as the waiter came up. The peach ice cream had taken the edge off his appetite. The uncle eyed him suspiciously.

"You eaten or something?"

"I was at a friend's. A little snack. You know how it is."

The uncle went back to eating his spaghetti. It was better he not know how it had been! Carlo was having trouble keeping his nerves under control after all the frustrations, and now if the old man was going to be on his back for the rest of the evening, he just might take a knife to him too. It was only talk, he knew. Attacking his uncle was the surest way to suicide. Later, maybe, when he had risen in the organization, shown how valuable and tough he was, won the loyalties of a few more people, he could make a move, actually defy the old man, assert his ambitions more openly. For the moment, he was making it as his uncle's nephew. He would show some respect, no matter how much it cost.

It was really costing him now after the day he had. He had been as thorough as ever. He had learned Becker's name, thanks to one of the students, Thomas Baskins. Standing across the street from the church, Carlo and one of his pushers awaited the exit of Becker and the students. The students came out first, and the pusher recognized Baskins from having dealt with him occasionally. A little conversation, and Carlo knew what name to put on the old man by the time he emerged. He would have gone for him too, except that Becker had kept to busy streets and stores, and for once, Carlo decided to be cautious. He would pay him a visit at home. He called Reggie, who needed money after being paroled from a five-year prison term for getting caught picking the lock on a midtown office safe. Carlo thought things were really going for him when Becker came out of his building with a woman around seven-twenty. They looked like a couple out for the evening. He would not have to get rough, not that he had objections, but he was feeling heat from several directions, not least from his uncle, for the episode with Sam. Carlo checked the names on the buzzers and found the floor and apartment. Reggie was preparing to work on the lock on the front door, but a delivery boy showed up with groceries, was buzzed in, and amiably held the door open for the two men behind him. They were greeted on Becker's floor by some loud disco music, which would mask any noise Reggie might have to make. The lock was a piece of cake, Reggie said. They were inside in a few seconds.

Carlo's good feelings did not last long. The two men went through every likely place, tempers mounting as the minutes stretched out and no money showed up, except a dollar in change Carlo found in one of Becker's pants pockets. Reggie nervously watched Carlo go from slow burn to tropical storm as he went through the place again, this time sparing nothing. Carlo was so angry he almost hit Reggie for suggesting maybe they'd better get out, the place was no gold mine. Carlo sat in the kitchen taking out his frustration on the ice cream, itching to get his hands on somebody. Then he remembered he was due downtown for dinner with his uncle, who had told him it was important. The uncle had this stupid habit of summoning him to dinners in the neighborhood where he had been brought up, presiding over corner booths of corny little restaurants with red-checkered tablecloths as if he were back in the 1930s.

They left Becker's place with the disco music still going next door, Carlo letting Reggie fend for himself while he climbed into the little gray Volkswagen, a substitute for the red Alfa Romeo, which was getting a little too conspicuous. It was a good half hour before he could get to the restaurant, park the car, and seat himself opposite his irritated elder.

Carlo's spaghetti came, and the uncle let him eat for a while. He was grateful for some respite and ate slowly and without his usual appetite.

"Listen," the older man said after a few minutes. "I won't go over the business with that nigger kid; I told you what I thought on the phone. You're still not out of trouble, you know. If he fingers you, you're not going to be much use; you'll have to lie low, maybe get out of town for a while. As a matter of fact, I'm surprised you haven't been picked up already for that Washington Heights crap."

"If he fingers me, he fingers himself," Carlo said. "I think he'll keep quiet."

"Maybe yes, maybe no," the uncle replied. He pointed a thick hand at Carlo. "But I don't want no more trouble. I'm telling you to forget about the nigger for a while. We got more important things to do."

Carlo kept silent. It was easy for his uncle to be so forgiving. He had gotten his money. Carlo had dug into his own pocket, so his accounts were even. A thousand bucks was a thousand bucks, and he didn't like being screwed that way. But he did not wish to start an argument. "So what's up?"

"I been to Miami. A shipment's come in. I got 10 kilos; we're talking about big money."

For the first time in weeks, Carlo looked at his uncle with something close to affection. Ten kilos of coke just when he had about run out! It hadn't happened that way for a long time. He wouldn't have to go back to grass. Coke was what everyone wanted anyway. Heroin was for jerks who didn't care whether they lived or died. He had lost a few customers who had OD'd on the stuff. With coke, there wasn't so much mess, the clientele could be very high-class and, depending on how you hit it, a gram went for a hundred bucks and up. Carlo left the chemistry to his uncle. All he knew was that the stuff cut with heavy borax was mostly for the sucker trade. The amphetamine mixes or the mixes cut with mannite, which his uncle also used as a laxative, were for the better customers. Maybe he would get a kilo. By the time he dealt it all out, there could be maybe $50,000 in it for himself.

The uncle interrupted his thoughts. "Sam's a good pusher, no? Why don't you make a little deal with him?"

Carlo shook his head. "He keeps saying he wants to get out. You won't believe this, but he wants to open a beauty parlor with that cunt he goes around with. On my dough."

"In the first place, don't talk like that about women, even if she is a nigger. Women should be respected, except maybe whores." He paused to allow the lesson to sink in, but nothing was getting past the hard, sullen face except spaghetti. He went on resignedly. "You're right. I don't believe it. Why should he get out when he's doing okay? Have you thought maybe the beauty parlor'll be only a front?"

Carlo's fork froze. No, he hadn't thought of that. He had to hand it to the old man for seeing things clearly. It would not be a bad setup. All those cunts getting their hair done, then buying a little something along with the perfume and spray. Carlo returned silently to his spaghetti and thought some more. What if the uncle was wrong and Sam really was going legitimate? In that case, he could still be persuaded to cooperate. Either way, he would have a talk with the nigger when he caught up with him again. He would try to keep his temper under wraps. Things would be friendly but firm. He felt for the knife in his pocket.

CHAPTER

Twelve

At five o'clock, Becker awoke to an unpromising day, unrefreshed and still bewildered. In a dream, his mother had gone completely out of character and descended on him like an avenging angel, but what she was screaming at him for, he could not make out. Had his parents ever suspected him of anything but "normal" behavior? He had said nothing to make them suspicious, not a word of his time in Tangier nor of his meeting in the washroom with the two students and his sympathetic treatment of them. When he was fifteen, he bought a body-building magazine at a newsstand, had leafed admiringly through it in an obscure corner of Prospect Park, then thrown it into a trash receptacle rather than risk bringing it into the house. Irreligion, the mediocrity of his life, these were things his parents might logically nail him for, although they did not call for screams.

He sat on the side of his bed in the dark, smoking a cigarette and shaking his head. It was no use invoking the reality of things. Dreams had their own logic. He thought he discerned in this one a manifestation of guilt. He had outwardly lived the life of a conformist, but deep within him, it was all a lie. Even so, had he ever really descended into what could be called debauchery after that one experience fifty years ago? So, the younger generation would ask, what was the big deal? He puzzled himself back to sleep, and his second awakening two hours later was calmer though no more joyful.

His eyes peered at the shaded room, painfully rediscovering the chaos he had left seven hours before. He had to clean up; there was no getting away from it. It would be a first gesture in straightening out his life. He went to the bathroom, stubbing his toe twice on objects he could not completely make out, then pulled up the shade, flooding the jumbled room with daylight. Not sure where to start, he put on yesterday's clothes, then got on his hands and knees and gathered the scattered books.

An hour later, his back and legs ached from all the bending, but the apartment was almost neat. Exhausted and perspiring—it was not quite eight-fifteen with most of his day yet to come—he sat in his easy chair and considered the rest of his crowded agenda. The time when he would get up wondering how to fill the hours seemed part of someone else's existence. The new Becker had started out innocently enough with a sign on a church gate, and now his life had become intertwined with people so alien they might as well have been from Mars. Poor drug-pushing blacks, white gangsters, he had read about them, seen them on television and in movies. Now he was so involved with them that his home—his castle—had been invaded and his life, his winding-down life, put at risk.

Against all the inertia of his existence, he had made a choice, not to help defend blacks, but one black, okay, maybe two. Even that was undoubtedly more than he could manage, but it was too late. It was as if he had been given a mission he could no longer refuse because his own survival was in jeopardy. Saving others, he would save himself. So he had no choice at all, he reasoned.

He began to feel better, if not safer. At least he would no longer waste time. He used to have so much of it! Now he was torturing himself with doubts or collapsing in wet-eyed jeremiads as he had done last night. Kvetching was an old Jewish tradition. It would have to go, although he had enjoyed it, and it would not be as easy to give up as the kosher salami he replaced years ago by the better flavor of the Italian kind. It was another mark against him among his bench companions. It didn't matter. He had no more time for benches either.

Carlo had left him coffee and an English muffin amid the kitchen debris. The toaster was working though dented from its fall to the floor. He ate breakfast and felt better still. He looked at his rumpled clothes and, frowning, took them off, showered, shaved with his still intact Gillette, and put on a suit, a shirt, and a tie. For the police, he would appear a person of substance.

Before then, however, he had one phone call to make and two errands to do. Until it was time to get out of the way, he read the paper distractedly. There was more killing in Lebanon, famine in Africa, and a tax scandal in Washington. Nothing to compare to his situation. He kept looking at his watch and remembered he had done the same thing after signing up for the church school. Well, things had moved up a few notches on the life-purpose scale. He was with the big boys now.

At nine o'clock, he called the Twenty-fourth Precinct and got Detective Mulvaney. Yes, the detective said, if he had some information, he would be glad to see him: two o'clock at the station.

Before Becker ventured out at nine-thirty, he surveyed the terrain with his binoculars from the window. It was no longer an exercise in idle voyeurism but the same fear-laden move Sam had made from the darkened room only a few nights before. When Becker emerged from the front door, he looked around again, half expecting Carlo or his army to be lying in wait. He was too hyped up, he told himself. Calm down! However imbued he was with a sense of mission, he could not, after all, say that he was really enjoying himself. In the street, he had never up to now watched for anything but cracks in the sidewalk, what dogs left, traffic, or, in certain areas, a possible mugger. There was at the moment no one he could see who looked threatening, but his pulse felt fast anyway. If Carlo didn't get him, maybe his heart would.

At the bank, he withdrew two hundred dollars. The bedding store was open and glad to sell him a new mattress for delivery in late afernoon, exactly when, they couldn't say. Did they have cots? If he was planning a camping trip, they had a nice, light folding one in canvas and aluminum, ideal for a tent, the clerk said with a dubious look at him. Another, heavier one was the kind he remembered from the one miserable summer his parents had insisted he spend in a camp for boys much more athletic-minded than he was. He took the flimsier of the two. It would be as good for a small studio as for a tent, easily put up at night and stowed away in a closet during the day. Becker paid and agreed to be home by five o'clock. No, there was no doorman to accept the delivery.

Becker had decided to take Sam in. Walking to the bank, with uneasy sideways glances, he told himself he needed company. Besides, Sam could not go home alone, at least while he was recuperating. Not that his own place was really safe anymore. It had all become a matter of degree. With a stronger lock and the two bound together by mutual interest, maybe they could better fend off the enemy. The locksmith, two doors down from the bedding store, said he would be at the apartment by six with a lock as close to pickproof as sixty-five dollars could buy. There had not been so much activity at the Becker residence in years.

At the bus stop, Becker felt the pressure mount. Waiting there were the Reverend Greenway in clerical garb and a young woman in a severe, gray maternity dress that could not hide a well-advanced pregnancy. Greenway was cordial, as if ready to put the strained dinner behind him. "Ah, Mr. Becker, enjoyed my evening with you. You haven't met my wife; she's been away for a couple of weeks."

"I'm going to the police this afternoon," Becker said without prompting. Greenway nodded with a cheerful smile, as if relieved of the need to ask a question. They got on the bus together. "I missed you last night," Greenway said when they were seated.

"Had to leave early," Becker mumbled. "I'm on my way to see Sam," Becker added as if in answer to another unspoken question.

Greenway's expression turned sober. "I thought about what you said the other night. I was too harsh. You're right;

he should be given the benefit of the doubt. When he's able, he can come back to class. Unless you've changed your mind about him?"

Becker assured him he hadn't. He wondered if Greenway's wife was behind the change of heart. She looked gentle and spoke softly, a countervailing force to her husband's chairman-of-the-board manner. Becker expressed thanks but without effusion, anxious to avoid reinforcing Greenway's idea of him as a man with the kind of desires only a Unitarian could tolerate. Was he imagining that the two were looking at him peculiarly? He could not help what other people thought. It seemed to take the bus forever to reach his stop and allow him to say good-bye.

Sam was sitting in a chair, looking more cheerful than when Becker had left him. "Hiya, Mr. Becker. I'm gettin' out at the end of the week. They say I'm havin' an amazin' recuperation." He pronounced the word with spelling-bee deliberation, having heard it for the first time this morning. "So how you doin', Mr. Becker?"

Becker forgot one resolution. He kvetched at length on the cyclonic visit to his apartment but tried to end on a strong note as the black dropped his grin and stared at him wide-eyed. "Don't you worry," he said, patting Sam on the shoulder. "I'm sure Carlo will be put away soon."

"Yeah," Sam answered without conviction. "If he don' put us away first."

Becker changed the subject. "I think it would be a good idea if you came to my place when you leave here."

Sam looked at him and smiled. Was it the same look he had gotten from the Greenways? He was getting awfully self-conscious. "You don' have to do that," Sam said. "I'll jes' camp out at Carolyn's."

"Carolyn's isn't safe!" Becker said so loudly the other patients turned to stare. "I mean, she doesn't even have a front door that locks." This time, Sam's look was definitely funny, Becker thought. He toned down the vehemence. "My place isn't so safe either, I guess, but I'm putting in a new lock, and you'll be recuperating some more, and you'll need someone to look out for you, right? I mean, Carolyn has to work, doesn't she?"

Sam waited to make sure the outburst was over. "Mr. Becker, you sure are a funny man," he said. "You wasn't so happy when I ask to stay over that night."

Becker's voice began to rise again before he regained control. "That was different. Now we're in this together. I didn't want it that way, as you probably guessed, but that's the way it is. So what do you say?"

"Why, sure, Mr. Becker. That's cool," Sam said with a placating smile. He looked wonderingly at the old man, as if discovering him for the first time. The black had one more thought on the subject. "I gonna sleep on the floor again, or you got somethin' else in mind?"

"No, no," Becker rushed to answer. "I have a cot for you."

"That's cool too," Sam answered with another long look into the old man's eyes.

"Good," Becker said and moved quickly to change the subject. "Now, Sam, another thing. Have you thought about what I said yesterday?"

"Ya mean about the police?" Becker nodded, and Sam became solemn again. "Yeah, well I jes' don' know. I mean I don' cotton to the idea of doin' time. Not with startin' the store and everythin'."

"Sam, it's not a sure thing you'll be doing time. I've told you that already. The police will be so grateful for your help, you'll probably be able to strike a deal. Anyway, Carlo's a menace; something has to be done about him. You may never get to start the store with him around. You as much as said so yourself."

"I know what I said. I jes' don' like gettin' mixed up with the cops."

Becker sighed and cupped his hands to rest his head, which was starting to ache. "Sam," he said after a pause, "I'm going to the police this afternoon. It's for me and for you and for Carolyn. Are you going to help or not?"

Sam went back to his bed, an exhausted look on his face. He tried a smile. "I guess I'm still a little weak." He spent some time adjusting his pillow and the covers, then turned to Becker, who was standing over him. "Okay, I trust you, Mr. Becker. But you not goin' to tell 'em about the money. We needs that money, ya unnerstan'?"

"I understand. I'll keep as much back as I can. But expect a visit from the cops soon, okay?"

Sam nodded. "Mr. Becker, can you bring that money to me tomorrow? I'll take care of it here. I got bills to pay; it ain't cheap gettin' knifed. And Carolyn is startin' to order equipment."

Becker did not even bother to wonder where Sam would keep the envelope. He suddenly felt light as air, and when he walked out, there was more spring in his step than most seventy-year-olds can manage.

The bank, the bedding store, the locksmith, and an unplanned visit with the Greenways thrown in. Not bad for a retiree's day, with the climax yet to come. Together with some stocktaking in his kitchen, he fixed himself a softboiled egg from a fresh supply, dipping small pieces of buttered roll into the yolk, French style. He would take another chance on his cholesterol count. He was taking a chance on everything else. He set his alarm, lay down on his eviscerated bed, and dozed off for a half hour. He awoke feeling stronger and walked to his next appointment.

Headquarters for the Twenty-fourth Precinct was in a plain, modern, yellow-brick building, constructed at a time when the city was obviously trying to save on architects' fees. Becker had the impression of being in the middle of a self-contained though alien village: a public health clinic and library branch across the way, a playground alongside, and large, equally unimaginative city-owned apartment buildings stretching for blocks around. The faces on the streets were black or Hispanic. The old man quickened his step and entered the station. He had to sign in and announce his business before being asked to wait in intimidating silence until Mulvaney was ready for him.

"Mr. Becker?" The detective loomed over him, looking even bigger than Becker had remembered. It seemed to Becker that he was not wearing the same suit, but so what? Even detectives ought to be able to afford two suits. Mulvaney led him into a room furnished only with a table and two chairs. Was it the interrogation room he had seen on television shows, where cops occasionally got rough? Becker looked nervously at a mirror, which he imagined served as a window from the other side.

"Well, sir," Mulvaney said gently. "You have something you want to tell me?" The question ended with a smile that Becker supposed was meant to dispel his inhibitions.

Becker recalled their brief encounter on Broadway, and Mulvaney remembered it well, not any of the people he had approached but the fact he had displayed a photograph and vainly tried to elicit information. "Well, I was not sure at that time," Becker continued as if to excuse himself for not having been helpful, "but certain events since lead me to believe that the man in the picture is named Carlo and he is in the drug business. That is all I know about him."

If Mulvaney would settle for that pompous but admittedly thin exposé, Becker was ready to leave. But the detective seemed in no hurry to end the conversation.

"We know his name is Carlo, Mr. Becker, and we know he is in the drug business. Tell me about the events."

So there would obviously have to be more since he had done nothing for Mulvaney except whet his appetite. "May I smoke?" Becker asked.

"Feel free," Mulvaney said ingratiatingly and produced an ashtray from the table drawer. Becker lit up and took a few drags before going on.

"A young man I know was attacked and knifed in Riverside Park a few days ago. It was Carlo who did it, as the young man is prepared to testify. Then there was a break-in at the Unitarian Church on Ninety-third Street, and there is reason to believe it was also Carlo's doing."

"This young man, what's his name?"

Becker told him, and the detective rose and left the old man to puff away in nervous solitude, wondering if he was being watched and trying to keep his eyes off the mirror. When Mulvaney came back, he had a file in his hand. "This case of Carlton White was handled by another precinct," Mulvaney explained, "but we got the reports on it because I'm coordinating antidrug activity on the West Side." He put the file on the table and looked closely at Becker. "According to what the victim told my colleagues, he didn't know his attacker," he said, almost as a question.

Becker shifted uncomfortably in his chair and stubbed out his nearly finished cigarette. "Yes, well, he wasn't in good shape when he was interrogated the first time. Maybe now that he's feeling better, he'll remember more."

"Yeah, maybe," the detective answered with a noncommittal tone. He looked through the file again. "I see my friends asked you a few questions too. This guy really a student of yours? What does he study?"

Mulvaney's incredulity was patent. Becker made an effort to keep his voice matter-of-fact. "I teach him English in a class sponsored by the church I mentioned, you know, the one they broke into. He wants to get his high school diploma."

"What for? To push dope?"

That's what I said once, Becker thought. How could he have considered the police so dumb they would not suspect Sam of being in the same business as Carlo?

"Mr. Becker, I asked you a question." The old man came out of his reverie with a start.

"Yes, I'm sorry. I was thinking of something. The boy wants to go into business, open up a beauty parlor with a girlfriend who's a beautician, and feels he needs to know a little better English."

Mulvaney was relentless. "We think he has a business already. Tell me what you know about his dealing in drugs."

"Well, he's never tried to deal with me." Weak, but why

compromise Sam more than necessary? Mulvaney tried another tack.

"Do you know why Carlo went after him?" Becker paused to take out another cigarette.

"Some misunderstanding about money," he said between quick puffs. "Maybe you'd better ask Sam."

"Sam?"

"Carlton White's nickname. His friends call him Sam."

"And you're a friend? Not just a teacher who sees him once or twice a week?"

For the third time today, he was getting that look. Did nobody believe in altruism? Perhaps cops had an excuse. They had to deal with too many ulterior motives to assume anyone was a good Samaritan.

"I've gotten to know him," Becker said. "He wants to improve himself, so I've tried to encourage him." He knew the answer sounded lame, and all it got from Mulvaney was an "Uh-huh." Becker wanted desperately for the conversation to be over but felt a need to go on, to defend himself. "I'm no friend of drug pushers. I'm no friend of drugs either."

"I didn't say you were, Mr. Becker," Mulvaney answered gently, with just the suggestion of a smile. He suddenly changed the subject. "Tell me why you think it was Carlo who broke into the church."

"Well, as I said, there may have been some dispute with Sam over money, and Carlo may have thought he could find it in the classroom." He was being too cute with his "mays," as Mulvaney made clear.

"Mr. Becker, are you sure you're telling me all you know?"

"I'm trying to cooperate, Mr. Mulvaney," Becker said with some exasperation. "After all, I called you; you didn't call me."

The detective conceded the point. "Have you been attacked or threatened personally by Carlo?" he asked.

"No, I can't say that I have," Becker answered. It was true, he reasoned to himself. His person had not been attacked, and he had not talked with Carlo. There was still a need to justify his actions. "This Carlo is a dangerous person for everybody, and I want to help put him away."

"You haven't talked to anyone else about Carlo?"

"Anyone else?"

"Yeah, you know, other people in the police department."

"You're the only one whose name I had," Becker answered. He wondered what Mulvaney was getting at. Maybe he didn't like competition and wanted all the credit for this case.

The detective stood up. The conversation was over. "Thank you for coming in," he said. "I have your name, address, and phone number, and I'll be in touch." He held out his hand, then had another thought. "One more thing, Mr. Becker. You spot Carlo, or you have any other information, you call me, okay? Don't try to do something about him yourself." For once, Becker felt sincere. He assured Mulvaney he had no intention of going after Carlo alone.

He felt washed out but relieved. He had imagined it would be worse. It had been more casual than he expected, no deposition to dictate and sign as part of the record that a district attorney might later examine. He thought Mulvaney had curiously let him off the hook at various points. The detective had not followed up, for instance, the question of friendship to where he would have had him answering red-faced and stammering. There was no crime to pursue there, Becker supposed, only a moral judgment Mulvaney tactfully kept to himself. As he said, it could have been worse, but he felt tired all the same. He walked into the street and headed toward Broadway. On one side of the playground, an empty bench beckoned, and he sat down to smoke his fourth cigarette of the morning.

Ten seconds later he found himself flanked, hemmed in, it seemed to him, by two large men, one white, one black, both in well-cut business suits. His heart began to beat wildly. The cops-and-robbers game he had involved himself in was moving so fast he felt dizzy. He was one hundred feet from the station, but it might as well have been on the other side of town. He tried to rise, but the black gripped his arm tightly. "Take it easy, Pop," he said, "or you tired of livin'?"

"You Becker?" the white man asked. All he could do was nod. It was the black's turn.

"What you tell the police?"

"What are you talking about? Who are you?" Becker asked. Try as he might, he could not keep the quaver out of his voice.

"Don't shit us, man," the white continued. "You just been in with the cops, right? You say anything about Carlo?"

"Who's Carlo?"

The grip on his arm tightened further. "Hey, didn' my friend here tell ya not to shit us," the black said, putting his broad face an inch from Becker's. There was liquor on his breath, and Becker turned toward the white, who was smiling at him as if playing the good guy. But the black was not finished. "So what did ya say about Carlo?"

"I don't know any Carlo," Becker protested. "The police just wanted to ask me about a break-in at a church where I teach." He had a sudden afterthought. "Did this Carlo do that?"

For an answer, the two men looked silently at each other. The white turned to Becker and resumed his smile. "We got a friendly message for you," he said. "We want you to stay away from the cops. For your health, ya know?" Becker didn't exactly know, but he had an idea. He nodded. The two men got up as precisely as they had sat down, and the black leaned over for a parting shot. "I don' know about you, man, but I wouldn' like both my kneecaps shot off." They walked off without looking back, then stopped at the playground exit and stood talking casually.

Becker waited ten minutes, but still they would not leave. He got up too and, steeling himself, walked past them without looking at either one. He wanted to go back to the security of the station, but sooner or later he would have to come out again. He looked down at his knees and decided to call Mulvaney from home. He had enlisted in the army of good to defeat the army of evil. So far, it was the enemy that was making points. Was it still possible to resign?

He walked shakily toward Broadway, feeling eyes boring into his back. It was not until he reached the neon lights and crowded aisles of his favorite supermarket that he felt a sense of security. This was the humdrum life he used to know, the one that had occupied all his time and depressed him so much that his mind constantly sought escape. Now he looked enviously at the other shoppers. All they had on their minds was eating tonight. All right, maybe they had problems too. All the same, how many of those cart pushers could complain of being wedged in between two hoodlums only a few minutes ago? Distracted, he turned a corner on his way toward the soup shelves and crashed into a cart. Mrs. Klein was on the other end.

"Why, Mr. Becker, I didn't expect to run into you." She giggled at her little pun. "Did I hurt you?"

"No, no harm done," he answered. "I wasn't looking. I'm sorry." He glanced at the cart. A sack of potatoes lay mixed with other fruits and vegetables and a carton of sour cream.

"They're having a sale on potatoes. Ten pounds for a dollar."

Becker could find no comment equal to the occasion. "Thank you again for the pleasant evening," he said.

"My pleasure, Mr. Becker." He started to walk past when she halted him.

"Mr. Becker, do you like latkes?"

Oh, Mrs. Klein, you temptress! First Mozart, now latkes. From the ridiculous to the sublime. He wondered at her taste for latkes, she who prided herself on her American upbringing.

Mrs. Klein's loud voice bored through his thoughts. "So Mr. Becker, why don't you come for a little light supper this evening, some vichyssoise and latkes."

That's a lot of potatoes, Becker thought, glancing at his

and Mrs. Klein's midriffs. Still, it was a better prospect than any other he had been offered today. "That would be nice, Mrs. Klein. Thank you."

"Seven o'clock?" She was off, charging up the aisle with her cart toward the checkout counter. She had rushed things a bit but had not scared him off. There would be a lot of grating and pureeing to do, but it was all for a good cause, she told herself. He looked a bit lost, even worried, she thought. Obviously, he needed someone.

Becker checked out his soup and headed home, a block behind Mrs. Klein. He saw her stop at a store window and hung back so as not to catch up with her. The evening ahead would be enough. He went down a side street he rarely took. A sprawling brownstone Lutheran church stood on the corner, a large sign covering one wall. "Christ died for you," he read. "What are you doing for him?" Plenty, he thought, more than was allowable to a Jew, even a bad one. He should stop reading signs on churches.

CHAPTER

Thirteen

True to Becker's word, the police were at Sam's bedside the next morning. The law was represented by Detective Mulvaney himself, abetted by a uniformed officer, who stationed himself at the entrance to the ward.

"I'm Detective Sergeant Mulvaney," he told Sam once he had noted that the only other black in the room was an elderly woman asleep.

"Nice threads," Sam said.

"What?"

"Nice threads. I like what ya got on."

"Thanks," Mulvaney said, carefully hiking up the trousers of his light-blue summer suit as he sat down. "But that's not what I came to hear. You didn't seem to know much the first time somebody talked to you." He looked solemnly at the black, who responded with a grin.

"Yeah, well, I wasn' feelin' good then."

"Feeling better?"

"A-okay, as the spacemen say. I'm gettin' out in a coupla days."

"I hope your memory has improved too. Tell me who you had the fight with."

"You gonna read me my rights?"

"What for? I'm not arresting you."

"Oh." Sam looked almost disappointed. "You got a cigarette?"

"Don't smoke. Who'd you have the fight with?"

"Yeah, right. It was a dude I seen a coupla times aroun'; he got a bad temper."

Mulvaney began to rap on the bars of the bed. "You wanna stop shitting me, Sam, if that's what they call you?"

"That's what they call me. It's a guy who goes by the name of Carlo. We were rappin' a little, and he got pissed off."

Mulvaney produced a picture. "Is this Carlo?" Sam nodded and the detective continued.

"What did he get pissed off about?"

"He loaned me a little bread a while back, an' I didn' happen to have it on me jes' right then and there, you know what I mean?"

"You're a pusher, right?"

"Hey, man, I don' have to answer that. That's, that's . . . ," Sam paused to get his tongue in position, "that's self-incriminatin'."

Mulvaney stared at the youth, who stared back defiantly before breaking into a grin again. The detective gripped the bars tightly as if to restrain himself from grabbing Sam's hospital gown and slapping him a couple of times.

"What did you borrow money from Carlo for?"

"I'm startin' a little business, a beauty parlor with a friend. I needed a little cash."

"And how were you going to pay it back?"

"From the profits, but Carlo, he not a patient man. I guess he don' wanna wait that long."

"What do you know about the beauty parlor business?"

"Not much, but my friend, she knows some things."

Sam had a feeling he was not being pressed too hard, as though Mulvaney was not very interested in him. For years, he had successfully evaded police interest, but now that it had shown up in the person of Mulvaney, it was not too hard to fend off. He relaxed. There were some questions about the location of the new shop, when it was starting up, who the girlfriend was. The detective jotted down the answers. He made another stab at identifying the source of the seed money for the business but gave it up when Sam stuck to his story of a loan.

"What you gonna do about Carlo?" Mulvaney asked.

"I don' know. What should I do?"

"I mean, are you pressing charges or what?"

Sam hesitated. Of all the answers he had rehearsed through part of the night, this was the hardest, the one he would have to explain the most if he was ever pinned down by Becker.

"Well, no, Mr. Detective," he finally said. "The way I figger, we was havin' a disagreement like, an' he jes' got a little hot under the collar, ya know what I mean? But we's still friends."

Mulvaney nodded and rose. "If that's the way you want it. But a word of advice. You keep your nose clean, you hear?"

"Hey, that's the story of my life."

The detective started to walk away but stopped for a last thought.

"Where you staying when you get out of here?"

"With another friend."

"Who's that?"

"A man who's helpin' me with my education."

For the first time Mulvaney looked surprised. "David Becker?"

"Yeah. You know him?"

"He came to see me yesterday. He said Carlo's no friend and you would testify against him."

"Mr. Becker an okay guy, but he gettin' a little old, ya know. He gets things wrong sometimes." Sam put a finger to his forehead.

"How come you're staying with him?" Mulvaney asked.

"He gonna take care of me until I get on my feet. Ain't that nice of him?"

"Yeah," Mulvaney said dryly and walked out, the other policeman behind him. Outside, he ordered the cop back to the station and headed downtown.

Sam's second visitor was Becker, carrying a briefcase and nervously surveying the room before he sat down.

"There was a cop here," Sam said.

Becker ignored the almost reproachful tone. "How did it go?" he asked.

"Okay, I guess."

"You guess? What did he ask you?"

"If I knew who knifed me. I tol' him."

"Good. He made you sign a statement?" Sam shook his head.

Becker looked at him puzzled. "He didn't take it all down or ask you to come to the station house and make a formal deposition?"

Sam continued to shake his head.

"Who was the cop?" Becker persisted.

"He say his name's Mulvaney."

Becker's mind went back to his own conversation with the detective. Mulvaney had a decidedly casual way of operating, he thought. Maybe that was the way things were done in the preliminary stages of an investigation. After all, what did he know? Still, here was one of Carlo's victims on whose testimony a case could be built, and why had nothing been put in writing?

Sam lay back on his elbows, staring at the point where his toes formed a small tent in the bedcovers. For an extrovert, he seemed extraordinarily taciturn to Becker.

"You feeling all right?" he asked.

Sam allowed himself a grin. "Why, sure, I feelin' better all the time."

The old man took a large manila envelope from the briefcase and laid it on the bed. "I brought what you asked for," he said quietly with a look around the room. Sam nodded, gave Becker another grin, and put the envelope under the sheets, his hand resting on the slight bulge.

Becker took out a sheet of paper from the envelope. "I've brought something you didn't ask for."

He handed the sheet to Sam, who held it as if it were a summons.

"Hey, what's this?"

"A couple of English exercises," Becker said. "You've missed a few classes. I'm supposed to be teaching you English, remember?'

"Yeah, I'll get right on it," Sam answered with no show

of enthusiasm. He laid the sheet on his night table and changed the subject.

"Carolyn, she call me. She been a busy girl. The shop's shapin' up; looks like we be in business in two weeks, maybe less."

"That's nice. I'm glad it's working out. Are you still getting out at the end of the week?"

"That's what they tell me. This place, it give me the creeps."

Becker got up. "So I'll come Friday morning to take you home," he said.

"That's cool. See ya Friday."

Becker walked out bemused by what he had just said. Taking Sam home. The father taking back the wayward son after years of separation. The thrill of expectation made him momentarily forget last night's scene with Mrs. Klein. He had tried to ward off a possibly embarrassing outburst later in Sam's presence by telling her over the latkes and sour cream about his future boarder. Her fork stopped halfway to her mouth, and she stared at him as if he had just confessed to rape.

She put her fork down. "David," she began. It was the first time she had called him by his first name, an idea for fostering intimacy she hit upon while grating the potatoes. "David," she repeated, "you know I don't like to pry into other people's affairs, but why are you bringing this ...," she searched for a word, "person into our building?"

She sounded like an aggrieved lover about to be replaced. Becker broke down and told her the story. She stared openmouthed, gulping when he came to the envelope full of money he had stored in her safe and ipso facto her own involuntary involvement in a filthy world she had sought all her life to ignore. She had so wanted the evening to go well. It was to have been phase two of Operation Seduction, but he was escaping her. The double life she had had so much trouble imagining was not only real but being lived just two doors from her and with what kind of person!

What was this obsession with blacks? Why blacks? She had all she could do to hold back the tears as she bit vehemently into her pancake.

"It will be only temporary, Mrs. Klein," Becker said, looking at her placatingly as though guessing her thoughts. "It's only to help him out for a while. He's been ill."

"You have always helped out your students that way, I suppose." If she meant to rile him with sarcasm, Becker thought, she would fail.

"I can't say I have," he answered evenly. "But I never really had students who needed that kind of help when I taught high school. I am doing what I can for a member of an underprivileged minority." Always when he became solemn, things came out more pompous than he intended. Mrs. Klein was not mollified.

"Yes, and endangering yourself and everybody else in this building. Why can't you leave the whole thing to the police?"

"I've brought in the police, but they're not going to give Sam protection."

"He has no family?"

"That's often the case with blacks," Becker answered.

"Yes, I know, but whose fault is that?" she said testily.

"I'm not sure. Maybe it has something to do with poverty and education." He wanted to end the subject right there. He was not sure why blacks had the family problems they had, with such a high proportion raised by single mothers. Jews had lived in poor ghettos and had kept a strong family tradition. He would have to study the question more before crossing swords again with Mrs. Klein. "Anyway, you'll hardly notice he's here," he said. "The latkes are delicious," he told her for the third time.

Mrs. Klein could not understand how an elderly Jew with a lot of time on his hands would want to spend it befriending young blacks, courting danger in the process, instead of caring for his own kind, working at a community center, for instance, or collecting for the United Jewish Appeal, anything that would keep his priorities straight and keep him out of trouble. She looked at him as a mother would at a perplexing teenager and decided it better to drop the subject lest harsh words alienate them forever. She regaled her guest after dinner with albums of family photographs and records of Richard Tauber singing Viennese operetta until, stealing a glance at his watch, he decided he could gracefully take his leave.

He had arrived for the little dinner party already unnerved by the afternoon encounter in the playground. Mulvaney had not been in when he called just after getting home and had not been helpful when Becker reached him this morning. "Those people play rough," the detective said, rather needlessly, it seemed to Becker, and in the offhand way he might use to describe a gangster picture he had just seen.

"But how did they know I'd been to see you, and so fast?" Becker asked plaintively.

He could almost hear Mulvaney shrug. "I don't know; they probably followed you from the house. We'd better not see each other for a while. If you have something to tell me, call."

Now, from what Sam had just told him of Mulvaney's visit, the detective had done little more than go through the motions again. Heading uptown from the hospital in the subway, Becker felt dispirited. He had enlisted the help of the police department, had indeed made a big thing of it with Sam. But somehow, he felt no safer than before. He might just as well have kept the whole thing to himself for all Mulvaney seemed to care. The police, Becker reluctantly concluded, evidently had bigger fish to fry. Since the day Mulvaney had canvassed the neighborhood, the capture of Carlo had dropped way down in priority.

"Not for me," Becker muttered. The plain, primly dressed young woman next to him looked up from her book. "You don't like *Death in Venice?*" she asked with a small smile.

He stared at her, then at the book, which he had always meant to read, with a lot of other books. "Oh, I was thinking of something else," he said. "I don't remember the book very well. It's been a long time."

The woman placed a mark in the book and closed it. "It's about the obsession of an older man, a writer and intellectual, with a young boy," she explained. "Perhaps you saw the picture?"

Becker shook his head. He could guess at how the story turned out. "He has a painful end, if I recall right."

Through dark-rimmed spectacles, she looked at him so sternly Becker had the feeling she was about to arrest him. "Serves him right," she snapped. "One should never become a slave to anyone or anything. With Aschenbach, it was like taking drugs."

"I guess Mann didn't like that kind of sex," Becker ventured.

Her hand impatiently brushed the observation aside. "That's not the point," she said. "You can be gay"—that word again!—"and control yourself, like anyone else."

Becker might have warmed to her, but she was competing with the roar of the train so successfully that the whole car was privy to the discussion. Across the aisle, a man giggled into his newspaper. He had close-cropped graying hair, a mustache, and skin that was starting to become leathery and creased. He wore the outfit of a younger man: jeans, a T-shirt, leather jacket (although the subway car was almost stifling), and running shoes the color of ten-day-old New York snow. Becker saw men like that on Broadway, including two who had strolled along with intertwined fingers. He marveled at their daring until he realized he was the only one taking notice of them. Now he stared without being aware of it at the man opposite him, only half-listening to the continuing lecture. He fidgeted until 96th Street came into view, signaling the end of the literary salon. He gave the Mann devotee a quick smile and nod and retreated to the door. "Nice talking to you!" she called out. He watched as the train pulled away, and she once again immersed herself in the book and the perils of obsession.

Maybe this was as good a time as any to catch up on deferred reading. On Broadway, Becker headed for the same bookstore where, with the help of a fat volume of French impressionists, he had scored his only triumph to date in the drug world. For $3.95, well within his price range, he found the Mann novella and seven other stories. The benches were strangely empty although it was not yet noon on a warm day. That's fine, he thought; I don't want to talk anyway. He opened to the first page. Aschenbach, he read, "was overwrought by a morning of hard, nerve-taxing work, which work had not ceased to exact his uttermost in the way of sustained concentration, conscientiousness, and tact." Becker smiled wanly. There are mornings like that.

A siren wiped out the turn-of-the-century quiet of Munich as it passed the intersection where Becker sat. He closed the book and watched an ambulance screech to a stop a half block further on. For the first time, he noticed a crowd gathered in front of a decrepit building. Becker recognized it as a hotel he had passed many times with indifference. Its entrance was decorated with a graffiti writer's obscenities, and curtains in shreds covered the unwashed windows. No traveler had stopped there for years, and it was now given over to permanent occupancy by men and women whose next sanctuary, Becker guessed from their looks, would be the streets.

He joined the crowd as a second ambulance drew up. Four policemen were trying to keep clear a passage for the ambulance attendants, who bore a stretcher on which lay a young, softly moaning black. Behind came other attendants bearing two bodies in plastic bags. A man in a white apron broke the respectful hush.

"They shoulda closed the place up a long time ago," he said. He pointed to a little cheese store next to the hotel and asked nobody in particular, "Howya supposed to carry on a business with what goes on here?"

"What happened?" Becker asked. The shopkeeper could only surmise.

"I run out when I hear shooting, and the next thing I see, two guys are running out and this black kid with a lot of blood on him is following 'em and waving his hands and yelling for help, and then he staggers back in, and there's some more shots and a couple more guys come scootin' out and head down the block. But I been telling 'em it hadda happen; it's a big hangout for junkies and dealers and every other kind of weirdo. It seems like every day there was a fight."

"Okay, let's move on! There's nothing more to see!" one of the policemen said loudly. The crowd retreated, then broke up into little knots of discussion. "Maybe you'll do somethin' now!" the cheese merchant yelled as he returned to his store. Becker followed him in and fished out a picture of Sam that Carolyn had taken in the hospital with a Polaroid.

Becker pointed. "Have you ever seen this man around here?" The storekeeper studied the picture and shook his head. "I don't know; they all look alike to me. Yeah, maybe. There was a lot of 'em like that comin' in and out. There was a police raid a coupla weeks ago, and I asked a cop why, and he said the hotel was a meeting place for dealers and junkies." He jabbed his finger at Becker. "I'll tell ya one thing; it don' do my business no good to have that scum next door. The other day one of them threw up all over the sidewalk in front of the store. That's nice for customers, huh?"

His voice grated on Becker. "It's not nice for anybody," he said. His voice rose. "The drug scene is all over the country. It's not just your store."

"Yeah, well, I'll worry about me, and the rest of the country can worry about itself."

He turned his back on Becker and began to arrange cheese in a display. But the old man was not finished. "Don't you see the awful waste?" he shouted. "There are so many people getting hooked, and there is so much greed and violence and death and corruption that comes from that, it's a nightmare. The whole country, the whole world, is going to hell, and all you worry about is your store."

Becker was waving a chunk of Gruyère as he harangued the startled cheeseman. Finally he subsided. His eyes moistened so that he could no longer see distinctly and he began to tremble. The merchant wondered if he should call the police to get rid of him. "Listen, buddy," he said, "don't make speeches to me. I ain't got nothing to do with the drug problem. You wanna buy somethin', stay. If not, I got things to do." Becker did not move. The merchant held out his arms, appealing for understanding. "If I don't look out for my store, who will? I got a family to support. I can't go out to save the world. I have to make a livin'. So what's with you?"

Becker calmed down. He had been getting worked up a little too often lately. There were good enough reasons but still . . . Almost in apology, he bought the Gruyère he had brandished. The storekeeper patted him on the shoulder and told him to take it easy and not worry so much. But heading home, he could not get Sam out of his mind. He would not be at all surprised if Sam was familiar with the sordid interior of the hotel. But for the fact that he was already a victim, he could have been the one on the stretcher. Becker decided he would recount the incident to his young friend as a lesson to buck up his determination to leave that part of his life behind him. It would help, of course, Becker thought, if Carlo would leave both their lives alone. But there was no way to guarantee that except to put Carlo behind bars or . . . Becker halted the line of thought there. He wondered where Carlo was and what the police were doing about him.

The newspaper account the next day informed Becker over coffee and rye toast that the police had found more than four pounds of high-quality cocaine in one of the hotel rooms. A gang from East Harlem had gotten word of the cache before the police had, and its attack on the hotel and the owners of the treasure explained the gun battle. Two lives were lost, one from each side, and one person, a defender, was in critical condition. Five people, all defenders, were arrested. Those attackers still alive fled empty-handed, some of them possibly wounded. The street value of the narcotic was put in the millions. Becker was used to reading of amounts like that, but the thought of that much lying about in a sordid hotel room made him swallow hard on his toast. As far as he could figure out, Sam's resolution to quit was based on the belief that wealth like that is of no use if you're dead. Still, he took scissors and clipped the story out as an aid to Sam's education.

By Friday, Becker had made a number of preparations for Sam's homecoming. He had looked at the cot, even lain on it, and felt he could not subject Sam's wounded body to the hard, unyielding canvas. He found a small mattress to fit it, then sheets that fit the mattress. Before leaving for the hospital, he made up the cot and nervously surveyed the cleaned-up studio like a hostess about to have her big reception.

Sam was dressed and sitting cheerfully in a wheelchair, Carolyn alongside him. There was a stop at the cashier's office, where the woman behind the window watched in fascination as Sam peeled off $1,200 in fifties and hundreds with the bored look of an important man forced to attend to details. Outside, he broke into laughter and waved the envelope in the air.

"Man, you see the look on that lady's face? She don' get to meet that much cash at one time."

"Sam," Becker said, looking around the street, "if I were you, I wouldn't wave the envelope around."

Sam gave the envelope to Carolyn, who stowed it in her capacious shoulder bag. "Right, Mr. Becker," he said. "Anyway, after the hospital's cut, it ain't that heavy."

"Whatever it is, let's be discreet," Becker said, and waved down a taxi.

"We's gonna be ready to open next week, Mr. Becker," Carolyn said as they rode uptown. "The plumber, he come this afternoon to hook up the washbasins, and they's deliverin' chairs and dryers Monday."

"That's nice, Carolyn," Becker said. He looked at her doubtfully. "Are you going to be the only beautician?"

"Got two friends who's gonna be workin' with me. They's from the place where I worked before. Ya shoulda seen the boss when we tol' her we's leavin'."

Sam and Carolyn found this so uproarious that all further conversation was halted for the rest of the way, and the driver kept looking nervously back at them. That was the wonder of young people, Becker thought. In the middle of all the problems, they could laugh. He could manage only a smile, then not even that, when they arrived at the door and found Detective Mulvaney in front of the building with another man.

For someone who so desperately wanted friends and allies, Becker found himself curiously unexcited by Mulvaney's unexpected appearance. There was something about the detective, whether it was his diffidence or his seeming lack of interest, that put Becker off.

"Hello there, Mr. Becker," Mulvaney said, with a curt nod to Sam and Carolyn, after the three had piled out of the cab. "We've been waiting for you." He pulled a piece of paper from the inside pocket of his suit. "I have here a search warrant for your apartment."

He smiled amiably at the three stunned faces and held out the court order to Becker, who stared at it without taking it.

"A search warrant?" Becker said. "You want to search my apartment?"

"You got it."

"What for?"

Mulvaney pointed to Sam. "This young man is a suspected drug dealer. We wish to verify that you have not stored narcotics on his behalf."

Sam came to life. "Hey, man, where you come off accusin' me . . . ?"

"Shut up!" Mulvaney cut in. "Just another word and we'll run you in." He turned to Becker. "You ready to go upstairs?"

The old man nodded. He felt drained of resistance. He could not seriously argue with Mulvaney about Sam. It was not surprising that the detective had not taken seriously the idea of the youth going straight. Yet he felt more uneasy than ever about the detective.

In the apartment, Mulvaney and his colleague moved quickly through drawers, closets, cabinets, and shelves but created surprisingly little disorder. An improvement on Carlo, Becker noted. Even doing this, the policemen seemed halfhearted.

Mulvaney signified they had finished by turning to Sam. "We'll be back, in case you got ideas of moving stuff in here."

Becker's normal deference for representatives of the law had been severely strained. "Mr. Mulvaney, I am a law-abiding citizen," he said in a choked voice. "Have been all my life. How could you have even thought I would have drugs here or would allow any in the future?"

"Sorry, Mr. Becker, but we have to cover all angles. You'd be surprised the kinds of people that are into drugs these days."

Becker continued with the same indignant tone. "Well, not me. Whose side are you on, anyway? And what are you doing about Carlo?"

Mulvaney remained unruffled. "Can't do much," he answered. "This one here ain't making charges." He looked at Sam, then walked out with his partner.

It was Becker's and Carolyn's turn to stare at Sam. "Did I hear right?" the old man asked between clenched teeth. "You didn't sign a complaint against Carlo?"

Sam held up his arms as if to ward off a blow. "Now don' go gettin' your balls in an uproar, Mr. Becker. I never said I would. I jes' don' know if the fuzz is gonna help that much, and like I said already, I don' like gettin' mixed up with them dudes."

"Why didn't you tell me?"

"Ya never asked."

Becker collapsed into a chair and sighed. "What about Carlo? He almost killed you. You'd rather be mixed up with him?"

Sam stretched out wearily on the cot and grinned. "I tell ya, Mr. Becker, now that I know what to expect, I'll be ready the next time." He reached for the envelope on the floor beside him, pulled out a sheet of paper, and thrust it at the old man.

"What's this?"

"Your English exercises," Sam answered. Then he went off to sleep, leaving his companions to gaze helplessly at him, then at each other.

"Did you know Sam wasn't going to do anything about Carlo?" Becker asked in a low, intense voice.

Carolyn shook her head and gave Becker a weak smile.

"But why?" he went on. "Isn't he afraid of him anymore?" He paused and stared at the sleeping youth. "Or does he plan to do some more business with him? You know anything about that, Carolyn?" She looked up startled and began to answer loudly. Becker motioned toward the kitchen.

"Mr. Becker," she said once they were seated at the kitchen table, "Sam's not in the business anymore. Besides, he couldn't get anythin' goin' again with Carlo even if he wanted to. That Carlo, he real mad. I know."

"I guess you do," Becker said gently. "I have to go teach my class in a few minutes. You'll talk to him, won't you, when he wakes up?" He made coffee, and they sat quietly drinking it until the telephone rang. By the time Becker could get to it, Sam was awake.

"Mr. Becker, you'll be by for your class in a little while?" Greenway asked. Becker said he certainly would; did the reverend doubt it?

"Not at all," Greenway answered hastily. "It's just . . . I was wondering if you could drop by the office afterward?"

Becker promised, silently wondering what was bothering Greenway. "I have to go teach the class," he told Sam. "We'll talk more later."

With Becker out the door, Carolyn came out of the kitchen and looked accusingly at Sam.

"What you up to with Carlo?" she asked.

Sam patted the cot as an invitation for her to sit next to him. "I ain't up to nothin' yet. I thought about talkin' to the cops, I really did, an' I decided I ain't helpin' out no cops and no DA. When did they ever give a nigger a break? An' supposin' Carlo gets sent away, how long will it be 'fore he's out and lookin' for me. I'll jes' take my chances now." He looked at his watch, then at her. "He gonna be gone about an hour. What we wastin' time for?"

She smiled. "What you mean?"

He pulled her against him and caressed her back. "You know what I mean."

"You sure you can do somethin' without bustin' a gut?"

Sam simply pointed to the daybed. "There's more room over there." They spilled clothing over the floor and Sam lay back, the bandages a white splash over the chocolate skin. "You're gonna do the work," he whispered. He took her breasts in his outstretched hands as she straddled him. She let herself down eagerly onto his stiff, upright cock, first pumping slowly, careful not to lose the hard, throbbing fullness within her, then speeding up until, in less than a minute, they both gasped and spent their lust in warm, liquid bursts. She remained impaled on him, ready for a signal to start again. He drew her head down and held it for a long tongue-penetrating kiss. "That was jes' a warm-up," he said after a while. He thrust up into her, and she giggled and began to move again like a locomotive getting under way. They had time to come three times, put their clothes back on, and straighten up before Becker's key was heard in the door.

It might not have mattered what they had been doing, so lost and preoccupied did he appear. He barely glanced at them as he dropped into his armchair with a grunt and passed his hand over his eyes repeatedly.

"You okay?" Sam asked from his cot.

Becker seemed to be considering the question. He stared lengthily at Sam, then at Carolyn, and finally answered, "If you must know, no, I am not okay. I saw Greenway after the class. You know what he told me?"

They shook their heads.

"He said that he was very sorry, but he could not continue to have me teach the class. Also that Sam could no longer be in it. Only a few days ago he told me the exact opposite. He said he was aware of that, but he had thought about it some more and decided that as long as we are there, his church is in danger, and he cannot afford that."

Sam and Carolyn were afraid that Becker was about to break down and cry. They sat in silence as he went on.

"All I wanted to do was help. Greenway seemed happy enough to see me when I came to volunteer. I asked him what danger we were causing him. He said we were mixed up with some shady elements. I told him that talk like that was totally unjustified; I did not deserve such a reputation." He leaned forward and looked intently at Sam, as if to say, "But you're a different story." He wagged his finger and said, "Don't lie to me, Sam. Carolyn says you're not, but maybe you're hiding something from her too. Do you still have business with that Carlo? Is that why you're not pressing charges?"

"I swear, Mr. Becker," Sam said, rising in his cot and sticking a hand up. "I ain't got nothin' goin' with that dude. I ain't pressin' charges 'cause it won' do me no good. That white boy be out and lookin' for me in no time at all."

Becker looked pensive. "You may be right. But what about now? What are we supposed to do now?" He got no answer, and a tear appeared on his right cheek. "I used to be a teacher, and I thought I could be a teacher again, just to help. Mind you, if I had known about the aggravation, I would have read the sign on the gate and then gone home and stayed there." Sam and Carolyn could not figure out what sign he was talking about, but they did not press him. Old people often went off into incomprehensible mutterings. He rose suddenly and asked, "Does anyone want some ice cream?" They shook their heads, again in wonderment. Ice cream, a half hour before dinner?

"Good," he said as he headed for the kitchen, "there'll be more for me." He turned and smiled at them. "A joke. That's all I have left to do—make little jokes." A tear rolled down his cheek. "You understand, when I die, people will find nothing in my life that really mattered . . . to anybody." He took in their blank looks a moment before turning back toward the kitchen.

CHAPTER

Fourteen

"Whose side am I on?" Mulvaney mused in a delayed echo of Becker's question. "I'm on my side," he answered as he headed into downtown traffic in the battered Chevrolet the City of New York provided him. At the end of the week, he was picking up a new Oldsmobile station wagon and taking the kids picnicking out on the island.

In the ten years since his graduation from Fordham University and his marriage to the plain-looking daughter of his father's best friend, a city sanitation inspector, Mulvaney had loyally slogged his way to sergeant and, three months ago, a place in the city-federal task force on drugs. He had wanted to go to law school, but mediocre grades precluded a scholarship that would compensate for his family's equally mediocre finances. His father, police lieutenant James A. Mulvaney, was not completely unhappy about being unable to help him. Instead of a career in law, son followed father into the police but, as it turned out, without the father's distinction. To the younger Mulvaney's frustration at slow promotion was added that of watching his best efforts go to waste. Dozens of pushers he had arrested were back in circulation weeks and sometimes days after he eagerly helped to convict them. The two large drug busts he had participated in had netted quantities of narcotics with impressive street values but nobody above a middle level against whom a case could be made.

In Astoria, the frame house acquired with his father-in-law's generous dowry was falling apart and had ten years to go on the mortgage. When his wife had graduated from Manhattanville College with a major in English, she thought of herself as a writer and was willing to stay home and even raise children as long as she had hopes of cracking the magazine market with her short stories. The rejection slips followed each other without a single break, and after three years, there were just the kids and the housework and the shopping and a husband who seemed little more brilliant in his career than she was in hers. At night, Mulvaney would find a tight-lipped wife with little enthusiasm for sex; in the morning, she would spoil breakfast by demanding more money than he ever seemed to have in his wallet. She was continually finding some expense he had not counted on: shoes for the kids, the first dress in a year for herself, a replacement for the broken iron. He would yell that he hadn't had a new suit in two years and storm out, his half-drunk coffee burning his stomach. A year ago, he came home to find only a note. His wife couldn't stand it anymore and was taking the children and herself to her sister's in Woodmere. Hidden behind the good dishes was a bottle of twelve-year-old scotch. He took three healthy belts, all the time repeating, "What about me? How much am I supposed to stand?" There had since been a divorce, devastating alimony and child-support payments, and moments in the still, empty house when he felt like taking his service revolver and putting an end to thwarted ambition and wounded pride.

Three weeks ago, the telephone roused him from his half-filled bed on a Sunday morning just as he was wondering what to do with himself. It was Frank Carlin, a colleague on the task force. Mulvaney had gotten to like him for his easygoing nature, a calm manner in accepting setbacks, and a sporty way of buying drinks. If Mulvaney wasn't doing anything, would he like to meet at two o'clock for brunch at the Plaza? Mulvaney was impressed. He had passed by the hotel many times, gone in once to stare at the public rooms and the expensive-looking people in them, and decided wistfully that the scene could never be a part of his life. Carlin's choice of the Plaza intrigued him. It occurred to him for the first time that Carlin was usually better dressed than the others, including himself. Nothing flashy, just well-cut, expensive-looking suits that would not be out of place at the Plaza.

Carlin was not alone. A short, round man, already well along in years, was introduced as Anthony, a friend. The friend, in fact, seemed to take over as host, seating himself between the others, urging dishes on them that Mulvaney had never heard of. He chose eggs Benedict because that, at least, he had heard of but had never ordered. He liked the slightly tart, lemony taste of the hollandaise sauce and felt comfortable with Anthony, who was obviously a man who knew his way around. He was thus more than attentive when Anthony offered cigars and asked Mulvaney what he liked to do on his time off. Mulvaney allowed as how he didn't mind spending a couple of hours betting at the track or being in the sack with a well-shaped broad. Neither happened very often because both could run into money.

Anthony and Carlin smiled and nodded their understanding. Thereafter, the conversation became more or less a monologue as Anthony launched into a speech on the foibles of humankind. People, he said, cannot be prevented from indulging in their weaknesses, whether it was horse racing or a little pussy. And why should they be? Life was meant for a little pleasure. Appreciative chuckles. Now take drugs, he went on. Keeping people from drugs was particularly futile. Anthony smiled at the cops. They of all people must know how hard it is to prevent cocaine, heroin, marijuana from reaching the consumer. For every ounce that was stopped, a ton got through. And besides, where was the harm? Liquor was also bad when taken in excess, but the one time it was made illegal, look at the mess that was made. Instead of the government and the police beating their heads against a wall, wouldn't it make more sense— here a pause that Anthony hoped was pregnant—and be more profitable for everyone concerned to control things and go with the flow? The older man laughed self-consciously; young people today had these crazy expressions, but in this case, it was pretty close to the mark.

To Mulvaney, Anthony's points seemed reasonable enough, but he could not shake an uneasy feeling about where the talk was heading. He looked at Carlin, who was sitting back in his chair, blowing smoke rings and acting as if he had heard it all before. No uneasiness there. Mulvaney decided to relax. He fingered the starched white napkin on his lap and dug his heel into the deep carpet. After all the paper napkins and tile floors in his life, he had not felt so comfortable for a long time.

Anthony took a swig of coffee and continued. If people wanted to spend money on drugs, it ought to be as much their business as drinking, gambling in Atlantic City, or collecting old cars. Anyway, no matter what the government or the police did, a lot of money was being spent, and—here another pause—a lot of money was being made. There was no reason why Mulvaney and Carlin should not be able to take advantage of a business opportunity instead of hitting their heads against a wall like so many others. For example, and this time, the lecturer gave his full attention to Mulvaney, he knew the detective had been on the trail of a kid named Carlo, who was a little hot-tempered, Anthony had to agree, but really wasn't worth all the time Mulvaney was putting into it. Carlo was a nephew who would behave himself, the uncle would guarantee that, if on his part, Mulvaney would see to it that the young man was left alone to do his work. Oh, the cops could go through the motions. He realized appearances were important, but if any big action was in the works against Anthony or Carlo or others associated with them, a little word to the wise could be rewarding to both sides.

Mulvaney again looked at Carlin, who had not batted an eye at the bribery proposal. He realized fully for the first time that the speech had been for him alone. From all appearances, Carlin had passed over to the other side some time ago, which explained a lot of things about him. His role today was evidently that of a go-between between Anthony and a man he had figured would react in a certain way. And indeed, Carlin had figured well. Mulvaney was at the point where the essential question was not whether what he was being asked to do was right, but whether it was safe. Anthony sensed his internal debate. He settled the bill, rose, and held out his hand. "I enjoyed talking to you. I hope we see each other again." And he was gone, leaving Mulvaney to reach, with the help of Carlin, the correct conclusion. This required only a few minutes of explanation from Carlin of the ins and outs of the operation and what was expected of them, which wasn't a great deal. Others would carry the ball. They would simply run interference.

So it was that soon after, Mulvaney had a second meeting with Anthony over a checkered tablecloth and plates of pasta in Little Italy, during which an envelope with $10,000 was passed, along with a promise of a weekly envelope of not less than $1,000. One immediate concern, not a big worry really, Anthony assured Mulvaney, was how to keep a young nigger who called himself Sam from making waves in a case involving Carlo's bad temper. A little misunderstanding really, but it could be messy, just when he needed Carlo's undivided attention, if Sam pressed charges for getting cut up a little. Besides, a little discussion Carlo was planning to have with the nigger would straighten everything out to their mutual benefit. There was also an old man, white and Jewish, believe it or not, who was befriending the kid, why it was not hard to figure out, Sam being not bad-looking for a black boy. Maybe the disgusting old queer needed a little scare so he didn't make waves either.

Mulvaney did not find any of this difficult or compromising to handle. When Becker had shown up at the precinct a few days later, he had phoned Anthony at the first opportunity. Becker had thus been efficiently taken in hand just after leaving the station. To add to the intimidation, Mulvaney had thought up the search of Becker's apartment as well as the visit to the Reverend Greenway, who had proved easily amenable to the suggestion that he let Becker go. As for Sam, the detective thought he had been really subtle in getting over the idea that the less the nigger had to do with the police, the better off he was. When Mulvaney was able to report that no charges were being pressed, he was rewarded with a bonus of $5,000. Mulvaney got the impression that something big was going down, as they say in the business, and it was worth a great deal to Anthony's organization not to be distracted by petty annoyances. Mulvaney was relieved that it was working out the way he had been told, and he was not really being asked to do anything, except protect those who were doing something.

Carlo thus had ample warning to get out of the East Side apartment before Mulvaney, anxious to demonstrate to his legitimate superiors that he was active, showed up with a search warrant. The red Alfa Romeo had been stowed in a little garage in Soho, an area where its owner also found refuge. An expensively furnished loft off West Broadway owned by Southern Imports, Inc., his uncle's tea-and-coffee business, became his base of operations. It was not as convenient to his pushers in upper Manhattan but safer because it was more out of the way. It was also easier for his uncle to keep tabs on him from Little Italy, but Carlo did not mind this so much because he discovered in the Soho loft crowd a dealer's delight.

Chastened by his uncle's repeated warnings to behave or be cut out of the action, Carlo had gotten his cocaine, expertly mixed and divided into packets so that it came to twice the original number of kilograms. Some of it he put out on the street immediately, but he kept some back for Sam. It would be the least troublesome way Carlo could figure of getting the debt repaid and reestablishing a business relationship that had been profitable in the past. The trick now was getting to Sam.

Carolyn's efficiency and Sam's resilience solved the dealer's problem. A week after Sam got out of the hospital, she had opened the shop. Sam had his bandages removed two days later and was taking short walks in the park, chaperoned by Becker. The youth was, in fact, finding Becker a bit burdensome. He hoped to find some smoke on his daily outings and recognized a pusher he could have done business with, except that the old man was beside him. The same omnipresence prevented him from doing anything with Carolyn when she came visiting. It seemed Becker was always there. Sam's annoyance was starting to turn to suspicion about all the attention with which Becker was smothering him. It reminded him of the looks Becker had given him at the very start of their relationship. Once, in the middle of a particularly warm night, he had awakened to find his guardian staring down at his naked body. He closed his eyes quickly and feigned sleep, afraid he was about to be touched, but after a few moments, Becker shuffled on to the bathroom, muttering something that Sam only partly caught.

"Who or what's Beshir?" he wondered, making sure Becker was back in his own bed before relaxing into sleep.

A week after that incident, Sam escaped to the beauty salon while Becker was out shopping. He was feeling almost as strong as he had before the knifing, and with his recuperation had come the old restlessness that made him such an enthusiastic denizen of the streets. He found Carolyn fussing with a rented hairdryer that stubbornly refused to work. There were no customers and two idle assistants.

"Things are kinda slow," she complained. "An' we got bills to pay."

Sam was down to his last $300. "We gotta get the word out," he said. "I'm gonna have some fliers made up, and we'll put 'em into people's mailboxes." He fixed the bad plug on the old dryer before going to a Harlem printing establishment he had looked up in the yellow pages.

Later, he found Becker sulking at home. "You might have told me you were going out," the old man said, trying to strike a balance between reproach and concern.

Sam flared up. "Mr. Becker," he answered, "I'm feelin' okay now, so you really don' have to be watchin' me all the time. I mean, I appreciate all you done, but you ain't my father."

The old man looked so crushed that Sam thought he

was about to cry. He put his hand on his shoulder. "I really can take care of myself now. An' I got this new business that needs tendin' an' you can't be with me all the time. That wouldn' be practical like, now would it?"

In the end, Sam agreed to stay on awhile at Becker's house mainly because he was still afraid to return to his old room. He was also making progress in his English with the daily tutoring he was getting. Becker in turn agreed to stop acting like a mother hen and allow him his freedom.

Carlo learned of Sam's return to circulation from the boyfriend of one of the shop girls, who had occasional dealings with him. Carlo spied Sam as he was entering a building on Manhattan Avenue to stuff the mailboxes with his fliers. The hallway suddenly fell into shadow, and Sam turned to find the door blocked by a massive backlit form nattily covered in light blue. Sam darted a look around him and found no other way out. He rolled the fliers into a stick and brandished it while backing against the brass-covered wall.

Carlo did not move. "Hey, that's no way to say hello to a friend."

"What you want?"

"I want to talk. Nice and friendly. You and me, we got some unfinished business."

"Las' time it wasn' so friendly."

"Yeah, well, that was last time. Let's sit in my car." Carlo held the building door for Sam, who moved glumly past, checking Carlo's free hand for any glinting objects.

"You owe me," Carlo said in the car. It was calmly stated as a fact. Feeling no immediate threat, Sam tried to brave things out.

"I paid ya off with my hospital bill, man. And what did ya do to my friend Carolyn?"

Carlo's tone got rougher, and it took an effort not to grab Sam's throat. "It was your own fucking fault for being such a smartass, so don't lay that on me. But if you'll listen to me a minute, we can work something out."

"I'm listenin'."

"How's your new business doing?"

"So-so."

"Yeah, I guess you wouldn't be out advertising if you were beating off the crowds. Maybe if the word got around the right places that you got other services, you'd start getting customers. You remember how easy it was to unload the last batch of coke I gave you? Well, you wrap it up with the beauty products, and it'll be even easier. In practically no time at all, you pay off what you owe me and, man, you're starting to make a nice little pile for yourself. A good deal, no?" Carlo looked inquiringly at Sam and waited for the one possible answer.

Since the shop opened, two customers, Carolyn had reported, had asked if something might be available besides eyeliner. Half afraid of being set up by a policewoman, she had vehemently replied that she was in the beauty business only. Recounting the incidents to Sam, she looked at him so fiercely he was afraid to open a discussion on opportunities they might be missing. Long ago he had decided that if he did some business on the side, it would have to be while she was looking the other way.

"I don't mind doin' a little dealin'," he told Carlo. "But I don' wan' nothin' big-time. The business is really legit, an' my girlfriend, she wants to keep it that way. You understand, man?"

In the interest of business, Carlo had resolved to remain as even-tempered as possible, but this was easier than he had expected. His uncle was right. The shop would be a front. The devious, hypocritical little fucker talking about his "legit" business!

Carlo suppressed a smile, said he understood, and handed over an envelope containing twenty packets for sale at $100 apiece. The debt would be liquidated for $1,500, and Sam could keep $500 for himself. A little encouragement wouldn't hurt. Then he released Sam from the car and drove away thinking that if Uncle Anthony was not satisfied with the way he had handled it, he could go screw himself.

Sam went back to his mailboxes. There remained the

problem of operating without Carolyn's knowing. In the shop, there was a large storage room. He had appointed himself in charge of supplies, so she had little reason to go exploring. It ought to be easy enough, he said to himself, to stash the stuff. As for the actual dealing, orders could be quietly taken at the cash register, which he also intended to man, for delivery elsewhere. As for the moral issue involved in going behind Carolyn's back, during his long hospital nights Sam had figured out an answer that neatly married morality to practicality. He told himself they had a few hard months to get through before they could start making money on the up and up. They could keep afloat on coke. He was really doing Carolyn a favor.

CHAPTER

Fifteen

The day Sam got rid of his bandages, he also got rid of Becker, two weeks after being taken under his wing. Having made up with Carlo, he felt no danger about now returning to Carolyn, whom he had sorely missed. Back from his last examination and treatment at the hospital, he declared his independence as gently as he could to the old man, who seemed unable to shake the depression that had followed his abrupt dismissal from the church school. While Sam packed the clothes Carolyn had brought him, he lengthily expressed his gratitude for being allowed to be in the way for so long. He swept aside the old man's stammering attempts to assure him that he had not been a burden and promised to come back. Mr. Becker could count on it, on Mondays and Fridays, he would continue the tutoring. He was, he said earnestly, still serious about getting his high school diploma.

Becker sat tight-lipped as Sam talked. He could find no serious argument to stop the black from leaving and consoled himself with the prospect of regular visits. He wanted to say that he loved him, that caring for him gave his life some purpose, and that more than anything else he was afraid of going back to the benches to listen to other aimless old men. But he said none of these things, certain they would make Sam flee even faster. Sam paused at the door, suitcase in hand, and smiling at the forlorn Becker, invited him to the shop the first chance he got. At the elevator, Sam joined Mrs. Klein, who took in the luggage with a rush of thankfulness. All was not lost with her bewildering neighbor.

Meanwhile, at the shop, Carolyn did not think auburn

was a particularly good color for blacks. But she was afraid to argue with a new customer, one of a dozen brought in by the fliers since they were distributed in houses and pasted to lampposts and trees a week ago. Sam more than once made the point that it was his idea, as if he felt the need to show how useful he was. Otherwise, his activity at the shop was confined to some cleaning up, reading the tabloids and, for about half the day, manning the cash register where his grinning, cajoling ways were effective in inducing customers to spend some more on cosmetics and perfumes. But there were also annoying moments, hours really, when Sam would disappear without explanation. Carolyn refrained from pressing him. Things were going a little better now at the shop, she thought, and since he had moved out of Becker's, he was always there for her in the evenings. She had welcomed him into her tiny apartment, going to bed with him almost immediately. Lying beside him after they had finished, she wondered what made him so much like his old self, carefree and assured, when danger seemed to her still imminent.

She put on the light in the back room and rummaged for henna rinse, an ear cocked for the sound of the door that would signal the arrival of a customer or, better still—given the uneasy feeling she could not shake or explain—the return of Sam from another of his mysterious errands. The bottle of rinse was in a carton of supplies on a low shelf, which forced her to squat to see what she was doing. Next to the carton was a toolbox whose cover did not quite close because of some protruding yellow paper. She raised the cover and tugged at what turned into a thick manilla envelope. It was much like the one she remembered Becker stuffing with the money found in the French grammar book, then bringing to Sam in the hospital.

"I'll be right out!" she called in answer to the sound of impatient throat-clearing and rustling in the shop. The envelope was not sealed. She drew out some small, clear plastic packets filled with a white powdery substance. She had seen and sniffed cocaine once before, at the end of an exhausting night in the bar when in the washroom the other waitress had offered relief to her tired body. She had felt a freezing sensation in her nostrils, then a diffuse exhilaration and the too-brief end of her fatigue. After her mother pulled her out of the bar, she had not gone back to the drug, preferring the gentler highs she dragged from one of Sam's cigarettes. From the toolbox, she took a small screwdriver, punctured a packet, and sniffed tentatively, then harder. There was the familiar numbing in her nose but not as much as she remembered it.

She was surprised at how calm she was, not the slightest trembling at coming upon a cache that undoubtedly only Sam could explain. They had talked so many times about their future and just as often had agreed—at least that was her understanding—that drug dealing would not be part of it, even if the beginnings of the business were tough. The feeling of betrayal was churning her insides. Her heart was pumping hard. She felt on the verge of panic. Yet her movements were deliberate and precise, as if she were dealing with some boyish prank of no consequence and easy to handle. She put the packets back in the envelope, cleared the carton of its bottles, placed the envelope at the bottom, and put the bottles back on top. She rose, straightened her smock, and strode back into the shop with the henna rinse. "Wouldn't you know," she said with a nervous laugh, "I hadda get to the bottom of things to find the rinse."

She finished in less than an hour and left the girls to handle two other customers. This was one of the best days yet, she reflected wryly, and returned to the storeroom. She removed the envelope from the carton, counted ten packets in all, and stowed one in her purse. She went into the bathroom and threw the others in the toilet. Then she vomited her lunch. Maybe bad mayonnaise in the tuna, she thought.

Sam had been on personal business. He was carrying a carton with a pair of pearl-gray slacks bought in a wood-paneled Madison Avenue shop, the kind he felt a man in his position ought to start patronizing. In his pocket was $400 from two deliveries he had made to women who had come to get their hair done and had been informed by him at the cash register, while adding cologne to their bill, that the shop offered other goods and services. Sam had disposed of half the supply Carlo had given him and paid off a third of his debt. Carlo had seen to that, relieving Sam every few days of some of his income, lest he be tempted to welsh again. "That's how we'll stay friends," he explained to Sam with the closest he could come to a friendly grin, his mouth opening on a slant just enough to show some teeth. Sam had been unhappy at having to pay $1,500 to clear a $1,000 debt, but there was the "interest" Carlo had insisted upon in a way that brooked no argument.

Sam needed more coke but not before tomorrow, so there was no point in returning to the shop. Carolyn would close it up and meet him at the apartment. Sam decided they would go out for a meal, maybe down to Columbus Avenue, where he noted a number of real cool establishments where white and black dudes who looked like they had made it took their equally classy-looking women. And you never know, a little business could be talked up in those places.

The apartment was empty. Seven o'clock, and Carolyn was not yet home. A little nettled, he tried the shop, but after five rings he hung up. She was on her way, the bus was slow in coming, or she stopped off for a little shopping. Nothing to get excited about, he thought. He took a beer from the refrigerator and turned on the television to a rerun of the Jeffersons, who had made it big in dry cleaning and had a chain of stores and an East Side apartment. He forgot his annoyance at Carolyn's absence as he saw his whole future right there on the screen. It was not like he was going to be in drugs forever, not when you had to deal with creeps like Carlo.

At eight o'clock, he heard a key in the door, and there was Carolyn on the threshold answering his broad grin with a sour look. She turned from him and went into the bathroom, closing the door behind her without a word. Sam stared at the door perplexedly. What was her problem? He turned back to the television set, but it was no longer fun to watch, and after five minutes he turned it off.

"Hey, baby, what's happenin'?" he called out. No answer.

"Carolyn, you okay?"

A full minute passed before the bathroom door opened. In nightgown and robe, her hair in curlers, Carolyn looked prepared for an evening at home and an early bedtime.

"Ya ain't feelin' good?" Sam asked. She barely glanced at him on her way to the refrigerator, where she began poking about. Her silence was draining all of Sam's good feeling.

"What's the matter? You lose your tongue? What's your problem?"

She whirled on him, a bottle of milk in one hand, a plate of ham in the other.

"You!" she shouted. "You the problem!"

"Hey, baby, keep it down. People gonna think we havin' a fight." He paused and asked softly. "What ya mean, I'm the problem?"

"You know where I been?"

"That's funny, I was askin' myself that jes' before you showed up."

"I bet you was. Well, I been to see Mr. Becker."

"Hey, that's cool," Sam said placatingly. "He okay?"

"Yeah, he's okay. You're the one got somethin' wrong with him."

"You mind tellin' me what you goin' off at the mouth about?"

Tears began to roll down her cheeks. She seemed to be crying with her whole shaking body. Sam stepped forward, his arms extended to enfold her, but she waved him away before they could touch. It was a full minute before she was able to stop her gasping and talk.

"I found your envelope."

"My envelope?"

"Yeah, the one you tried to hide in the storeroom. I also saw what was inside."

Sam sat down again in the easy chair, casually swung one leg over an arm, and took a long swig of beer. "That's what you goin' on about?" he asked in a calm voice. "What's the big deal?"

She sat down hard on the bed, her mouth agape. "You askin' me what's the big deal? I know coke when I see it. What you doin' with coke when we supposed to be runnin' a business on the up an' up?"

Sam sat down beside her and put his arm around her shoulder. This time she did not reject him but refused to look him in the face.

"Baby, that's what we doin'," he said, pushing the words out hard to emphasize his sincerity. "That's exactly what we doin'. But I supposed you noticed the customers ain't been beatin' down the door." His arms went out as if he were pleading. "Didn't I spend days gettin' the word out? Now things gettin' a little better, but we got rent to pay, Baby, don' forget, and those two girls, they gotta be paid too, and we don' have it unless we got a little extra income. Baby, you diggin' me?" She kept looking off into space as if what he was saying did not concern her. When he seemed to be finished, she glanced at him before turning away again.

"You connected up with Carlo again?" she asked.

Sam hesitated, seeking the least explosive answer. "Yeah, well, it was the only way to get him off my back. As long as I play ball, he don't pull no knife on me, ya dig?"

Her voice rose again. "I dig. It's you who don' understand that you'll be playin' ball with him forever. You'll never get out from under."

"Hey, you got that wrong. Jes' as soon as I pay off what I owe him, we home free, and we drop him. By that time, we'll have the business rollin' so we don' need to do no dealin' anyhow."

She turned toward him and seized him by the arms. "He'll never let go!" she said intensely. "Never as long as you does what he tell you. You gotta split now. You was gonna do that a long time ago. We agreed, remember. Anyway, you ain't got no more coke to sell, so you might as well get used to the idea you ain't dealin' no more."

He looked at her fearfully. "What you mean?"

"I mean, I flushed the coke down the toilet."

He doubled over as though hit in the stomach and began to sway back and forth, his arms folded over his middle. "Oh, lawdy, you done it now," he whispered. "You done it now. Ya jes' lost your Sam. I'm not gonna last twenty-four hours." He was shaking and crying almost as hard as she had been a few moments before.

Carolyn felt about to break down too. Pity overcoming anger, she stretched out her arms toward him. As soon as she touched him, he shook her off and slapped her hard, furious at her for reducing him to tears. Now both cried together in wordless misery. In a few moments, they calmed down, and Sam walked toward the door. "I'll be seein' ya, Baby," he said just before opening it.

"Where you goin'?"

"I don' know. I jes' don' know."

"Then why you goin'?"

" 'Cause jes' twenty minutes ago, I wanted to screw the hell out of ya, and now I don' even wanna look at ya no more." He was gone before she could say a word.

Only a few minutes before, Carolyn was certain she had done the right thing. Now she sat bewildered, unable to come up with any thought in which she could take comfort. She wanted to keep Sam from destroying himself, and now he was accusing her of being the agent of his destruction. Even her visit to Becker seemed ludicrous. He had been the first person she thought of turning to, but what could an old man do for them when he could barely look out for himself? He had looked appropriately concerned, but nothing in his words carried a promise of help. She had given him the cocaine packet she had saved from the toilet with nothing precise in mind except to offer evidence of Sam's perfidy, and he had looked at it blankly as if to say, "What am I supposed to do?"

An hour after her visit, Becker was distractedly stirring the noodles in his chicken soup, no clearer in his mind about his future course. The soup grew cold, and while it reheated, he poked at the little packet Carolyn had left on the table. He was feeling the same pangs of betrayal and of personal affront as she. He too had wanted to help somebody who was turning out to be a hopeless, unreformable case.

To be honest, had he not brought it on himself? What had he felt when Sam arrived for the first time, in the middle of the night, frightened half to death? The picture of the long, sensuous body that later curled up on the floor flitted through his mind. That night, he now realized, he had fallen in love with a young black and had become committed to his well-being. It was incongruous, and to others, including the object of his love, unavowable. But what was he to do except keep a tight grip on himself? He had allowed Sam to take advantage of him, to abuse his goodwill. He rememberd how indignant he had become at the Reverend Greenway's doubts about Sam. He had been amazed that a man of God could be so cynical. Now, he was furious at Sam for justifying Greenway's assessment.

Supper finished, he retired to his easy chair, and in a half-doze his mind traveled from Sam back to Beshir. He tried to imagine what the Moroccan was like these days. If he were still alive, he could only be a broken-down hophead, perhaps a gardener for the Europeans in the villas outside Tangier, making titillating centerpieces, so titillating that elaborate receptions would be conceived around his *pièces de résistance*, people journeying from all over North Africa and Europe, eager for an invitation. . . . He started at the sound of the downstairs buzzer but instinctively knew who it was.

"Sam?"

"Yeah, it's me. Can I come up and talk?"

Becker allowed him in and, waiting for the elevator, dragged nervously on a cigarette and thought about the appropriate things to say. He could say, "Sam, you'd better not come to me for help anymore. It's all over, and you're on your own, and if you want to be mixed up forever in drugs and maybe get killed someday, that's your business." Not bad, and amply justified. The old man assumed a severe look as he went to open the door.

If not quite the hunted animal of a few weeks before, Sam looked frightened enough. He managed a weak grin, sat down on the daybed, took a tissue from the side table, and wiped his face.

"There's a lot of trouble, Mr. Becker."

"Whose trouble?"

"Mine, I guess. You know what Carolyn done?"

"She told me. Can you blame her?"

Sam jerked his head back as if he had been hit again. "Hey, man, don' you start on me too. You don' understand; she don' either. I meets up with Carlo an' I'm as good as dead."

"Who told you to get mixed up with Carlo again? Wasn't once enough?"

"He tol' me, that's who tol' me. I still owe him some bread; everybody knows that, and he don' let go. So when he got me alone a coupla weeks ago, what was I supposed to do? I figger, I sell what he give me to sell, and I get him off my back. All I needed was another coupla days. Carolyn, she really done it to me." He sat shaking his head mournfully. Becker softened his voice.

"Do you really think you'll ever get rid of him? As you say, he doesn't let go. You get the debt paid off, and he'll be back wanting you to sell some more. You're a good pusher, aren't you?"

Sam winced. "Mr. Becker, I don' wanna be a pusher," he said.

"You say that, but you didn't mind keeping a little money for yourself from the stuff Carlo gave you. I mean, you didn't turn it all over to him, did you?"

"The shop wasn't hardly payin' its bills. We needed a little extra to keep us goin'."

Becker was getting exasperated.

"And that's the way you plan to stay in business? By pushing drugs on the side?"

Sam shook his head vigorously. "The business is goin' better now." For the first time, he broke into a grin as he explained his advertising campaign. "In two or three months, we'll be makin' money," he said. "I even got a location for a second store in mind."

"Good," Becker replied dryly. "So what do you want from me?"

Sam shifted his feet and began to reach in his shirt pocket for some grass, then glanced at Becker and changed his mind. "I still owe Carlo a thousand," he said. "I can't put him off no two or three months. He likes his money right away, ya dig? I was supposed to meet him tomorrow, and I ain't gonna show 'cause I ain't got nothin' for him. But sooner or later, that dude gonna catch up with me." He hesitated and mopped his forehead again. "Mr. Becker," he finally said, "could you like lend me the bread? I promise to pay it back in a coupla months. Like I said, the shop's goin' better now."

So there it was. Sam had come to put the bite on him, which was probably the least surprising thing he could have done. In turn, Becker thought, he would not be surprised if he agreed to the loan. It is what any Aschenbach worthy of the name would do. Except that, except that . . . and he closed his eyes and thought of ways of not being a complete patsy. There must be a way of salvaging something from the wreckage. It was as if his brain had suddenly been given a shot of adrenalin; his mind was working unusually fast while, his eyes shut and his hands folded over his stomach, he pursed his lips like Nero Wolfe from his mystery-reading days.

"Mr. Becker, you okay?"

"I'm okay, Sam. Tell me, why should I help you?"

Sam blinked hard. He had been expecting hemming and hawing, a few mild protests, finally surrender. That was the way cajoling worked with most people.

"What you mean, Mr. Becker?"

Becker looked steadily into Sam's eyes. "What I said. Give me a good reason why I should help you."

Sam composed a serious face and kept his voice calm. " 'Cause," he said, "there ain't nobody else I can ask." He walked over and sat on an arm of Becker's easy chair and looked down at the old man. " 'Cause we's friends." He had never looked so earnest, Becker thought. "Mr. Becker, you don' wanna see me dead, do ya?"

"No, of course not," Becker said, putting a hand on Sam's thigh, then hastily withdrawing it. "I don't want you to die. But how long is this going to go on? Do you really think you'll ever be rid of Carlo? Be honest?"

"He won' wanna bother with me if I don' play ball."

"Bullshit!" The word barely out, Becker blushed and covered his mouth as if afraid someone would wash it out with soap. Sam looked at him, startled.

"Let's be serious, Sam," Becker went on after a moment. "The money's easy, right? You never refused an offer from Carlo before. Why should anyone believe you now? You need $1,000 to pay him off? I'll help you if you'll help yourself and everyone else. Is it a deal?"

Sam chose not to address the question of his credibility. He was torn between elation and wariness. "What deal you talkin' about?" he asked.

"The deal you agreed to in the hospital but chickened out on. We go to the cops together and nail Carlo. He has to be gotten out of the way, at least for a while."

"Like you say, for a while. Then what I got to look forward to? He comes out and starts gunnin' for me, and maybe you too, you thought about that? And then things is worse than ever."

Becker had thought about it and decided that, with luck, he might be dead by the time Carlo was in a position to threaten him again. Right now, there was an immediate problem that needed an immediate solution. It had to be better for Sam, Carolyn, himself, for all of society, if Carlo was put away as soon as possible.

"Mr. Becker," Sam was saying, "what cops you got in

mind? It ain't that Mulvaney who came around the other day, is it?"

"No," Becker answered almost vehemently. "This time we go higher, right to the FBI or the Drug Enforcement Agency."

Becker was gratified by Sam's awed look. For young men like him, and those not so young, and Becker included himself, the Feds still carried an aura of majestic power that plain cops, the city variety that Sam saw every day, did not have.

"So what's your answer?" asked Becker.

"Ya gonna give me what I need to keep Carlo quiet?"

"Yes, but not until we see what the federal agents say. In the meantime, keep out of his way."

Sam nodded vigorously. "Oh, I'm gonna keep out of his way, all right," he said. He paused and looked ingratiatingly at Becker. "Okay with you if I stay here tonight? Carolyn, she's a little pissed off at me, and I don' wanna be on the streets too much tonight, ya dig?"

Becker pointed to the closet where the cot was stowed. "I dig," he said.

Sometime in the middle of the uncomfortably warm night, Becker got up for a trip to the bathroom. He stubbed his toe on a leg of the cot and gasped from the pain. Sam's naked body stirred. He had thrown off the top sheet, and the moonlight made the sweat of his smooth, dark skin glisten. Becker stood transfixed, the ache in his toe forgotten. Sam opened his eyes and smiled. He reached out and took Becker's hand.

"You can have anythin' you want," he whispered.

The old man tightened his grip on Sam's hand, then suddenly dropped it and stepped back. "I . . . I only want to go to the bathroom," he mumbled. When he came back into the room, Sam seemed asleep.

In the morning, over breakfast, they were too embarrassed to speak, aside from a perfunctory greeting, and even managed to avoid each other's eyes. When he finished his coffee, Becker glanced at the kitchen clock. It was eight-forty-five. "I'm calling the FBI in fifteen minutes," he said and for the first time looked at Sam as if making sure he had not changed his mind. But the black simply nodded and, wordlessly went off to take a shower.

Becker looked up the federal listings in the phone book. He came across the Drug Enforcement Agency first. It seemed like a likely place to call. People were always calling the FBI. This sounded different. If he was wrong, they would tell him. He was taken aback when, asking to speak to an agent, he was asked by what was obviously a switchboard operator to state his business. He had imagined being connected immediately with someone of authority eager for information from a dutiful, law-abiding citizen. "I don't know whether I should talk about this on the phone," Becker said. "It's a delicate matter."

Whether the operator was impressed, he could not tell. "Will you call back at ten, please?" she said and hung up.

He should have known, Becker thought. When you're dealing with bureaucracy, it's always more complicated than you figured. When he called back an hour later, he was told that Agent Schofield was expected momentarily.

Sam made up his cot, helped Becker straighten up the room, and sat on the daybed, submissively waiting for the old man to make the next move. Becker skimmed through the *Times*, studiously ignoring Sam but all the time exulting in the unusual feeling of being in control and calling the shots. It was wonderful what money could do. The embarrassment of last night's incident, when he almost lost control of himself, faded.

Becker got through to Schofield at ten-thirty, rather laboriously explained that he had information on drug dealings, and paused, waiting to be told to rush down. He was given an appointment for two-thirty, Schofield welcoming the prospect of a blow against crime with surprising patience and calm. So they would be home for both lunch and dinner, and Becker, inspecting the refrigerator and the shelves, found he had to do some shopping. Sam was not anxious to appear on the streets, and Becker left him with the English exercise book, whose return Greenway had un-accountably neglected to demand.

Ten minutes later, the bell rang. As Sam swung the door open, Mrs. Klein opened her mouth for a cheery greeting and left it gaping as she stared at the young black man. She peered behind him into the studio and became flustered when she failed to spot Becker.

"I . . . I was looking for Mr. Becker," she said. "I'm his neighbor."

"He not here right now," Sam said cheerily. "Ya wanna wait?"

"No, no," she answered hastily, alarmed at the thought of being alone with him. "It's not important. I'll talk to him later. Don't let me disturb you." She threw a stern glance at him and walked off. Fumbling with the lock of her own door, she felt Sam's eyes boring into her back. What was with her David again? She had wanted to invite him for cof-fee and cake, but now it would be awkward with the other one there. David's sympathy for underprivileged minori-ties—his expression—was getting out of hand. It was, in fact, more bizarre than lofty. She shook her head. She did not like what she was thinking.

"So what did she want?" Becker asked when he put his packages down on the kitchen table.

"I don't rightly know. She say it weren't important." Becker didn't doubt it. He would deal with her later.

After lunch, he and Sam arrived at the Drug Enforce-ment Agency's Fifty-seventh Street office early, than were kept waiting twenty minutes beyond the appointed time because Schofield was late getting back from lunch. Becker passed his hand back and forth over the packet of cocaine in his pocket until the agent appeared, looking as if he could use a few more lunches. His gray suit hung loosely on a tall, spare frame. He seemed to Becker amazingly young, no more than thirty-five, but the pepper-and-salt crewcut and the cold blue eyes behind the rimless glasses reassured him. The man looked the part. The agent barely nodded before disappearing into his office. Another ten minutes passed until he ushered Becker in, Sam nervously bringing up the rear.

Somewhat remote behind a large desk, Schofield spent little time in introductions and preliminary explanations. He was acting director, filling in for the director, who was on vacation. He looked, in fact, bored, as though he had had his fill of patriotic citizens. His eyes shifted from Becker to Sam and back, registering the unusual makeup of this particular delegation. Taking down names, he asked them what was on their minds, then sat back expressionless with his note pad. Placing the packet of cocaine on the desk, Becker launched into the menace of Carlo while Sam fidgeted beside him.

"That's it?" Schofield asked.

Becker nodded. The question unsettled him. It made it sound as if he had just wasted valuable time.

"We've known about this Carlo for some time," Schofield resumed. "His last name is Rosetti. The police have tried to pick him up, but he always manages to stay a step ahead. We thought we had him located a few days ago, but when the cops got to his apartment, he had skipped. Anyway, the main thing is that he's dangerous all right but small-fry. For our purposes, he's valuable only if he can lead us to people higher up, the ones he takes orders from and who supply him."

He picked up the packet, opened it and sniffed. "It looks heavily cut," he said. "That's the way they make money." As poker-faced as ever, he looked at Sam as if for corroboration. "How did you get to know Carlo?" he asked.

Sam was afraid of this moment. On the way down, he had rehearsed his story with Becker, but nothing they could think of completely made him an innocent victim. "I bought a little grass from him once. Nothin' much, ya know." He paused and looked at the agent, but the latter continued to show no reaction. "I owed him some money, and he come after me and want me to use my shop—I got a beauty parlor I run with my girlfriend—to sell some heavy stuff like what ya got there." Sam pointed to the packet and became silent.

"And that's what you did?" Schofield asked gently.

"He cut me up once, and he say he gonna do it again to me and my friend if I don' play ball."

"So you played ball?" It was more a statement of fact than a question.

"Yeah, well as I say, he's a mean dude, and I'm not that tired of livin'."

A smile flickered faintly before Schofield put it out. He gazed at both Becker and Sam for a while. "Does either of you have any idea who Carlo works with?"

When he got no's from both, he sat tapping his pencil on his desk, seemingly lost in thought. "You've been to the city police, haven't you?"

"I went to see a detective at the Twenty-fourth Precinct," Becker said. "I got a funny feeling that he didn't care. He even conducted a search of my apartment, as if we were the criminals."

"Did he find anything?"

"Of course not!" Becker said more vehemently than he wished.

"Well, he might have had a good reason for being suspicious," Schofield said, with a glance at Sam. "By the way, what's the detective's name?"

"Mulvaney."

Schofield looked up quickly, then wrote the name down. He went back to thinking, as if all alone in the room. Becker found the silence a little unnerving. Suddenly, the agent put down the pencil and pad and leaned forward.

"How do you feel about helping us and helping yourselves at the same time?"

"Mr. Schofield, that's why we came," Becker answered.

"Yes, I know, and I thank both of you. But I'm talking about something different, something that might be . . ." the agent hesitated. "Well, let's say there are a few risks. If you can't, I'll understand." He turned his full attention to Sam. "But you'll have to understand that if you can't cooperate with us, you may be liable to prosecution for trafficking."

Neither Sam nor Becker liked the drift of Schofield's conversation. "What do you have in mind?" Becker asked with a slight waver in his voice.

"A small scam," the agent said. "You approach Carlo with an offer to buy big, but you make it plain you won't deal except with the big boys. Otherwise it's no go."

Becker's sense of duty was cooling quickly. "Carlo might get suspicious," he suggested.

Schofield nodded. "Maybe, but we're dealing here with very greedy people. I'm talking about big bucks."

"What's big bucks?" Sam interjected.

"Say a hundred grand."

Sam drew in his breath. "Where do we get that?"

"Don't worry about it. We'll handle that. What I figure is that Carlo won't say yes right away but will relay the offer. We're sure he's working for someone. As a matter of fact, we have a pretty good idea who it is, but we've never been able to pin anything on him. Anyway, whoever it is is probably just as greedy as he is. That's what makes the drug business run. At least, that's what we have to hope for in this case. If there's a deal, you get back to me, and we set up something. As I said, there's some risk, but we'll have plenty of people around to make sure nothing goes wrong."

Schofield looked at both men for a reaction. It did not come quickly. There's plenty that can go wrong, Becker thought to himself. He suddenly remembered an old movie. A sheep is tethered to a tree to draw out a mountain lion, which has been laying waste to the flocks in the region. The herders lie in wait with high-powered rifles. The predator comes, circles the bleating sheep, and attacks. The herders open fire, and the mountain lion is killed. So, Becker remembered with a shudder, is the sheep, who is half eaten by the time the predator finally succumbs.

He looked at Sam. A black sheep in more ways than one. Then he glanced at Schofield, who sat patiently behind his desk, looking as unconcerned as if he had just asked them to join him for a round of golf.

Schofield was, in fact, more concerned than he let on. In charge for a few weeks, he had yielded to an impulse. If the idea worked, he would be taking a big step up the administrative ladder. If it failed, and either of the two in front of him was a casualty, his ass would be in a sling. The more they seemed to hesitate, the more he was assailed by second thoughts. He decided he would look stupid if he withdrew the offer, but if they refused, and he now almost hoped they would, he would make no big issue of it.

Sam was no more confident than Becker, but was feeling more squeezed. He had not confessed to much, but it seemed like enough to get him a prison term. He grimaced in disgust at the choices suddenly thrown at him. It was jail or play ball in a very dangerous league. He looked at Becker, but the old man seemed lost in his own thoughts. Schofield resumed tapping with his pencil.

"How are we going to make contact with Carlo?" Becker asked timidly.

"I'll leave that to you," Schofield answered, looking at Sam. "It hasn't been a problem up to now, has it?"

Sam remained silent. "No, I guess not," Becker said, answering for him.

Schofield rose. "Good. Keep me posted. Here's a phone number you can call day and night." He handed Becker a sheet torn from the notebook. "Memorize it, then destroy the slip." He paused, then said, "If you don't feel up to it, that's all right too."

But Becker felt he had taken another step down a slippery slope and he could not go back. Schofield had a nerve, really. So why didn't he say no? Because it was his idea to go to the police, first to the local cops without much result, then to the Feds. He had to show Sam the way toward being a proper citizen. Becker grimaced. He was quite the educator. Except that this time it was not nouns and pronouns. This time, they could get their heads blown off. They took a taxi home, Becker no longer feeling any safer in the streets than his pupil was.

The next morning, he drew $1,000 in hundreds from his savings account and handed it to Sam, who was scheduled to meet Carlo in the afternoon. Most of the evening, he and Becker had rehearsed the scene, what he should say to Carlo that would arouse his interest but not his suspicions.

But seeing, from a block away, the short, powerful figure waiting on a corner of Amsterdam Avenue, Sam felt only fear. He ducked into a doorway and tried to calm himself, fingering the wad of bills in his pocket as if the strength of the money would flow into him. He glanced out. Carlo was looking at his watch. He had better not keep him waiting too long.

"So what's happenin' man?" Sam asked with a grin.

"I was starting to figure you wasn't gonna show. You got the money?"

"Yeah, I got it."

"Okay. C'mon in the car." The Volkswagen was parked a hundred feet away on a side street.

When Carlo finished counting the bills twice, he turned amiable. "Glad to see the shop's working out. You want some more merchandise, right?"

"Yeah, well, me and a friend, we're thinkin' of somethin' a little bigger."

Carlo frowned. "What friend?"

"He's an old dude, used to be my teacher. He's interested in dealin'."

"The old fart on Riverside Drive?"

"That's him."

"What's somebody like him doing in this business? And what's between you and him anyway?"

"Ain't nothin' between me and him," Sam answered self-consciously. Carlo allowed himself a crooked grin, and Sam tried to control his temper. "He needs some bread, man, fast. His buildin' goin' co-op, and he wants to buy his apartment. You remember, you was in it."

Carlo glared at him, and Sam thought he had better drop the sarcasm.

"Yeah," Carlo said. "But what does he know about dealing?"

"What he don' know, I'll tell him. It's a good setup, an old teacher who the fuzz never heard about and who got neighbors interested in a little blow."

Carlo seemed to be thinking, and Sam, taking the silence as a good sign, waited patiently.

"What kind of money you talkin' about?"

"Fifty thou, maybe a hundred."

Carlo let out a laugh.

"Where does he get that much?"

"Don' worry, he's good for it. He saved his money all his life."

"So if he's so interested, how come he didn't come with you?"

"Hey, man, he's seventy. He don' like doin' business out in the street."

"Yeah, well, you'll have to give me a coupla days. I'll see what I can do."

Sam shook his head. "For this kinda bread, he don' wanna deal 'cept it's with somebody important, ya know, men around his own age. Don' get mad for tellin' you this, but he don' wanna do business with you."

He held his breath. This was the crunch. He glanced down to see what Carlo was doing with his hands. But one rested placidly on a thick thigh and the other on the wheel. It was hard to tell whether Carlo's feelings had been hurt. He stared out the windshield in silence. "I don't know," he finally said. Sam could not remember seeing him so unsure of himself. Sam was certain he had started wheels turning in his mind. "I'll meet you here Friday at the same time," Carlo said calmly as he started up the engine.

For once Carlo had kept his head. Driving downtown, he congratulated himself for not following his normal instinct, which would have been to stick a knife into Sam's heart. The black bastard's bullshit story about the old man wanting to deal big with big people deserved that. Except that if, as he thought, there was an effort at entrapment, you could bet your ass there would be cops close by. There wasn't much chance that Sam and what's-his-name would be trying something like that on their own. One thing had puzzled Carlo. Why would Sam go along with a police bust and kill a source of profit? The cops had forced him to play ball; that had to be it. It was too whacky to think they had money like that, but what if they did? While Sam was still in the car, Carlo had decided he had better lay this one on his uncle, who had his little network of police informers.

Accomplishing this took an hour of annoyed waiting in an outer office and five minutes of succinct retelling after he finally was admitted to his uncle's presence. Leaning back in his leather chair, the older man blew rings of cigar smoke through the capacious room, gratifyingly pleased with the way his nephew was learning to handle difficult matters. But Carlo did not expect the next words.

"When you see Sam, tell him I'm inviting his friend for dinner and a little business discussion Saturday night."

"You haven't been listening."

The smoke shot out in short, quick blasts. "Don't talk to your uncle that way."

"Maybe someone's trying to set us up. The old man don't look like he has a hundred grand."

"Don't you think I thought of that? But I want to find out who's doing it. Don't worry about it. The old guy—what's his name, Becker?—won't be going back home after dinner. Besides, I'd like to see who goes in for black boys."

Carlo was placated. The uncle was talking his language for a change. "Okay," he said. "What about the nigger?"

"If this is a setup, and I think it is, he has to disappear too." The uncle looked stern. "But I don't want him found on some street. Thanks to the last time you used a knife on him, the cops will know who to come looking for. When I say disappear, I mean disappear. You see he gets quick-limed out in Jersey like the old man."

Carlo was positively awed. The uncle was talking like the hard-nosed operator you had to be to stay alive in this business. Up to now, he had seemed like a bumbler who got squeamish when brutal action was needed, as, in Carlo's opinion, it often was. But now he was talking even tougher than his nephew. Carlo had never actually set out to kill someone, although, as Sam would attest, the result of his blind rages was not much different.

They discussed the dinner arrangements and decided that Sam should be invited along with the old man, there being little point in having to look for him separately. The two would be fed and eliminated together after being questioned separately. They would, of course, have no advance knowledge of the site of the dinner. Carlo would pick both up in a chauffeured limousine, rented under an assumed name, and escort them to the quiet back room of Uncle's favorite little trattoria off Mulberry Street. Carlo would make sure he was not being followed. If he was, he would drop them off at another restaurant and disappear after promising to return with the man higher up. But the meal would be on them, if they were still in a mood to eat after being stood up. They would be found and driven to Jersey later. Mulvaney, in the meantime, would be asked to find out exactly who was trying to play cutesy.

The uncle's phone call made Mulvaney uneasy. He was sure that if a scam was under way, it was the Feds' doing. Up to now, the city narcotics police had not only been kept informed of federal operations but had been brought into them. So how come neither he nor Carlin nor any of his other sidekicks had heard of this one? Unless, of course, Sam and Becker really were getting into the business in a big way. It was hard to believe, but stranger things had happened in the drug business. When Mulvaney suggested that it was altogether possible Becker and Sam were on the up and up, the uncle got irritated. He hated to be argued with when he had acquired a certain conviction.

When Carlo conveyed the dinner invitation to Sam, he became more worried than ever. It sounded too easy. He had always figured that whoever was behind Carlo would be very careful about the people he met. Now, not only had their offer been accepted, but there was an invitation to dinner and a limousine to pick them up! That was class, except that he had seen *The Godfather* and its sequel three times each and, as he remembered, when big cars showed up, sinister things happened.

He hurried to tell Becker, whose pulse rate rose precipitously as he rushed to the telephone to fill in Schofield. The agent did not like the smell of it either. The invitation was all too elaborate, but he kept his misgivings to himself. In a matter-of-fact way, he told Becker to meet him Saturday with Sam for lunch in the back part of a delicatessen opposite Lincoln Center. Wear a suit, Schofield said.

By then, the agent had organized a surveillance team that would try to keep the limousine in sight without being sighted itself. It involved several anonymous-looking cars that each would follow for a few blocks, then drop out to be replaced by another. Not knowing the route nor the final destination made the operation complicated but not impossible. To the lunch, Schofield brought a colleague, Ed Burns, as big and rugged as Schofield was slight, who wired Becker up in the washroom so that the device would emit long-distance beeps on his journey through town. All the time, Schofield spoke calmly and soothingly, trying to contain the panic the old man showed every sign of giving way to. If only Becker were a little younger and a little more courageous! Sam was holding up better, although his grin was weaker than usual. The old man came close to falling apart when Schofield gave him an envelope with $10,000 in thousand-dollar bills. If he wished to appear serious about making a deal, Schofield said, he needed something to back him up. Nothing was more serious than cash up front. Examining Becker, Schofield had second thoughts and turned the money over to Sam, who fingered the envelope almost with the same thrill he felt at having sex. Becker revived slightly after washing his face and hands and the back of his neck in cold water, but Schofield urged him to lie down after he got home and take it easy until dinnertime.

"Remember, you'll never be very far from our people," the agent said back at the table while Becker was fortifying himself with boiled chicken, matzoh balls, and celery tonic. Sam wanted a second beer to go with his hot dogs, but Schofield vetoed it, figuring he and Becker would be plied with plenty of wine in the evening. He wished he knew where the food and drink would be served, but the enemy was playing his cards close to his chest. That was par for the course, but it was not making things easy. That, too, he kept to himself.

Also unmentioned was the visit he had gotten in the morning from two members of the city task force, Carlin and Mulvaney, who seemed at first to have nothing better on their minds than to chew the fat. It soon became clear that they were on a fishing expedition, but Schofield refused to bite. He needed no help from the city people on this operation. If there was a manpower problem, he could always call on the FBI. Besides, doubts about the two cops had begun to gnaw at him ever since the joint operation that had failed to nab Carlo. When the agents got to the East Side apartment just after dawn, Carlo had already cleared out, leaving nothing behind that could be used against him. Two other pushers were caught in their beds, and a little searching uncovered sizable supplies of heroin and cocaine.

In the case of Carlo, the biggest operator of the three and seemingly the best connected, was it bad luck or forewarning? Schofield could not be sure, but he reached the point at which doubt turned to suspicion when Becker had mentioned going to Mulvaney and gaining nothing from the experience except harassment. Schofield had nothing really to go on except his instincts and the precedent of corruption among city drug enforcement officers. He had to admit, in fairness, that corruption was not unknown among the Feds either, but it was rarer.

"Whatever they're after," he thought to himself as Mulvaney and Carlin chatted away on the other side of the desk, "these guys are going to be kept out." So Schofield chatted back at them, talking of affairs they seemed already to know about but adding nothing to their knowledge. They took leave a half hour later, a little stiffly, it seemed to him.

He made a note to talk to the FBI about surveillance on both men.

Uncle Anthony was not happy when Carlin reported drawing a blank. He had been so sure he was being set up that he snarled denunciations of Carlin's and Mulvaney's incompetence for minutes on end. He hated to abandon his instincts, which had served him well for thirty years. When he was able to get a word in, Carlin assured him that he, too, and Mulvaney, for that matter, had also been suspicious, and still were. After all, where did an old man with nothing more than a schoolteacher's pension, as far as he could tell, get off dealing that big? But they had gotten not the least hint out of Schofield that something was up. And stranger people than Becker had gotten into the business.

"Play it by ear," Carlin said. "If there's some dough in this, why pass it up? You can handle Becker and his nigger friend anytime."

It was the kind of talk that appealed to Carlo, whose lust for money was beginning to overcome his own suspicions. He sided with Carlin. "What we got to lose?" he asked. "Maybe they're playing this straight. The nigger knows what I can do to him if he isn't."

The dinner would proceed as planned, the uncle finally agreed. If a fairly large quantity of green stuff was produced, he would hold off on the mayhem. But that, too, would proceed as planned at the first inkling of a trap.

CHAPTER

Sixteen

"Can you call Carolyn and explain things?"

Sam sat across from Becker in the studio, watching the old man eat ice cream as a preliminary for a nap. Becker could think of nothing else to calm the fear that was bordering on terror as the afternoon wore on. Sam turned his thoughts to sex, then to Carolyn, to distract him from the approaching meeting. The arrival of the limousine to take them Lord knows where was two hours away, and he was becoming as edgy as Becker. The imaginary lovemaking stirred him almost to a frenzy, and he longed for the one who was always ready to give his cock a warm, moist home. He began to think of what they would do when they made up, excitedly rubbing his crotch until he realized Becker had stopped eating and was staring at him.

He got up, awkwardly twisting his head to avoid Becker's eyes, and went to the window. "Can you call Carolyn?" he repeated as he looked into the street.

"We'd better keep this thing to ourselves until tomorrow anyway," Becker answered. "The fewer people who know, the better." He paused. "I guess you miss her."

Still casually inspecting the scene outside, Sam nodded. Suddenly he leaned forward, and his body tensed.

"What's the matter?"

"I ain't sure, but I thought I saw a dude I used to know. But when I knew him, he didn' hardly never leave Harlem, 'cept maybe to hustle around Times Square. So if that's him, what's he doin' here?"

A good question, Becker thought. His pulse, which had calmed after the stimulus it got in the restaurant, was back to racing as he went to the window and pulled the shade down. Again he lamented the passing of afternoons when his biggest decision was between a bench in the park and one on Broadway.

"Did he see you?"

"No, he weren't lookin' up this way," Sam answered, this time drawing aside the shade a couple of inches to peek out. "He jus' was leanin' on the buildin' across the street, watchin' the traffic on Riverside Drive."

"Where's he now?"

"I don' see him no more."

"Maybe you're imagining things," Becker suggested hopefully.

"Yeah, that's it, jes' my imagination," Sam said, taking another look before turning away from the window.

Becker finished his ice cream in the heavy silence while Sam picked up the sports pages of the *Times* and read an article on the New York Nets. There was a photograph of a player jumping for the basket. Sam studied it. If things had been different, that might have been him. At six feet, he was not big for basketball, but he was quick and agile and handled the ball well in Harlem schoolyards against most other kids. His head filled with memories; he had gone out for the high school team in his freshman year. He did not last long. "We're not interested if you can't show some discipline," an assistant coach warned him after he had arrived late for practice twice in a row. Then he and three others were dropped from the squad when they were caught smoking grass in the locker room, and no amount of promising and pleading could keep his fancied career alive. That was only four years ago. He had not touched a basketball since, except for a rare game of one-on-one. He put down the paper and sighed softly.

Becker, who sat dozing in his chair, was not good company. Bored, Sam returned to the window. The same guy again, languidly smoking a cigarette while propped against the building across the street. Sam studied him. He was short and compact like Carlo but less husky. Sam had not seen him in two years, but he was sure he was the pusher who had worked some of the same Harlem neighborhoods and had given him strong competition. He was one of the reasons Sam had decided to try the Upper West Side. Either the guy was branching out too, or something else was on his mind, Sam thought. He looked at Becker, who was now snoring. He took the keys the old man had left on the kitchen table and quietly let himself out.

"Hey, what's happenin', Luke?" Sam raised his arm in greeting. The other, who had been intent on the traffic, turned to him in surprise. It took him a second for the flash of recognition to come; then he managed a smile and a firm slap of Sam's hand.

"So you been doin' yourself some good, man?" Sam said, keeping the patter relaxed.

"Ain't complainin', brother. How about you?"

"Same. Didn' figger on seein' you around here, though. Nice surprise. You used to like to stick to Harlem for business. Or you got somethin' else goin' down?" Sam was leaning against the building and grinning as if what Luke was doing didn't matter nearly as much as the pleasure in seeing him.

"Yeah, that's right, man. I usually stay out of honky neighborhoods, at least for business."

"So you fixin' to get yourself a little white ass for a change?"

Luke slapped his thigh and laughed. "Don't give me no ideas; ain't got the time."

Sam decided to take the plunge. "So Carlo got you workin' too." Luke's smile vanished, and he jerked his head from one side to the other searching for eavesdroppers. He glanced at Sam reproachfully. "Hey, why don' you go on TV, man. Keep it down." His looked turned suspicious. "What you mean, 'too'?"

"I mean, Carlo ask me to watch this corner for cars, you know, the kind the fuzz like to drive. He pickin' someone up here, and he don' like nobody followin' him."

Luke scratched his head, perplexed. "He ask you?"

"Yeah, man," Sam answered. "He ask you too?"

Luke nodded a little sadly. "I guess he don' trust me much."

"Nah, that ain't it," Sam assured him. "He figger four eyes is better than two."

While Luke considered this, Sam went on. "Right now, even eight eyes wouldn' do no good here. Carlo ain't gonna show until seven o'clock. That's an hour and a half away. So if the fuzz is got plans, they ain't gonna be here for another hour, so why don' you and I go have ourselves a drink in some nice air-conditioned place? Maybe we find ourselves some pussy too."

Luke was tempted but doubtful. "If we miss somethin', Carlo sure gonna have our balls."

"What we gonna miss, man? We'll be back here in plenty of time."

Sam moved off with an encouraging smile, and Luke followed. They went to a Broadway bar where Sam used to do business and occasionally find women. He was in luck. A girl he'd been to bed with two or three times and who, each time, had begged him to stay a little longer, was sitting at a table alone. She was a mulatto, the next best thing to white ass, Sam told himself. He greeted her effusively and introduced Luke. It took only ten minutes for him to fix the two up with each other, the girl more than willing to use her place on Amsterdam Avenue, although a bit disappointed Sam was not coming too. Despite a hard-on, Luke was still worrying about Carlo.

"Hey, man, no sweat, take your time," Sam said. "I'll cover."

Sam left them finishing off screwdrivers and rubbing knees, and made it back to the house just as a somewhat battered blue Chevrolet was pulling into a space on Riverside Drive. From there, the driver had a view of the entrance to Becker's building. Sam recognized Schofield's assistant, Burns, despite his sunglasses and open-neck, short-sleeve sport shirt. They nodded at each other before Sam went upstairs to find a forlorn Becker, frazzled by worry over his absence and looking as if he had just been orphaned.

Carlo was waiting downtown for a phone call. When none had come by six-thirty, he concluded no police surveillance had been spotted, although with Luke, as with any other nigger, you could never be sure. You pay them good money, and you take your chances. All the more reason to keep a close watch on the rear-view mirror. He looked out and saw the long, black limousine, its driver hidden by the tinted glass, waiting. Carlo got into the front seat beside him. In the heavy traffic, the drive north took thirty minutes, time for Carlo to reflect on what he could do with maybe ten grand or more if a bullshitter like Sam was on the level, which was not likely, he had to keep telling himself. To his uncle, fifty grand, even one hundred, was maybe only routine for the week. He was not sure because he was never allowed to share in more than a small part of his uncle's business. The miserly bastard probably had millions salted away by now, with no sons to leave it to, while his only nephew, his only family really, was just another employee who had to hustle all the time for his bread.

The car double-parked in front of Becker's house, and Carlo looked carefully around before getting out and ringing the bell. Becker answered, and Carlo told him he would wait downstairs. Five minutes later, the old man and the young black man appeared, Becker in a rumpled blue summer suit, Sam in a tight-fitting yellow sport shirt and neatly pressed light-gray slacks. A real oddball couple, Carlo thought, avoiding their eyes as he held the rear door for them. Sam swung both ways, he figured, but why swing with an old fart like Becker? Some people will do anything for money.

Savoring his disgust, Carlo paid no attention as the limousine drove off and the old Chevrolet swung in from Riverside Drive fifty feet behind. On Broadway, Carlo told the driver to go right, and Burns radioed that they were heading downtown. At Seventy-second Street, he almost lost them when he was stopped by a red light the limousine just managed to make, but he caught up with them by the time they reached Columbus Circle. Then he sped ahead as a second car, a dirty black Ford with rusted fenders, took up the tail. Carlo was idly noting it in the rear-view mirror when the crash came.

A huge fuel truck they were passing on the left suddenly veered and caught the limousine on the right side. The car swerved crazily, and Becker was thrown to the floor alongside Sam. In front, the driver struggled to regain control while fending off Carlo, who was sprawled half over him, half over the wheel. Behind them, the Ford screeched to a halt, and the breathless driver watched the limousine careen left and right before coming to rest, half on the sidewalk, half out into the middle of traffic.

The occupants untangled themselves and felt themselves for broken bones. Becker's head and left shoulder, the first to make contact with the floor, were hurting badly. He raised himself to the seat and touched the lump on his head, then rubbed his shoulder. Old people had brittle bones, everyone said, but nothing seemed broken. He knew there was a good reason for all the ice cream and cheese he ate. They were full of calcium. He wished he had something for nausea.

Beside him, Sam seemed to have suffered no more than some dishevelment. He tucked his shirt back into his slacks, then shrank back as Becker doubled over and began vomiting. In front, Carlo felt the slight rip in the sleeve on his jacket and cursed the frightened chauffeur. He ranted on and on until the driver got out and inspected the damaged car. The tanker truck, its driver evidently unaware of what he had done, had long gone. Carlo looked back at Sam and Becker and grimaced at the smell of the vomit.

"Both of you okay?" Carlo asked. They nodded grimly. A crowd had gathered, some trying to peer inside, and pretty soon there would be cops. "Let's get the fuck outta here," he said. His stoved-in door was jammed. He jumped out on the driver's side, pushed his way through the onlookers, and hailed a passing taxi.

"Hey, what do I do?" the chauffeur called.

"Tell your boss what a fucked-up driver you are!" Carlo

yelled as he almost shoved Becker and Sam into the taxi. He gave the cabbie an address on Mulberry Street. The Ford followed, its driver radioing the incident and the changed vehicle. In the last of the five cars he had been furnished by the FBI, Schofield pursed his lips and worried about a loused-up operation in prospect.

The taxi got to Mulberry Street only five minutes later than had been planned, thanks to Carlo's constant badgering of the cabbie. So intent was Carlo on making up the lost time that he forgot to keep an eye out for a tail. With Becker continuing to beep despite the accident, Schofield picked the taxi up at Chambers Street and followed it into the crowded streets of Little Italy. He halted thirty feet ahead when it stopped to let out its three passengers and dispatched the agent beside him to watch as they walked to Hester Street and a nondescript restaurant advertising in neon northern Italian specialties. It was named Il Duomo, and neon tubes gave a rough version of the Milanese cathedral in the window.

The three men were ushered into a small room in the rear where Uncle Anthony greeted them first with joviality, then with mother-hen concern as Carlo explained their mishap. Still shaken by the accident, one pant leg stained and smelly from the vomit, Becker excused himself and went to the bathroom to clean up. On a motion of his uncle's head, Carlo followed to help, even wetting a cloth to remove some of the stain. Becker, remembering the chaos Carlo had created in his apartment, forgot his nervousness and became infuriated at the sudden solicitude. He snatched the cloth abruptly and did his own rubbing, Carlo looking on, then following him back to the dining room almost meekly.

"We'll skip names," Uncle Anthony said, the peremptory tone tempered by a gracious smile as he seated everyone at a large square table already loaded with platters of antipasti. "I am Carlo's associate. That is enough."

He began pouring wine but was stopped short by Becker. "I'm sure you know our names," the old man said. "Why shouldn't we know yours?"

He was being argumentative again, but at least for a purpose this time. The uncle put the bottle down and considered how to handle the outburst. Why sour things before he had a chance to see what there was in the old man's offer? He had a large stock of aliases he dipped into for various circumstances, mostly to confuse things when law enforcement officials tried to follow his trail.

"You are right. I am Anthony Bellini, like the composer. You like opera, Mr. Becker?"

The latter shook his head while Carlo struggled to keep a straight face at hearing "Bellini" for the first time. Sam searched his memory but could not recall that Carlo had ever named anyone further up the chain of supply. In drugs as in music, "Bellini" was a first for him too. Thoughts of the accident and the near unpleasantness over names faded as the dinner proceeded from the antipasti to a thick minestrone, then to fettucini, veal piccata, and salad, washed down with white and red wines. Becker spilled red pasta sauce on his pants twice but wine only once. He noted consolingly that Carlo was none too neat either. Through it all, the uncle kept up a patter of small talk as if it was a family reunion. To Becker he made oblique references to Carlo's misconduct, remarking on how wildly impatient young people could be, as though, Becker thought, this was enough to excuse brutality. For dessert, there was tortoni in the classic white cups, and Becker and Carlo each had two, the host watching them through a cloud of cigar smoke while drumming his fingers on the table to signify that at least he was ready to get down to business. Finally, when the coffee was served in little espresso cups, it was time to end the festivities.

"So," he said, looking at Becker and ignoring Sam as he had during almost the entire evening, "you're thinking maybe you'd like to make a couple of bucks?"

Becker had rehearsed the moment. "I think so. I don't indulge in such products myself, but I've said to myself, why fight it? If others want it, there'll always be someone to satisfy them, so why not me?"

Becker was rewarded with approving nods. "You're right not to indulge, Mr. Becker, but why deprive others if that's what they want, am I right? Alcohol and tobacco are also bad, but are there laws against them?" He held up a hand as though warding off an objection. "Yes, of course, I know there are some laws to protect children and young people. But adults should be allowed to make their own choices. When they're not, you get Prohibition, and you know the trouble that caused." With a glance at Sam, he added, "I want to make it clear I do not approve selling drugs to kids in school yards."

"I don' do that," Sam said. "Not no more." This time, Becker looked at him, and Sam corrected himself. "Not anymore."

The uncle continued to ignore him. "So tell me, Mr, Becker," he said, "what do you have in mind?"

That's getting to the point, thought Becker. He had been afraid the uncle would go on about how they were actually performing a public service, and he would then interject some comment that would queer things, as so often had happened with him.

"For openers," Becker replied, pausing to relish an expression he had heard in movies but never had the occasion to use, "I'm prepared to put up $50,000 for good-quality merchandise."

"My quality is always good." The uncle sounded almost hurt. "You talking about coke?"

"That's the best market these days," Becker said with the assurance of one who knew.

The uncle nodded. "You been studying the market?" he asked.

"I know what my friends want," Becker answered.

The uncle poured himself more coffee and relit a cigar. "I have to know who I'm dealing with," he said finally. "I need something up front; otherwise it's not serious business."

"You want something in advance?"

"That's it."

"That's easy," Becker said with a smile. He reached inside his jacket. Nothing. He reached again, exploring every corner of the pocket as if the envelope were only a small ball of paper. Nothing. He felt in all the other pockets, then looked below him around his chair. No envelope. Nothing. He began to tremble. Uncle and nephew stared at him. Sam looked down at the table and broke out in a sweat. Becker tried to remember. For an hour before they left the house, the envelope had lain on the table. When Carlo had rung, he had put on his jacket, then picked the envelope up and put it in his inside pocket. He was sure of that. He appealed silently across the table to Sam, but the black continued to look down at his empty coffee cup. Then the accident came back, the sudden lurch as the car was sideswiped, his sprawling on the floor. . . . He was sure he was going to be sick again.

"What's the matter, Mr. Becker?" the uncle asked gently.

Becker wiped his face with his napkin. "I . . . I had an envelope with $10,000. I don't have it anymore. There was the accident. It may have fallen out when I was thrown, and I didn't notice. It may still be in the car."

"An envelope with $10,000, and you didn't notice it was missing?"

"There were ten thousand-dollar bills," Becker said, not reassured by the uncle's unbelieving look. "It wasn't very thick."

"So what should we do?"

"Find out where the car is. Was it rented?"

The uncle nodded. He turned to Carlo. "Call the agency."

Carlo used the telephone at the little bar in the front of the main dining room, now empty except for two men sipping coffee. He got the garage, where a highly disturbed employee wanted to know what had happened. The chauffeur, he said, took off seconds after driving the bashed-up car in.

"Never mind that," Carlo snarled. "Just look in the back and see if you see an envelope on the seat or the floor."

He waited while the employee went off, glancing idly at the two late diners, who seemed little interested in him. Then he leaned forward into the receiver. "Nothing? You sure you looked good? Okay, okay."

He returned to the table and shook his head in answer to his uncle's inquiring look. Mr. "Bellini" turned solemnly to Becker.

"No envelope in the car, Mr. Becker. You wouldn't be playing games with us, would you?"

Becker and Sam looked helplessly at each other. The old man tried to think. If he yelled, would Schofield or someone with him hear? If he ran, how far would he get before Carlo stuck a knife in him? He had to get hold of himself. He could not count on help, in spite of Schofield's assurances. The beads of sweat on Sam's brow confirmed his feeling that he was on his own. And for what? How did he let Schofield talk him into this? For the agent, he was just another expendable weapon. Some weapon! He heard himself talking as if it were someone else.

"Well, then," he said, "it must be that I left the envelope home." He placed his hands on the table to steady them and looked directly into the uncle's eyes. "Why would we play games, Mr. Bellini?"

"I don't know, but it would be very foolish. Unless you're working with the cops. Are you, Mr. Becker?"

For once Sam spoke up. "Cops and us don' mix. Like you say, Mr. Bellini, we're fixin' to make a coupla bucks, that's all."

Becker was grateful to Sam for taking over the lying. He was sure he would have done it so transparently that he would have driven another nail into his coffin. Sam, he reflected distractedly, had had much more practice.

"So what do you suggest, Mr. Becker?" asked the uncle, who seemed determined not to talk to Sam.

"We go to my place and find the money."

The uncle pondered this for a full moment, Becker trying not to squirm under the cold gaze. "You don't need me. You go with Carlo," he said.

The last thing Becker wanted now was to be alone with Carlo. He shook his head. "I've been talking serious business with you. Why don't you finish what you started? I'm sorry not having the money on me. It'll be just a few minutes more." He was surprised at the steadiness of his voice.

The uncle glanced at his watch and rose suddenly. "Let's go," he said and began to stride out of the room, then stopped and turned. "I don't like to waste my time, Mr. Becker. I'm sure you know that."

The uncle was seething. He was being had, as he had suspected all along, and by whom? An old kike who was probably a pervert, and a nigger punk. He could barely restrain himself from strangling the two right there. But for the moment, he was keeping his self-control. There was still an outside chance Becker was not lying and that there was money to be made. The organization hated to pass up such opportunities, however slim, especially because of someone's hot temper. The two would be done away with a little later if, as he thought, they were trying to screw him, and he personally would give himself the pleasure of overseeing this act of "justice." He gave them an intense look and walked on.

Becker smiled weakly and followed him out, Carlo motioning to Sam to precede him. The main dining room was now empty. A large black Cadillac pulled up in front of the restaurant. The uncle looked around the deserted street, gazing intently at the parked cars. Evidently satisfied, he motioned the other three into the back while he sat with the driver, a huge man with thick features and a bald head that almost touched the top of the car.

In his car, the long wait and the steamy night had made Schofield drowsy. Hunched over the wheel 50 feet down the street, he became alert as he watched the group emerge and get into the Cadillac. He recognized everyone but the heavy-set, middle-aged man who got in beside the driver. Was he Carlo's superior? If so, an operation intended to draw out whoever was behind Carlo looked as if it might do just that. The two diners he had posted in the restaurant had reported on their walkie-talkies during their occasional trips to the bathroom. The dinner had been quiet. He would have raided it only if there were sounds of violence. Otherwise, he had intended to hold off on the theory that there would be no merchandise produced on this first contact and therefore nothing with which to nail anyone.

He was uneasy about Carlo's call, to which the men posted inside had cocked a careful ear. The report he had gotten made it look as though Becker had lost the envelope in the limousine, perhaps during the accident. He had put everyone on alert after that for fear there might be dire consequences. There were none, so far, but what had Becker done with the ten grand? And where were they going now? As the Cadillac pulled away, he started his engine and followed, alerting three other cars in the neighborhood.

Half an hour later, the evening was back at its starting point—Becker's building. Schofield arrived in time to see Becker, Sam, and Carlo alight, but not the two men in front. He felt in his pocket for the keys Becker had given him: one for the building, another for the apartment. What had led him to take that precaution was not exactly clear to him, but he thanked his instincts. Now there was a man leaning into the front car window on the passenger side, in conversation with the one who interested Schofield the most. Then he straightened up, and from his double-parked position on Riverside Drive, the agent got a good look at him. It was Carlin. Could Mulvaney be far behind? Again Schofield thanked his instincts. He gripped the steering wheel tightly as though to anchor himself from flying into a rage and doing something he would regret later. He reminded himself that such betrayal of trust was not new to him, even in his short career, but each time he encountered it, it churned his stomach and made him reach for his revolver, the first step in the summary execution he would not carry out but felt men like that deserved. The drug business generated seemingly infinite amounts of money, which, in turn, had an infinite power to corrupt. But not everyone succumbed. He was still living on his salary. What would happen when his five-year-old reached college age, he would worry about then.

Never mind now about morality and self-righteousness. He had to worry about how much the renegade cops had picked up of the operation. Had they tailed the tailers? Neither had been reported around the restaurant, so where had they spent the evening? He watched Carlin, his conversation over, station himself across the street, while Topman—so Schofield had dubbed both him and the operation—got out of the car and entered the building.

"Burns, Michaels, Gross, be prepared to move in," Schofield called over his radio.

Up the street came two elderly women, one short and wide, the other a little taller and thinner. The fates were not being kind tonight. The women stopped at the door, deep in a conversation that wrapped up all the loose ends of an evening out, plus the seemingly endless last thoughts that occur at leave-taking. The taller woman finally said good night, and the other fished in her purse for her key to the inner door.

She did not have to use it. The door swung open, and Mrs. Klein was facing Becker and Sam, with two other men so close behind they seemed to be almost leaning on them. She opened her mouth to greet Becker, but the words froze in her throat. A thin line of blood was trickling from a lump on his forehead and mingling with the sweat on his face. His eyes stared straight ahead like those of a blind person. She glanced confusedly at Sam and caught his look of wide-eyed terror before turning back to Becker.

"What's the matter?" she cried. "David, are you all right?"

"He's had a little accident," Carlo said behind him. "We're taking him to the hospital." He pushed Becker forward almost on top of the woman. "Get out of the way!" he snarled.

Behind her, the outer door opened, and four men rushed in with drawn guns. Becker heard a shot and the glass in the front door shatter. He ducked and pulled away from Carlo. Suddenly without a shield, Carlo grabbed Mrs. Klein, spun her around, and pointed a pistol at her head.

"Drop your guns or she's dead!" he called to the four agents. But Schofield watched Sam break free from Topman. With a blow from behind on Carlo's arm, Sam sent his pistol clattering against the tiles. Mrs. Klein collapsed in a huge heap. Two agents fell on Carlo and tried to wrestle him to the floor. A third agent made a flying leap at Topman before he could get off a second shot. Carlo was still fighting. He got a hand on an agent's revolver and twisted it around until the barrel was facing his attacker. Becker looked at the ground and saw Carlo's gun beside his left foot. He picked it up, pointed it at the back of Carlo's head, and fired. Through watery eyes, he just had time to watch blood mix with thick black hair before he fainted atop Mrs. Klein.

In the street, two other agents got to the Cadillac just as its engine began to turn. One ordered the chauffeur out while the other crossed the street and grabbed Carlin just as he was breaking into a run. A crowd was collecting, people running down the street, and from Riverside Drive and the park, windows were opening, and the ever-louder sounds of sirens signaled approaching police cars and ambulances.

CHAPTER

Seventeen

After the cut on his forehead was closed with three stitches, Becker was kept overnight at Roosevelt Hospital for observation for a possible concussion. Mrs. Klein was administered an electrocardiograph and given strong sedation after she regained consciousness and went into hysterics at the sight of the dead and bloody Carlo next to her on the floor. If not hysterical, Becker was horrified when he came to and realized he was a "killer," as he put it. The doctors could do little for his moral pangs except to counsel rest.

Mrs. Klein and Becker were released in the late morning with assurances they were at least in good physical health, and Schofield drove them home. Sam was also waiting in the hospital lobby, and Mrs. Klein was by then effusive.

"I have you to thank for my life, young man," she said, smiling at Sam for the first time that either Sam or Becker could remember. "It was a little confusing, but this gentleman," she pointed to Schofield, "told me what happened. You were so brave. Thank you, thank you." And she actually patted him on the arm. Then she turned to Becker. "And you, David, what a wonderful thing you did!"

"Never mind that!" Becker snapped. "I have killed a human being. Not even during the war did I do such a thing."

Schofield put an arm around his shoulder. "This is a kind of war too. You did the right thing. Just think, if you hadn't fired, one of my agents might have died instead of Carlo. Forget the guilt trip."

Maybe Schofield could kill without qualms, Becker thought morosely as the agent drove through traffic. He probably had. But this was not the way he had wanted things to turn out. Becker tried to recall those confusing moments in the lobby. He had only a vague memory of picking the gun up and aiming at Carlo. He acted without thinking, like a robot. This is what frightened him the most. At least, his instincts had been correct. He had hit the best possible target.

At home, Becker and Schofield filled each other in. A fingerprint check on the uncle showed him to be Anthony Calabrese, a member of one of the New York crime families, albeit one not in good standing with his associates because of his difficulty in keeping people like Carlo in line and of his own tendency to fly off the handle, despite all his lecturing to his nephew.

Looking a bit embarrassed, Schofield said the U.S. government was grateful to Becker for his help, but there was the matter of the $10,000 that had to be accounted for. With Sam's help, Becker gave a description of the dinner up to the ominous shake of Carlo's head when he returned from his call to the garage.

"I was sure I had the envelope with me," Becker recalled, "but how could I explain its disappearance except to say that I had probably forgotten it at home? When we got there, Bellini, I mean Calabrese, told Carlo he would wait in the car. Well, the envelope wasn't on the table or the floor or anywhere else Sam and I looked. Carlo was getting more and more agitated."

Sam broke in. "Yeah, I was expectin' him to pull a knife. But he takes out a gun and starts wavin' it at us."

Becker nodded. "I told him to take it easy, maybe the limousine chauffeur took it. But he said, 'Maybe you never had any money.' Then he yelled, 'The bullshit's over' and took his pistol by the barrel and hit me on the side of the head. He was going after Sam when the buzzer for the downstairs door rang, and Carlo answered it. He was talking and pointing his gun at us and looking grimmer and grimmer. Then he hung up and told us to move out. He took us down the stairway. Maybe he was afraid of meeting people in the elevator, I don't know. Calabrese was waiting in the lobby."

Schofield explained that Carlin had made a full confession when interrogated during the night and had implicated Mulvaney, who was picked up in his Astoria house while packing a suitcase. Both men had been posted by Calabrese in an apartment overlooking the street where the restaurant was. It was not until after the four diners had gotten into the Cadillac and pulled away that they had spotted the tail car, too late to warn Calabrese. Mulvaney had chickened out by then and had gone home. Carlin made a lucky guess about where the four were headed and finally got to Calabrese when the Cadillac arrived at Becker's building.

The police had gotten little out of Calabrese, on advice of his lawyer, but it was Schofield's opinion that the gangster had allowed his emotions to get the better of him. When, through the car window, Carlin had confirmed his suspicions, he had evidently gone a little berserk.

"That's when he made his big mistake," Schofield said. "He could have gotten away and left Carlo to handle the two of you by himself. Maybe it was pride, but I guess he wanted to take charge of the execution. Where you were going to be taken, I don't know, but it obviously was going to be your last ride." Becker let out a nervous laugh.

"That's funny?" Schofield asked plaintively.

"Excuse me, but it sounds like a gangster movie, and I never figured to be in one," Becker said. But the laughter did not come from mirth. His nerves, which he had controlled to a degree that flabbergasted him, were now beginning to unravel. He assumed again a properly solemn expression and looked at Sam, who seemed undecided whether to grin or frown. Becker took his hand, and Schofield, pretending not to notice, rose and left after saying he would talk to them again later.

Sam gently withdrew his hand and also got up. "Mr. Becker, can you call Carolyn now?" he asked. There was the slightest of sighs, as if the old man was resigning himself to the fact that Sam's attachments and interests were elsewhere. He picked up the telephone and got Carolyn in the midst of washing a customer's hair. She sounded impatient, and Becker told her only that Carlo was dead, thanks to Sam's courage in working with the police. There was a moment of silence on the other end.

"He there?" she asked.

Becker put on Sam, who almost blubbered into the receiver, then paused for blubbering from Carolyn. "Yeah, but Mr. Becker was in on it too," Sam allowed generously. "Yeah, right. You go back to your customer. See ya in a while." He hung up and stuffed his few belongings in a tote bag. He began to walk toward the door, then stopped, and returned to Becker's chair. He leaned down and kissed him on the top of his head. "You take it easy, you hear, man," he whispered.

Becker nodded. "You stay out of trouble, you hear, man," he whispered back.

"Yeah, I'll do that. Shouldn't be hard, now that I ain't got Carlo hasslin' me." And he was gone with a grin, leaving Becker forlornly wondering, What now? He picked up the *Times*. There was a short item on a shootout in a building on the Upper West Side, in which a drug trafficker was killed and another arrested. The address was given but not the names of anyone involved. The police had obviously kept this one close to their chests. A minor skirmish in Schofield's "war." Not even a footnote to history. He was heading for the kitchen when the doorbell rang.

Mrs. Klein was in a shapeless bathrobe, looking lumpier than usual. She had taken a nap and was feeling fine. "How about you?"

"*Comme ci, comme ça,*" he answered. "That's French for 'so-so.' "

"I'm sorry," she said. "Did you see the paper this morning? Drug traffickers, it said. Is that what those men were?"

Becker merely nodded.

"So how did you get involved with drug traffickers?" she went on. "It was that young colored boy, I'll bet. It's all

— 222 —

good and well to want to help people like that, but most of them are not worth helping."

Becker was getting annoyed. "He helped you last night," he snapped. "You even thanked him for it."

Mrs. Klein recoiled slightly. "I know, and I'm grateful," she said placatingly. "Maybe he's better than most of them, but that doesn't mean I have to associate with him."

Becker wanted to end the visit before he got nasty. "Mrs. Klein, I'm sorry you got involved. Is there something I can do for you?"

"Yes, that's why I came. I want you should come and have some dinner tonight. I'll make something nice, and you'll feel better. Say you'll come." She smiled and gave him an imploring look.

"Fine, fine. I'll come. Seven o'clock?"

She nodded happily, and he watched her walk down the hall to her apartment. "Boiled chicken with soup and vegetables and matzoh balls, David," she announced like a siren call.

The rest of his life was already unfolding. Fattening dinners with Mrs. Klein. Afternoons on a bench to get away from her. He was sleepy, and the wound on his head was throbbing. He stretched out on the daybed. Lots of naps, too, were in the cards again. Remember, he thought to himself, a few hours ago such prospects did not seem so dismal. You were even getting nostalgic for the old days, remember? Well, they're back. His eyes closed.

He was sitting with Sam at a marble-topped table on what looked like a café terrace. Around them were other tables peopled by slim, swarthy young men. One of them rose and came up to him. It was Beshir, and he was carrying a sharp stick, the kind he used to make his sculptures in the dirt and sand. He pointed it at Sam. "Who is that?" he asked. Becker was about to answer when Beshir cut him off. "Never mind; I don't want to know. It is enough to see him with you." Beshir plunged the stick into Sam, who fell forward, bleeding profusely. Becker screamed, and Beshir fled in a great clatter of upset tables, glasses, cups, and saucers. In the distance, an alarm went off, like the fire bell that used to interrupt classes in school.

The telephone jarred Becker awake. Shaken by what had just happened in the café, he had difficulty focusing on what Schofield was saying. "Press conference?" he repeated stupidly.

"Mr. Becker, are you listening? I'm trying to explain that we are going public with this affair. Some of the reporters at New York police headquarters have gotten wind of the bribery in the drug enforcement division—don't ask me how—and it's been decided that it would be a good thing to tell the whole story, including what happened at your building. Besides, we expect grand jury indictments shortly against the two cops and Calabrese."

"So?"

"So you're a star, Mr. Becker. We're going to put you on show as an enlightened and courageous citizen who has helped fight the drug problem. I'm not saying we're proposing you as an example because we don't enlist people like you every day." He was going to say "as bait" but stopped himself in time. "But still, maybe it will encourage others to come forward with what they know. There'll be a certificate of commendation from the Drug Enforcement Agency. The TV stations are going to eat it up."

Someone was proposing fame to him for the first time in his life, but there was no rush of exhilaration. Schofield was, in fact, making him uneasy. The reason came to him quickly.

"I don't want to interfere with your plans, Mr. Schofield," he said, "but I think I'd rather stay anonymous."

Schofield was astounded. "But why, Mr. Becker?"

"Because, what if Calabrese's friends come after me?"

Now Schofield sounded relieved. "Is that it? Don't worry. Calabrese doesn't have any friends, at least nobody dangerous. Carlo's dead, as you know better than anybody, and the others who worked with him are in custody. We've got pretty good information that the rest of the mob had no love for him. As a matter of fact, if we hadn't gotten him, they might have rubbed him out. They thought he was a dangerous pain in the ass. His old family might give you a commendation too." Schofield chuckled at the thought, but Becker was in no mood to share his mirth.

"Mr. Schofield, I killed someone. I feel bad enough about it already. I don't want to relive that again, not in front of television cameras."

"You still have that on your mind?" Schofield said with a note of exasperation. "I told you, you have nothing to be ashamed of. It happened for the best, I assure you. What are you afraid of, that people are going to take you for a blood-thirsty killer? Forget it. You're a hero. Accept it."

Becker winced at the word "bloodthirsty."

"There's another thing, Mr. Schofield. If you're going to make a hero out of me, how about Sam? He helped get Carlo, didn't he?"

Schofield took a moment before answering. "No charges are being placed against him for trafficking. That's his reward. We thought we'd keep him out of this because there might be"—more hesitation—"well, there might be awkward questions about how the two of you got connected, you know."

"That wouldn't be so hard to answer. He was a student of mine."

"Yeah, I know, but some people don't have the cleanest minds in the world. They're liable to think all kinds of things. You know what I mean?"

Becker did not like this conversation. It was clear, to him anyway, that Schofield was among the "some people." Who else? Well, there was Greenway and probably Mulvaney, although he no longer could give moral lessons, and maybe even Mrs. Klein, who seemed ridden by anxiety every time she saw him with Sam. Did he still care what people thought? Yes, he did. He always had. He no longer felt like fighting Schofield.

"Where and at what time is the press conference?"

"Right!" exclaimed Schofield jovially. "Ten o'clock tomorrow morning here at our offices. That'll give us plenty of time to make the six o'clock news."

There was not only the six o'clock news. There was a short item on the national news at seven, a repeat in late evening, and stories in all the papers the next morning. "A quiet-living, seventy-year-old retired schoolteacher has helped to expose a Manhattan drug ring and two New York City detectives working for it, federal drug enforcement officials announced yesterday," was the way the *Times*'s account started. "David Becker," it went on, "who used to teach French in the city's high schools, posed as a drug buyer and succeeded in luring two prominent members of the ring into a trap set by the Drug Enforcement Agency. Mr. Becker was slightly injured and one of the traffickers was killed in a shootout with federal agents. The head of the ring, identified as Anthony Calabrese, along with six associates and the two policemen, will be arraigned in federal court today."

The story was not exactly accurate, but at least he had avoided embarrassing questions about his gunplay. It was he who had prevailed on Schofield to obscure his responsibility for the one death. His encounter with the press lasted an hour, a confusing time of strong, hot lights and rapid-fire questions, which left him perspiring and exhausted but not displeased with himself. "I did my duty as a citizen," he watched himself modestly explain on the screen, the prominent bandage on his head eloquently expressing his courage. He stumbled a little when asked how he got involved in the first place. Schofield came to the rescue before Becker's meandering sentences could involve Sam, explaining that the old man had been approached several times by pushers working for Carlo.

Sprawled half naked with Carolyn on the couch in front of their set, Sam calmly took in his consignment to anonymity. Carolyn frowned.

"How come you don' get no credit?" she asked.

"It's all right, baby. I'm not lookin' for that kind of publicity. Word gets out that I was playin' along with the cops, and some brothers may not like it."

Carolyn pushed his hand away from her breast and looked at him accusingly. "What brothers you talkin' about, man? You still pushin' the stuff?"

"Hey, cool it, baby. When I said I'm out of it, I wasn' jivin' you, you know that."

"That's just it. I don' know that. So what you talkin' about?

"Listen, there's a lotta guys around who used to do things for Carlo. Not everybody's in the slammer. I figger some of them is not gonna like what happened to Carlo, he bein' dead and all that, and might come after me if they knows I had somethin' to do with it. Ya dig?"

"It was Mr. Becker who did it to Carlo. That's what you tol' me."

"Yeah, well, you notice he ain't takin' no credit either. He no fool. But I gotta say he got more balls than I thought."

Carolyn appeared mollified. She curled up again beside him. "Jes you be careful, ya hear? And don' go gettin' ideas again about usin' the shop for somethin' else. I swear, the next time'll be the last time, ya dig?"

He grinned and rolled over on her. "Hey, I wanna see the rest of the news!" she protested. Then she giggled, turned away from the screen, and opened her mouth for his tongue.

Three times the telephone rang while Becker was dressing. Someone called for the producer of a morning talk show, wanting to know if he could appear later in the week. The second call was from a free-lance writer, who proposed they collaborate on a quick paperback. His agent had assured him it would sell. Becker took both numbers and promised an answer. The Reverend Greenway was the third caller.

"I don't know what to say, Mr. Becker, except, I feel I owe you an apology," Greenway said. "I guess it just shows that when you don't know what's going on, you shouldn't make judgments."

To Becker, the apology tasted as sweet as vanilla ice cream. Nothing had galled him as much as the peremptory banishment Greenway had pronounced on him. He savored the deferential tone a moment, before assuming his own note of generous forgiveness.

"Don't worry about it, Reverend," he said. "I wasn't at liberty to say much anyway. With all the trouble you had at the church, I could understand why you were a little upset at the time."

"Well, it's nice of you to say that, Mr. Becker." Greenway hesitated and then went on. "I don't suppose that I could lure you back to the education program. We'd be proud to have you."

"I might want to do that in a few days, reverend. I enjoyed the few sessions I had. Of course, you'd take Sam back into the program too?"

"Well, I guess," Greenway answered hesitantly. "Was he involved in the case?"

"He was instrumental in breaking it, I can assure you. You don't believe me?"

"Oh, yes, of course I believe you," Greenway said hastily. "It's just that I didn't hear his name mentioned."

"It was kept quiet," Becker explained, "to prevent reprisals."

"I see," Greenway answered in a hushed voice as if he had become part of a great secret. "Of course, tell him to come back."

So, Becker thought after he hung up, he would have an excuse to see Sam again. Why did he want to do that when it was such a dead end? Because he could not get Sam out of his system. He had clung to Sam as if he were a prolongation of the Tangier experience, which, all his life, he had alternately evoked and suppressed. "You can have anything you want," Sam had whispered, but even then, he had not dared to succumb. Sam's offer had been made out of desperation, anyway. Once he got what he was looking for, namely money, that was it. The young man sought love elsewhere.

Becker had fame instead. Walking home from shopping, he told himself he must have no illusions. The fame would be momentary; then he would be back to the same anonymity that had enveloped Sam. But while the notoriety lasted, he could not deny that it was more than pleasant. Each time he saw or heard his name, a delicious thrill went through him. In the store, the manager gushed and made him richer by two pounds of vine-ripened tomatoes from Israel "on the house." Two customers shook his hand, and at the checkout counter, the girl offered *"muchas felicidades"* and then told the sad story of her brother, who "fooled around" with marijuana and would surely get caught one of these days.

He could not resist passing by the benches in the middle of Broadway. Those people who had virtually ceased talking to him were gratifyingly respectful. A few of them renewed the long-dropped effort to recruit him for the synagogue with the thought that his presence would be a magnet to others. One man eyed Becker as a prospect for his widowed sister, whom he wouldn't mind seeing on someone else's back. Would Becker come to dinner some evening? Perhaps soon, Becker answered. Three asked for advice from an obvious expert on how to deal with teenage grandchildren who took drugs. Discipline, he said. They must not be coddled. There were nods of approval. Then he had enough and moved on.

Later, at his apartment, the telephone began to ring as he was putting his key in the door. Maybe he would change his number for an unlisted one when the thrill of all the attention wore off, which he thought was already starting. He used to get a call a week. This morning alone, he had already had several weeks' worth. He ran to the phone. It was his sister, wanting to know if he was crazy.

"I really mean it," she said. "You have to be crazy to do a thing like that at your age." She started to blubber. "David, you could have been killed. You could have had a heart attack. How did you get mixed up in something like that? Never mind, I don't want to know. David, you come down to Florida this instant, you hear? I saw you on television with that horrible bandage. Oh, David, I was so proud. You'll tell us all about it when you get here, but it's obvious you can't take care of yourself. You need peace and quiet. David, are you listening?"

The storm subsided, and Becker put the receiver back against his ear. "I'm listening. It's too hot in Florida."

"We're air-conditioned."

"Collins Avenue is air-conditioned?"

"So who goes to Collins Avenue except in a car? The car is air-conditioned. David, are they after you?"

"Who's 'they'?"

"These gangsters, these low-lifes. How did you get mixed up with them? Never mind, you'll tell us later. David, say you'll come."

For one of the few times since his sister had moved to Florida, he was receptive. At least he would be away from his telephone for a while and have time to think. A week in Florida couldn't be too hard to take. He needed to figure things out. After all the congratulations, misgivings had begun to gnaw at the edges of his enjoyment of the sudden notoriety. It had not been neat, this little onslaught of his against the forces of evil. For one thing, the forces of good he had sought to mobilize were not ideal crusaders. A cop he appealed to had been crooked. Another, a federal agent, was young and probably so driven by ambition he had been willing to sacrifice anyone. A churchman had worried only about his church and had not lifted a finger. And the object of all this? To save a young man he was not sure wanted to be saved. For all he knew, Sam would be back peddling his dope in no time at all. The more he thought of it all, the messier it sounded. Messy and ambiguous, like the inner self he kept hidden from the world.

"David?"

"All right, Beverly. If I can get reservations, I'll be down tomorrow. I'll call you. There's a problem, though. In a few days, I have to get the stitches out of my head."

"So in Florida, we don't have doctors?"

Becker finally got his sister to hang up. An idea had come to him to help Sam keep to the "straight and narrow," an expression his moralizing parents had often used with him. He rummaged through his desk drawers until he found the document he wanted and some blank paper. After a trip to the bank, he spent the rest of the day writing and packing.

Several times, he picked up the telephone to call Sam at the shop. Each time, he put the receiver down. He wanted to tell him he was leaving but would be back. He wanted to tell him a lot more than that. That he cared for him. No, even more than that. That he loved him. Had he not proved it by going out on the most dangerous of limbs for him? He would, mysteriously, add that someday Sam would find another proof. And all Sam had to do in return would be to live an upright life and sometimes come to see him, not just in the classroom but at home, which, in a way, was Sam's home too, whenever he wished. Was that asking too much? Once he actually dialed Sam's number and let it ring twice before hanging up. It is no use, he told himself. I cannot force myself on him like some lovesick swain. Sam would not accept it. Why should he? It was asking too much. Long ago, Becker had stopped resenting Carolyn as an intruder, probably the day he had found her face deformed and her apartment nearly wrecked. She was Sam's natural, "normal" lover, the only one who ought to play that role.

Becker was in Miami early the next afternoon. Eastern Air Lines was only too glad to take him, and at cut-rate prices. Seats to Florida in early July were not in demand. Becker found the plane half empty. There was nobody in the next seat, or in front or back for that matter, leaning over to congratulate him. The hostesses either had not read the newspapers or had missed the newscasts. He was of two minds. The quiet suited his solitary nature, but he felt let down by the sudden falloff of attention. He had called his sister to tell her he was coming, then forgot about the freelance writer and the television station. He was sure they would forget him too, another depressing thought.

Outside the Miami terminal, it was as hot as he had feared. His brother-in-law, Ben, was a small, wiry man for whom Becker had an envious dislike because, after supposed retirement from his law practice, he had grown even more affluent selling advice on wills and estates to dozens of aged Floridians. Ben had never thought much of Becker after learning he had turned down a lawyer's career, but today he respectfully carried his suitcase. His sister gushed solicitously all the way to the parking lot. The long, gray Lincoln did not cool off until they crossed the Julia Tuttle Causeway into Miami Beach.

"This is Arthur Godfrey Road," Beverly said. "You remember Arthur Godfrey?"

"Of course I remember Arthur Godfrey!" Becker snapped. "He drank."

"Never mind, he was a very good entertainer." Beverly lapsed into silence, wondering whether it was going to be such a good thing having her brother. He looked out the window as the car turned into Collins Avenue and headed north. Few people were out braving the sun. Even the palm trees looked droopy. It was siesta weather, and he was feeling drowsy himself. But it was a long, slow drive past luxury hotels and shops—where his sister's instinct to play the tourist guide reanimated her tongue—to the expensive-looking, high-rise apartment building in Bal Harbour. He would have only a few minutes for a nap, according to his sister's plan for the evening. There would be cocktails with just a few friends starting at five o'clock; then they would be off to a nice French restaurant around seven. Becker remained glumly taciturn throughout the party. At least the air-conditioning was working, as promised. As for the dinner, his effort to show off by ordering in French came to nought when it drew only blank looks from the Cuban waiter.

Beverly, Becker came to discover in the days that followed, was born to be a social director. Her urge to plan his days and nights was as relentless as the heat. Only breakfast was eaten at home. Scarcely more than a few minutes were available for Becker to read the paper, and naps were hard to come by. Everywhere, he was shown off as "My crazy brother! You heard what he did?" He had to be nice to three times as many people as he would normally meet in a year in New York, and who "Oohed" and "Aahed" and asked him what Mafia gangsters were like. "Family men," he would answer, and he would be slapped on the shoulder and told, "Hey, that's funny!" while others exclaimed in tones of awe, "Such a modest man!"

"Maybe we should let him relax a little," suggested Ben as he climbed wearily into bed one night after a day he had found as trying as his brother-in-law had.

"Don't worry," she said. "Believe me, I know my brother. You leave him to himself, and he gets bored right away. He's always been like that."

Beverly made full use of the local Jewish community center's considerable resources. There were exercise classes, lectures on the proper life-style for the golden age, pinochle, bridge and Mah-Jongg tournaments, bingo sessions, movies and amateur plays, Spanish lessons. Becker had hit a particularly strenuous week, most of the members being reluctant to venture outside for more than a few minutes for fear of sunstroke. That had not stopped Beverly, who had insisted on going to the beach, which they left only after a couple of enervating dips in the warm ocean.

At the end of four days, Becker decided he had had it. He had enjoyed only one bingo session, at which he won $100. For once, they were eating dinner at home, a light meal after a heavy lunch in Miami Beach's most famous deli. But at dessert, he discovered that dinner was not meant to be the highlight of the evening.

"The Schwartzes upstairs have asked us over for bridge," Beverly announced.

"I don't like bridge," Becker answered.

"So what's the big deal? You'll watch."

"You go. I'll stay in and watch a little television."

"You are going to stay home alone?" Beverly asked more as a protest than a question.

"Beverly, if the man wants to relax by himself, let him," Ben interjected with the vehemence of a man who longed to do the same. Becker looked at him gratefully.

"All right," Beverly said reluctantly. "We won't be too late. There's fruit in the refrigerator, and if you want a drink, you know where to find it."

Becker dozed off over a rerun of *Miami Vice*, full of characters who led an even more exhausting life than he had done for the past four days. It was all about the drug trade, and he had had his fill of that too. A protracted and noisy shootout brought him out of a doze, and he turned off the set. He browsed through the small library in the den but found nothing but paperback romances and detective stories, for which he had no patience. In the way of fruit, he found two peaches and munched on one. It gave him a sudden hunger for peach ice cream. He rummaged through the freezer compartment but could find no ice cream of any flavor. In fact, there was precious little of anything anywhere in the refrigerator. Evidently, eating out was a way of life even when he was not there.

"So I won't have ice cream," he said aloud. But the idea gnawed at him as he wandered through rooms whose silence was broken only by the whir of the central air-conditioning. He vaguely remembered, during all the goings and comings, that they had passed a convenience store on some side street, which his sister said stayed open late. "I guess that's why it's called a convenience store," he had remarked, and his sister had shot him a quizzical look as if to ask, "Why do you always have to be a wise guy?"

He glanced at his watch. His sister and brother-in-law had been gone less than an hour and would probably not be back for another hour. He felt in his pocket for the key his sister had given him "in case we get separated, and you get home ahead of us." Until this moment, Beverly had seen to it that it never happened. He also felt the almost intact bingo money. As though caring for a waif, his hosts had let him spend nothing, except for cigarettes and, once, an ice-cream cone. He decided to look for the store. If he didn't find it, at least he would have had one of the few walks he had been allowed to take.

Even now, with the sun gone, few people were out in the steamy evening. Doormen stood listlessly in front of their apartment buildings, casting suspicious looks at the solitary stroller. He turned into a street but found it bound on both sides by high hedges and thick iron fences that protected spacious grounds and mansions. There was a shopping mall, but all its stores were dark and quiet. He saw lights down another street. He came to two restaurants and, wedged in between them, what seemed to be a bar with only a tiny window cut into a heavy mahogany door and a small red neon sign above that spelled out "Fiesta" in script. The door opened as Becker passed, and in addition to feeling the cool air, he caught a glimpse of a long, dimly lit bar with only a few people seated against it. Two young men came out, looked at him, and walked off, so close together, it seemed to him, that their shoulders touched.

He had been walking for fifteen minutes, with little idea of where he was going. He was thirsty. He opened the door and hesitantly peered inside. A young barman was pouring a beer. He looked up and smiled.

"Come on in," he said. "We don't bite."

Self-consciously, Becker closed the door behind him, took the nearest stool, and tried to make out his surroundings. Three middle-aged men shared the bar with him while two youths in blue jeans and T-shirts lounged on stools set against the opposite wall. There were no women. He peered into the mirror behind the bar. The low light softened the lines of his face. He did not look young, but he did not look old. He began to relax.

"What'll it be?" the barman asked.

Becker considered the question. He would have settled

for a lemonade. He decided a bar was not the place. "I would like a gin fizz," he said. The barman looked at him as if hearing of the drink for the first time.

"A gin fizz?"

"You don't make them?"

"Oh, yeah, sure. Haven't been asked for one in a long time."

Right away, Becker thought, he had established a generation gap. The barman did not look much older than Sam and was strongly built, like Carlo. He wore a body shirt, and Becker stared at his heavily muscled body and arms as he mixed the drink.

He could barely taste the gin and downed the drink in seconds. He was still thirsty and ordered another.

"You new around here?" the barman asked as he set the second gin fizz down. "Ain't seen ya before."

"I'm just down visiting from New York for a few days."

"Well, welcome to the Fiesta. My name's Manuel. It's a little dead in here right now, but it'll liven up in a little while if ya lookin' for company." He leaned toward Becker and designated the young men across the room with his head. "They're good kids. Won't give ya no trouble, if you're interested," he said in a low voice. Becker looked over at the youths, who stirred at the sign of interest and smiled at him. He hastily turned his back on them.

So he was in one of those places. He had never dared enter what people persisted in calling a "gay" bar in New York. All of a sudden, he was out of the closet. He always knew Florida was dangerous. He giggled. It's ten o'clock. Ben and Beverly, do you know where your child is? He called for another drink.

The door swung open, and a large, heavily made-up woman in a low-cut, red-flowered dress walked in. "You can all relax, dears, your mamacita's here," she said in a loud, husky voice. The two young men laughed. She parked herself on a stool beside Becker, her back to the bar, and looked at him severely.

"Well, are you going to buy your poor mother a drink, or are you going to let her die of thirst?" Long, dark eyelashes fluttered at him, and a manicured hand reached out and stroked his arm. Becker knocked over his glass. The barman came over and scowled. "Countess, leave the customers alone, okay?"

She looked pained. "You don't have to get huffy. I'm just trying to breathe some life into the place."

"Hey, countess, come here and breathe some life into my dick!" one of the young men called.

"Impossible!" she shot back. "It's been dead too long."

She looked pleased with herself after the laughter subsided. But when an inquiring look at the other men at the bar aroused no interest, she got up and headed toward the door. "Ain't no fiesta in this Fiesta," she said and left.

"The countess got stuck with no dough to head north for the summer," Manuel explained as he replaced Becker's drink. "She must be the only drag queen left in Miami Beach."

A night for firsts! His first gay bar, and now his first drag queen. He had been flustered by the queen's advances, but with the return of quiet, Becker found he was actually enjoying himself. He was feeling lightheaded but not unpleasantly so. He got up, a bit unsteady on his feet, and headed for the bathroom that Manuel pointed to in the back. When he returned, a young man all in white was sitting on the stool next to his. Becker looked at the stools against the wall, but they were peopled by the same two youths who had smiled at him before. Besides, they were wearing blue jeans, right? So his companion was a newcomer. Elementary. The man was smiling at him. White, even teeth shown out of a handsome, swarthy face. He was slender and broad-shouldered and looked tall, even on the stool. Becker did a double take and looked away quickly. If he were casting a play about Tangier, this one would do as well as anybody for Beshir's part. He felt his pulse quicken and grasped his glass tightly to steady his hand and studied it intently. Would he ever stop seeing Beshir every time some tall young man entered his life?

"So what's happening, man?" He was being addressed. He had wanted it to happen and was afraid it would. "Apprehensive hope," he murmured. Boy, are you drunk!

"What?" the young man asked.

"Just having a drink. Would you like one?" The invitation had slipped out, just like that.

"Sure, thanks. I'll have what you're having." And because he was nearly finished again with his own, Becker ordered two drinks.

"My name's Kim," the young man said, holding out his hand. Becker took it. "David," he said. "My friends call me Dave." Take it easy, he told himself. What friends call you Dave? What friends call you anything? There had to be more gin in those drinks than he was tasting.

Kim was looking at him. "Hey, ain't I seen you somewhere?" the youth asked suddenly. He snapped his fingers. "I know! You're the guy that was on television, the drug bust in New York, right?"

"Yes, that's right, but it was nothing really," Becker answered with an embarrassed smile.

"How'd you get mixed up in that?" Kim asked. "Ya know that's a big business down here. Ya shouldn't oughta go gettin' mixed up." Becker looked at him apprehensively, and Kim laughed and slapped him on the back. "Only kiddin'! I won't hold it against ya."

Becker noticed for the first time that Kim was perspiring heavily. Beads of sweat hung below the ring of dark, curly hair on his forehead. His hands were shaking.

"You feeling all right?" Becker asked.

"Yeah, sure. It's hot outside."

"You live in Miami Beach?" Becker went on.

"In Miami. How about you?"

"Just down from New York for a few days."

"Stayin' in a hotel?"

"With some relatives."

Kim looked disappointed. He took a gulp of his drink, then put an arm around Becker's shoulder and whispered in his ear. "I know a place we can go. Just ten minutes by taxi."

"What kind of place?"

"You know, a little motel. They don't ask no questions. We can be alone for a little while. I know how to give you good time." He had a slight accent. Becker was noticing things about him in bits and pieces.

"Are you Cuban?" Becker asked.

"Yeah," Kim answered with a smile. "Cubans know how to make love. So what you say, man?"

Manuel was leaning against the bar a few feet away and frowning. "Wait here," Kim said. "I gotta take a leak. I be right back." He walked away, then returned and said in a low voice. "Ya wanna check it out, I won't lock the door." Becker watched the gracefully swinging body until it disappeared into the bathroom. He lowered himself clumsily from the stool and pointed himself toward the back. Manuel came up quickly. "The guy's a junkie," he said. "I seen him in here before, and he's bad news. I know one guy he rolled." He moved away as Kim came back and put his arm around Becker's shoulder.

"So what you say, man?" The voice sounded urgent.

Careful, Becker thought. He's beautiful, but he's trouble. Don't want to get rolled. He gently removed himself from Kim's embrace and sat down again. "I'd like to, but I have to get back. My relatives are expecting me," Becker answered. His voice was full of regret. Fifty years ago, he had passed up an opportunity. Another was here challenging him. He was frightened. Get hold of yourself. You're not that drunk. "Maybe another time. Okay?" he said placatingly.

Kim's smile was wan. "Sure, maybe tomorrow night. I can be here anytime you say." He leaned over and whispered again while caressing Becker's thigh. "Can ya lend me a little now, ya know, maybe five bucks? Ya won't give me so much tomorrow."

Becker decided this was as good a way as any of ending things amicably. He wanted it to end that way despite what Manuel had said. When had he felt such longings? Kim was dangerous. Manuel had said so. And yet he wanted to be nice to him. That's what desire did. He had to battle to keep control. That's what drinking did. He pulled out his money. Kim stared at the fistful of money while the old man searched for a five-dollar bill. He found one after going through the whole roll and handed it to Kim. The youth kissed him on the cheek.

"Thanks, man. So what about tomorrow night?"

"I hope I can make it," Becker answered vaguely. "If I can, it'll be about this time."

"Sure," Kim answered.

He had to get away, or he would be lost in lust. "Lost in lust," that's good. A real phrasemaker you are. He walked to the door, swaying a little and leaning on stools as he progressed. At the door, he turned and looked back. He had forgotten to say good night to Manuel. But Manuel probably didn't care. No, what you really want is another look at Kim, isn't it? Maybe let him twist your arm a little until you say yes. But he's "bad news." That's what Manuel said. He smiled at Kim and walked out.

At the corner, he looked up at the street sign but did not recognize the name. Lost in the fleshpots of Miami. There are worse places to be lost. Kim really looks good. He should get home. Not really home. If he were in New York, he'd know how to get home. It was late. He would never hear the end of it. What was the name of his sister's street? Bal Bay Drive? Bal Harbour Drive? Why the British "u"? Probably to raise the prices. Someone will give him directions. The street was deserted. He tried to remember all the turnings he had made to get here. Nothing came back to his befogged brain.

Footsteps behind him. He turned. Kim was flashing another smile. "Hey, man, what's the hurry?"

The opportunity was following him. He wanted to welcome it. He felt excited. He wanted to say, "Okay, let's go."

He looked at the vacant, slightly hooded eyes. Like those of the blond who had pushed him in front of a taxi one day. Kim was talking.

"You smile at me. You like me, no?"

He had made a mistake. He shouldn't have smiled. Had to keep a grip on himself. "Of course I like you, Kim. It was just to say good-bye. Got to get home."

"Sure, where ya live?"

Kim was not arguing with him. Thank God. He looked at the young man, who continued to smile. "You know a Bal Bay Drive? Or maybe it's Bal Harbour Drive."

None too steady himself, Kim put his arm around Becker's waist as if to prop him up. "I know that. It's not so far. I know a shortcut."

They walked on, passing a high gate. Beyond it, at the end of a winding, slightly rising road, a few lights gleamed from a large, three-story house. "Hey, man," Kim said admiringly. "How'd ya like to live in that?"

Becker looked at the house dubiously. "Too big. Who's going to clean it? You like to clean house?"

"You live in a place like that, you don't worry about cleaning it. You get Cuban girls."

"Too big," Becker insisted. "A little cottage, maybe. I wouldn't mind that. For the winter. Too hot here now. Need to be rich to live in that place."

"You not rich?"

"Of course not. What makes you think I'm rich?"

Kim's voice harshened. "Hey, don't go shitting me, man. I seen the bills you got."

They were under a tree whose leaves cut the streetlights into crazy patterns and spread a semidarkness over them. Becker tried to make out Kim's features. The perspiring face was no longer smiling.

"Bingo," Becker explained. "Won a little at Bingo." He reached in his pocket and withdrew the first bill he came to. It was ten dollars. "For you, Beshir," he said haltingly. "I can say it now. I love you. I always loved you."

"Who the fuck is Beshir? Why you jiving me, man?"

The beautiful face was now distorted by a grimace. Kim took the ten dollars. "Need more than that, man. C'mon, I know ya got it."

Becker broke into a run. Have to get away, he thought. Why did he call him Beshir? Beshir never asked for money. Beshir was gentle. Except for that time he stabbed Sam. No, that was in a dream, stupid. His lungs were bursting. Haven't run in forty years. Have to give up cigarettes. His leg, the one with the blocked artery the doctor constantly warned him about, was hurting. A few more steps and it gave way. He fell to the pavement. He saw a glint of metal, then felt the sharp pain as a knife entered his stomach. It withdrew and entered him again, struck a rib, withdrew, and came in close to his heart. Someone was leaning over and rummaging in his pocket. Then a sound of running that quickly receded. Yeah, you'd better run. You're dealing with a killer.

The street was quiet again. He lay there for a long time. Hours, it seemed. He felt his body and gazed fascinated at his bloody hands. Be careful. Always get sick when you see blood. Then he was looking at faces above him. Dimly he heard the word "ambulance." He groped in his empty side pockets. "Can't even get a little cottage," he moaned. He was sinking into blackness. Then he saw and felt and heard nothing more.

CHAPTER

Eighteen

Ben and Beverly identified the body at the morgue of the hospital where Becker had died as he was being wheeled in. Beverly was quiet now, too exhausted to sustain the hysteria that had built up when first she found the apartment empty, then vainly waited an hour for her brother to appear, then learned of his fate from Ben's calls to the local police station and to the closest emergency room. She was still incapable, however, of completely coherent answers to a detective's questions.

"Weird thing," the detective was saying. "If I got it right, he helped bust a drug ring in New York and was on television. We have a lead on a junkie who may have done it to him. It's almost like revenge, if you think about it. There's a gay bar a few blocks away from where the body was found, and your brother answers the description of someone who was seen there with the hophead. He followed him out."

Beverly stared at him. "A gay bar? A gay bar? What would my brother be doing in a gay bar?"

The detective shrugged. "You'd know better than me," he said.

"My brother was a respectable Jewish man, a schoolteacher," Beverly said. She began sobbing again, and Ben tried to comfort her.

"You have any idea what he was doin' out?" the detective asked when she had calmed down again. Beverly shook her head and said, "Just to take a walk, maybe."

"He have any money on him?"

"I don't know. He won a little something at Bingo the other day. Maybe he had that."

"His pockets were empty except for a Medicare card," the detective reported. "It looks like a case of robbery. He was mumbling something just before he lost consciousness. It was hard to make out. The person who heard him thought he was saying something about a little cottage."

"A little cottage?" Ben repeated.

"Yeah, that make sense to you?"

Sister and brother-in-law shook their heads helplessly. The detective had no more questions and left.

"So now what?" Ben asked in the car as they drove home.

"We have to make funeral arrangements," Beverly answered and broke into another fit of sobbing. "I used to get so mad at him," she said when she got over it. "Every time I asked him to come down, he would say he wasn't ready for the graveyard yet." More sobbing. "He must have had a premonition."

"So where do we bury him?" Ben asked, his mind on immediate problems.

"Just before his wife died, he bought two plots in New Jersey. That much I know. The least we can do is bury him beside his wife."

"Flying a body up to New York is expensive," Ben objected.

"Ben," Beverly said, putting a gloved hand on her husband's shoulder, "it's the right thing. After all, we insisted he come down. If he'd stayed in New York, he'd still be alive."

"You insisted."

She looked at him indignantly. "Ben, are you going to argue over a few dollars to fly him up." A thought occurred to her. "He had a round-trip ticket. I'm sure we'll be able to use the return for part of the expense. The rest we can deduct from the estate."

Ben was only partly appeased. "What kind of estate can a schoolteacher have?"

"So maybe he has a few thousand dollars put away. That's enough. We'll see if he's left a will. And if he doesn't have any money, what's so terrible if we pay? Are we starving?"

The irritation in her voice made Ben turn to other matters. "What kind of funeral? He was an atheist, no?"

She became indignant again. "He was not an atheist. He just didn't like rabbis. I'm sure deep in his heart was a love of God." Ben thought it better not to continue the argument, and they drove on in silence until Beverly suddenly shouted "Ben!" so loudly he nearly drove into another car. He braked to a stop, breathing heavily.

"What's with you?"

"Ben, I just figured out something. He didn't say, 'A little cottage.' He said, 'A little kaddish.' I'm sure. You see, he felt he was dying and wanted to make his peace. That's what he was saying." She smiled for the first time since the ordeal began. "So we'll have a rabbi say a little kaddish."

Ben looked dubious. "Deathbed conversions, that's for novels. He wouldn't allow a service for his wife. Why would he want one for himself?"

She shrugged. "Go figure. A change of heart. Everybody's entitled. Look, all his life he was a quiet-living man. All of a sudden, he gets mixed up in drug busting and becomes a hero. You couldn't expect that either."

"Why 'A little kaddish'? Either you say kaddish, or you don't say it. Besides, you need a minyan."

Beverly was getting annoyed with Ben's peckish ways. "Who knows? He was making a concession but couldn't bring himself to go all the way. So he said a 'little' kaddish to show he still had some doubts. You can take the boy out of Judaism, but you can't take Judaism out of the boy."

"Where'd you get that?"

"I don't know. Maybe in some Philip Roth book, that wise guy."

"And the minyan?"

"Don't worry. There'll be enough people for a minyan. Why do you have to argue all the time?"

Becker's body was flown to New York the next morning after an autopsy that showed three stab wounds and a fatal loss of blood. A little violence would be done to the Jewish rule about burial within twenty-four hours of death. It could not be helped. Riverside Chapel could not take them until a day later. At least, this gave time for a funeral notice in the *Times*. It and the other papers carried dispatches from Miami about the death of a man who only a few days before had been cited for helping to break a drug ring. All the articles dwelt on his ironic death at the hands of a dope addict. In late afternoon, in Little Havana, the police arrested a suspect, Pedro Elisondo, who thought "Kim" was an American-sounding name and who had a long police record as pusher and addict. He was nineteen years old.

At Becker's building, Ben and Beverly got the key from the superintendent, who, when they identified themselves and told him what had happened, broke into a rapid stream of Spanish condolences and crossed himself. He and Becker had exchanged few words all the time the old man had lived there. But after the bloody scene in his front vestibule and then a day later, the television news and the story in the *Daily News*, the superintendent, who was as surprised as anyone at Becker's role, had knocked on Becker's door and shaken his hand.

Now, he made Ben and Beverly uncomfortable by breaking down and crying. He showed them up to Becker's studio, then returned to his basement apartment and found the story of Becker's death in the *Daily News*. It was a Cuban, like himself, who had done it, and he thanked the Virgin Mary for giving him the good sense to move from Miami to New York ten years ago with his wife and four children. Not that New York was a safe haven. The smashed glass in the front door showed that. He read the story a second time, then carefully clipped it and put it on the bulletin board in the elevator next to where tenants were signing up for the exterminator's next visit.

Mrs. Klein found it as she was coming up from the basement with a load of wash. She dropped her basket on her foot and screamed, whether from pain or shock she did not know. She was moaning as she came out on her floor, so loudly that the young couple next door stuck their heads out and asked if she was all right. Beverly stopped rummaging in her brother's closet and opened the door to find out what the commotion was about.

Mrs. Klein looked at the unfamiliar face and went toward it in a limping waddle.

"Who are you? What are you doing in David's apartment?" she blubbered.

"I am David's sister," Beverly answered, and she looked as though she would break down too. "You know what happened?"

"I just saw it in the elevator. I didn't listen to the news this morning. My God, I gave him dinner a few nights ago. And now he's dead? How could it happen?

"It's hard to believe, I know. I still don't believe it myself. You knew him well?"

"Yes, of course. We saw each other every day. Such a nice man, a quiet man, a little shy maybe. Didn't talk much. And then that big thing he did without telling anyone, without boasting. And now this." She halted a moment to catch her breath, and Ben hoped she would go away so they could continue going through the apartment. But Mrs. Klein was not finished. She broke into a coy smile. "We had plans," she said. "We were thinking maybe it would be nice to get together and not be so lonely."

"You mean marriage?" Beverly asked incredulously.

"Oh, it wasn't firm. It was just an idea."

"He never mentioned it to us."

"Just like him. The dear man wanted to be sure, I suppose. In a few weeks, it could have happened." The tears began again. "And now this. Excuse me. I have to lie down." She hobbled off, picked up her laundry, and disappeared into her apartment.

"The funeral's tomorrow morning at ten o'clock at the Riverside!" Beverly called after her. She shut the door and asked Ben, "Did you get that?"

"Yeah, something tells me the plans were all hers. Hello, what's this?" He pulled out a sheet of paper from a stack he

held in his hand. "I think we found it. 'Last will and testa-
ment,'" he read. He looked at the bottom of the page.
"Wouldn't you know!" he exclaimed. "He signed it, but
there are no witnesses. It's dated July 12, only seven days
ago.

"So what does it say?" Beverly asked excitedly.

Ben read silently and looked at his wife. "He left
$10,000 to somebody named Carlton White, 'sometimes
known as Sam.' The rest, he says, should be enough for funeral expenses. Who the hell is Sam?"

"How do I know?" she snapped. "Who knows what he
had in that head of his, my brother. Is the will legal?"

"Of course not. It needs witnesses. I guess he didn't
have time to find them. Maybe there's an earlier will."

Beverly hesitated. "This one may not be legal, but it's
his last desires. Don't you think . . . ?"

"I don't think anything," Ben answered sharply as he
resumed searching the desk. He pulled out more papers and
leafed through them. "Ah!" he exclaimed triumphantly.
"Here's another, dated four years ago." He looked at the
bottom. "This one's signed and witnessed."

"And?"

"'All my earthly possessions I leave to my beloved sister, Beverly. These include all the furnishings in my apartment and any funds that may be left in a savings account,
number 06-21953, at the Chase Manhattan branch at 2410
Broadway, and a checking account, number 06-479530.'"

Beverly looked with wet-eyed disdain around the room.
"They're not much, the furnishings."

"So we'll give them to the Salvation Army or something," said Ben, putting the older will in his pocket. "We'll
file this for probate." The newer one he began tearing up
until Beverly restrained him. "We should find out who
what's-his-name is. Maybe David had a good reason to
want to leave him something."

"Sounds like a goy. How could he get so intimate with a
goy that he'd want to leave him everything instead of to his
own flesh and blood?"

Beverly shrugged. "Go figure. If you ask me, he was always a little meshuggah, my brother, especially lately. Maybe that woman, his neighbor, would know."

Mrs. Klein insisted they join her for coffee and cake. She spilled her cup when Ben asked her who Carlton White, or Sam, was.

"He's a young Negro man," she said. Ben and Beverly stared at her. "I know, I thought it was strange too. He started out as a student of David's, but there was more to it than that. As a matter of fact, David told me a little one night about this Sam being mixed up in the drug business, and he, David, was trying to get him out of it. Can you imagine? A nice, quiet man, he should be entitled to a little peace and quiet at his age, getting so involved with this colored boy that he even slept in David's apartment a couple of times, and David held money for him. It's not to be believed! And then they were together in that horrible business with those gangsters, and he even helped save my life. So he's not so bad, but still I always felt there was a part of David I did not know, like there were two Davids, and one was practically secret."

The mention of a "secret David" took Beverly's mind back to the gay bar the detective had mentioned. She looked at her husband. He had listened solemnly to Mrs. Klein and now seemed lost in his own thoughts. How could it be? He had been respectably married for so long, never a hint there might be—what could she call it?—another side to him. If there was one, he had certainly kept it bottled up. Go figure. Beverly sighed and drained her cup.

"It just shows," Beverly said, "you think you know a person, and you find out you don't know him at all. Even your own brother. Thank you, Mrs. Klein, but we have to be running along now. You'll come to the funeral?"

"Of course," she answered. "We all owe David that. I want you to know how sorry I am his life had to end this way."

Her guests agreed it was a real tragedy, each silently trying to dismiss the idea of being responsible for it. Some things were better left unsaid. Actually, Beverly thought, some things were unspeakable.

The number of people at the funeral home bewildered Beverly. "I'll bet David never would have imagined this," she remarked to Ben. "And you were worried about a minyan!" Extra folding chairs had to be brought in. Most of the mourners, she thought, hardly knew him. The better part of two block associations came to pay homage to a man who had contributed to the fight against street crime. Most of Becker's fellow tenants were there with the superintendent. The Reverend Greenway was in one of the front pews, turning over in his head an idea for naming the basement classroom the David Becker Memorial Room printed on a brass plaque. Maybe he could hold a little ceremony that the local stations might be persuaded to cover. It would help with the fund drive.

The principal and five teachers from the high school where Becker had taught also got seats up front. The owner of the cheese store whom he had harangued one evening decided he would open his shop a little later. Becker might have been strange, but he practiced what he preached, you had to hand him that. Schofield and three other agents sat behind Greenway, along with a representative of the city police. Ten people with whom Becker argued on the benches came as though for a send-off to a club member, albeit an unpopular one.

Rabbi Kirschbaum refused to limit himself to kaddish. A year out of Hebrew Union College and still looking for a congregation, he had taken on the dreary work of eulogizing hardworking fathers and devoted mothers with unchanging formulas that made mourners wish he would get it over with. Now he had something he could sink his teeth into, embroider on, soar to the oratorical flights he had been complimented on in school. He drew Becker's sister and brother-in-law into a little room to press them for details on Becker's life. They were strangely reticent, he thought, as he perspired through a series of questions on Becker's exploits.

With embellishments, the rabbi resigned himself to twenty minutes worth, enough to earn his fee. Becker's seeming lack of piety except at the very end of his life, and even that wasn't sure, bothered him a bit. But his sister insisted he had finally come to terms with God. Perhaps, he said comfortingly, this was all that mattered. He decided to leave out the part about teaching in a church basement, lest the question of what God Becker had in mind might lead to ecumenical confusion. When they returned to the crowded chapel, Beverly looked around anxiously. Her eyes swept along the rows until, reassured, she sat down in front and faced the casket and the pulpit. All the faces were white.

Rabbi Kirschbaum cleared his throat, and the mourners quieted down.

"Friends," he said, "we have come to say farewell to an exemplary man, a good man who lived a quiet life of service to his community and who did not deserve to die the way he did. He was not wealthy the way we often think of wealth, but he imparted wealth to others. Yes, my friends, he was a teacher, and that is someone to be honored. He gave to the young something more precious than gold. Learning, knowledge, they are the tools of life. Ah, if only the young could understand that." There was a stirring among Becker's former colleagues, who nodded approval at each other. One of the older members of the romance languages department wondered how many of Becker's pupils could now remember even *bonjour*. Could any of his own students, for that matter?

When the rustling died down, the speaker resumed, satisfied he had stirred his audience. "I am sure our departed friend deplored with all of us what is happening in the schools he served so well: the disorder, the dropouts, the wasted lives. Perhaps he was more sensitive than most to the state of education because he was not only an educator but a Jew." It was Greenway's turn to stir. Just like a rabbi, he thought, to think nobody else worries about education. The gall of the man. And what about the opportunity his church had given to Becker? he wanted to shout. He was getting upset.

With a sense for the dramatic, the rabbi moved on quickly to more exciting things. "This man, David Becker, devoted as he was to serving his fellow man, did more than his bit to combat another scourge. Yes, my friends, I am talking about drug abuse. You all read or heard about his bravery, how he unhesitatingly, and with no thought to his safety, confronted the gangsters who prey on men's weaknesses. He defeated them only to fall prey himself to the violence of a drug-crazed world, an innocent victim doing the most innocent thing in the world: he was out taking a walk. An absurd thing. You may well be asking yourselves how God could let this happen." He paused and looked around inquiringly.

Beverly wished he would drop the subject. Why does he have to bring God into it? Behind her, she heard the noises of restless people. But Kirschbaum was determined to finish with a moral lesson.

"It was meant as a warning to be on guard against the temptations that threaten us all, especially our young people," he said. "Yes, my friends, David Becker's death was meant to have a sense, a meaning. We must all of us, public officials and private citizens, dedicate ourselves to fighting this terrible thing as he did. That must be the meaning of his death. He did God's work and died as a martyr. Let that be his memorial."

In the very last row of folding chairs, Carolyn turned to nudge Sam. "You listenin'?" He nodded glumly. He fingered the cigarettes in his shirt pocket. He was dying for a drag.

Carolyn and Sam had come in, breathless and self-conscious, just as the rabbi embarked on the subject of drugs. Around them, people stared at them curiously, as if they had ventured into the wrong funeral. They looked resolutely ahead, pretending to ignore the attention they were getting. Sam noticed that the men were wearing skullcaps.

A man nodded at a box next to the door, and Sam got up and fished out a paper yarmulke and put it on.

For two days, he had fretted and paced through Carolyn's little apartment. She had never seen him so down, except perhaps when she had told him of washing the cocaine down the toilet. They had learned of Becker's death on a late news telecast. Carolyn's mind had gone back to the time she listened to the news of Sam's knifing. She broke down first.

"They's just no end!" she cried. She turned on Sam as if it was his fault. "Ya see? Ya don' need no Carlo for folks to die. They's lots of assholes like Carlo out there jes' waitin' to kill people. You understan' that, man?"

But Sam was already thinking too many dark thoughts of his own to listen to Carolyn's outburst. Dimly he perceived, like her, a link between himself and Becker's death. In the drug business, the stakes were high. You could make plenty of bread, but you could also get yourself killed or locked up. He had always told himself that but had gone on anyway. Chastened more than usual by his brush with death during the drug bust, he had quietly helped to manage the shop, and at the end of the day had gone home with Carolyn, helping to cook meals and staying put. He had smoked a little pot, but so had she. So did a lot of people. No harm in that. He was feeling relaxed. Business wasn't that bad; he had even looked a couple of times at a location for a second shop, and had begun to think again about his high school diploma. As he kept reminding himself, there was no Carlo to bug him, and he was clear with the cops. But he had that restless feeling, wondering what was happening out there on the street. He was bored.

Now this. Mr. Becker didn't have it coming to him, no way. He was white folks, and maybe a little queer, the way he would stare at him sometimes, but he had never met anyone who had been willing to help him like Mr. Becker. He had involved the old man in his drug problems. Now he was dead from a junkie's knife, the man on the program said, like he had almost died from Carlo's murderous shiv. What one had to do with the other, he wasn't sure, but the connection was there somewhere. He sat down on the couch, took Carolyn in his arms and cried with her.

They shared an equally vague feeling that amends had to be made. They went by Becker's house, learned from the superintendent's wife of the funeral, and rushed to Amsterdam Avenue in time for the rabbinical sermon on drugs.

Maybe he could be a cop like Schofield, Sam thought, as Kirschbaum droned on. Images flipped through his mind: speedboats giving chase to drug runners, a whispered stakeout in a dark, cavernous warehouse, kicking in a door and rushing into a room with his gun drawn, screwing the hell out of women who would fall adoringly into the arms of their hero. He thought some more and frowned. "Nah," he said aloud. Carolyn hushed him as people craned to see who was disturbing the peace. Oh God, Beverly thought, he came after all. She looked quickly at Carolyn before turning her attention back to the rabbi. He's got a wife? Probably not; those people don't marry. Must be his girlfriend. At least he likes girls. She stole another look at him. He was very young, and he was kind of good-looking, for a Negro. He had an unhappy expression on his face. Perhaps he did have feelings for David. The thought unsettled her.

In the midst of his adventures as a drug-busting Fed, Sam remembered that those guys were all college men. He could not see himself going through four years of higher education when it was not so easy even getting through high school. That would be all the education he could take. He let out a sigh, and Carolyn hushed him again. He was worse than a child, she thought.

Even Rabbi Kirschbaum knew when to stop. It was getting late, and there was still the cemetery. He had noticed the brother-in-law looking at his watch several times. He launched into the kaddish, and all over the room men picked up little cards from the racks in front of them with the prayer in Hebrew and Roman letters and a translation.

Self-consciously, Sam rose with the others and tried to follow silently. He found he could read the English pretty well.
He was not sure what it all meant, especially all the references to Israel. He had thought Mr. Becker was an American. Anyway, he was reading better than he used to. The
old man had taught him something.

The rabbi finished and announced that two limousines
were available for those without cars who wished to accom-
pany the family to the grave site. Then the Reverend
Greenway jumped up.

"Excuse me," he said to the startled rabbi. "Can I say
just a word before we go our separate ways?" He cleared his
throat while mourners stole quick glances at their watches.
Beverly wanted to say something, but Greenway was already launched.

"I know this is unusual, and I apologize," he said to the
rabbi. "Your tribute to an old schoolteacher was most moving. I am the Reverend Eliot Greenway. I just want to add
that David Becker cared so much about education that he
came into a house of worship not his own to carry it on
among disadvantaged young people with ambitions to get
ahead in life. We have examples with us today." Greenway
paused and pointed at Sam and Carolyn. "Carlton White
and Carolyn Rogers are here to pay tribute to a man who
tried to help them." There was a great shifting of heads, and
the two smiled weakly. Greenway grasped the pulpit, as if
officiating at his own church. "In a way, in the upright life
they live, they are memorials to him. I want to announce
another memorial. We will shortly be dedicating the David
Becker Memorial Room as a reminder of his dedication to
education and to true ecumenism." Greenway would have
liked to have gone on with the ecumenical part, but the
rabbi and the family in the front row did not look happy. "I
just wanted to say that," he finished lamely. "Thank you."

Barely acknowledging such chutzpah, Kirschbaum regained control and repeated his announcement of the limousines. Mrs. Klein, who took her mourning seriously, was

a taker. The high school principal sighed and decided it was the least he could do, particularly after getting knowing looks from the teachers, who had to get back to classes.

Schofield decided he had better get back to his office. He caught Sam's eye and motioned him over. "So how are things going?" he asked. "Staying out of trouble?"

"Yes sir, strictly legit now, Mr. Schofield," Sam answered. A thought struck him. "You ever get back that $10,000?"

"Yes, as a matter of fact. At least, most of it. The cops picked up the limousine chauffeur at Kennedy Airport buying a ticket for Aruba. Had $9,000 on him. The rest went for clothes, a watch, and a suitcase."

Sam, it seemed to Schofield, was looking wistful. The agent studied him a moment. "You know," he said, "maybe I've already said this, but you handled yourself very well the other night. Pretty cool. Did you ever think of getting into government service?"

"I thought of it, Mr. Schofield. But all you dudes are college men, and I ain't even got my high school diploma yet." Sam shook his head. "I don' think I can make it through college."

Schofield patted Sam on the shoulder. "Well, think about it," he said. "You're not any dumber than a lot of others that have gone through college. If you are interested, give me a call."

Schofield walked off. "I'll do that!" Sam called after him. He stood there pensively until Carolyn joined him. "The cars is gonna leave," she said.

When she spied the principal getting into another car, Mrs. Klein motioned to him to join her. A nice-looking man, she thought. But Sam and Carolyn piled in before the principal could make his move. Flustered, the old woman shrank into a corner and looked at them warily.

"Mornin', ma'am. How ya doin'?" Sam said cheerfully.

"You're going to the cemetery?"

"Yes, ma'am, we think that's the right thing to do. Don' you?"

"Yes, well, obviously since I'm here." She let out a nervous laugh. "I suppose you felt close to . . . uh, the deceased."

"Mighty close. You heard the reverend. Mr. Becker, he done help me a lot when I was in trouble; not many white folks do that for blacks. And then we went through a lot together, you remember?" He looked at her intently as though to make sure she was remembering.

She shuddered. "Oh, yes, I remember. Have you been all right since then?"

"Yes, ma'am. Me and my friend here, this is Carolyn, we're in business together. We operate a chain of beauty shops. Well, it's just one so far, but it will be a chain real soon."

"That's very interesting." Even if he was not telling the whole truth, she wanted to believe, on the day she was helping to bury David, that there were good things in him as in all people. She silently conceded that some Negroes undoubtedly tried to get ahead in life with honest work. Her cleaning lady, for example. And some of the delivery boys were nice. She had been as startled as anyone by the Reverend Greenway's impromptu speech, but she had found herself moved by it. It would be a tribute to David to try to be more generous-minded, which, she also conceded, was not a bad thing in itself, although why he had never worried more about his own kind of people, she could never figure out. She also could think of nothing else to say to her fellow passengers, and the rest of the hour's trip to New Jersey passed with hardly a word more between them. Sam asked who was taking care of the funeral, and Mrs. Klein explained about his family in Florida.

Riding in the front car with Ben and the rabbi, Beverly had paid no attention to who was accompanying them. She had arranged for only two extra cars because she did not imagine there would be a crowd. She also had not imagined who would be among the mourners. She alighted from the car at the cemetery and froze as she watched Sam bound out of the last car, followed by Carolyn and Mrs. Klein. Out of the other car came the sole passenger, the principal. There would be six besides the rabbi. A very peculiar six.

Beverly grabbed Ben's hand and motioned with her head. "Do you see who came?"

"I see. That goy Greenway must have told him to come."

She walked ahead to the plot, ignoring the others. The sun was almost as hot as in Florida, and everyone stood around the grave perspiring. Kirschbaum was all business, and in ten minutes the ceremony was over. There was an awkward moment she could not avoid. Each of the mourners came up to her and offered condolences. For Sam and Carolyn, it was the first time.

"My name's Carlton White. Guess you know that already from the Reverend Greenway. My friends call me Sam, and this here is Carolyn," the youth said. "Me and Mr. Becker was good friends. We're sorry about what happened."

"Thank you," Beverly said. She wanted it to end right there, but something egged her on.

"How did you and my brother become friends?" she asked. "I mean, wasn't he your teacher?"

"That's right. He helped me with English. I wanted to get my high school diploma, but he done more than that. He helped me and Carolyn with our business. We got a chain of beauty parlors, or we will real soon, I hope. And then we helped each other make that big drug bust. I guess you heard about that."

He grinned at her. Beverly had to admit he had charm, and close up, he really was good-looking, for a black. She wanted to ask how he and David became allies in a drug bust when he was selling the stuff himself. She had pressed her brother several times, but in his taciturn way, he had offered only vague explanations. Sam didn't look like someone in the beauty parlor business. Had he reformed, or was he still a pusher? The question seemed desperately important, but she could not bring herself to ask it. There had been a bond between her brother and this young black man, and there was nothing she could do about it now. Except, perhaps, respect it.

Everybody was getting back into the cars for the return trip to New York. The chauffeur of the family car started the engine when Beverly said suddenly, "Hold it a second. I'll be right back."

She walked quickly to the car carrying Sam, Carolyn, and Mrs. Klein, and leaned in the window.

"I almost forgot," she said to Sam. "My brother left you a little something in his will. To be exact, $10,000." She fished in her pocketbook and took out a pen and a piece of paper. "Here, write your name, address, and phone number down, and we'll be in touch."

Hot dog! Sam had not figured on this. Tremblingly, Sam scribbled on the paper and handed it back. "That's nice, ma'am. Thank you."

"Don't thank me. Thank my brother." She started back to her car, stopped, and returned to where Sam was leaning out. "I forgot something. You are to get the money in six months, provided there is no evidence or reports of illegal activity on your part." Her stern gaze moved from Sam's startled face to Carolyn's. "My brother said the Reverend Greenway would keep tabs, but he expressed the wish that you be responsible too for Sam's conduct."

Dumbfounded, all Carolyn could think to do was nod. Beverly gave both another stern look and walked quickly away before Sam could protest his innocence.

Ben exploded after she returned to the car and told him what she had done. "What the hell got into you?" he shouted as the car drove off. "I told you that goddamn will was not legal!"

"Please don't swear. All right, so the will's not legal. But David wanted to leave something to that boy. There was something between them. What can I say? Don't you see, if we don't respect David's will, there'll be no point to his dying."

Ben started to say there was no point anyway, not the way David had died, but he thought better of it, and they drove back to New York in sullen silence. Beverly considered how to break the news to Greenway of the added pastoral duties she had conferred upon him. Behind them, Sam allowed his injured pride to be soothed by the balm of impending wealth and kept up such relentlessly cheerful banter that Mrs. Klein considered getting out and hitchhiking. She was looking forward to a strong cup of coffee and some conversation with friends on the strangeness of some people's tastes. All that money left for what purpose!

"Hey, baby," Sam said to Carolyn when they had left Mrs. Klein and were riding uptown in a taxi. "There'll be enough to put down some money on a second shop. What ya think of that?"

"That'll be real nice. But maybe we should go slow and make sure the first shop is gonna work out."

"Hey, no problem, baby. It will. I know it will. We're on our way. It's jes' a question of a little capital. And now we got some."

A wave of fear passed through her as she thought of all the other capital. "You gotta remember you ain't gettin' this capital unless they's no more funny stuff. You hear?"

"Hey, after what me and Mr. Becker been through, what you worried about? You heard the Reverend Greenway. We's memorials to the old man. I want you to know, woman, that I even thinkin' of becomin' a G-man. Mr. Schofield, he say I can do it."

Carolyn looked at him as though sizing up a stranger. He sure knew how to jive, and most of the time she had to admit she liked it. But this time, things had to get serious. She snuggled up to him, and he put an arm around her. "We're on our own now," she whispered. "We ain't got Carlo to bug us, but we ain't got Mr. Becker to run to either."

He nodded. "I know that. Don't you worry." A plaintive note came into his voice. "Why they makin' us wait six months?"

You know why, and I know why, she said silently. Mr. Becker may have been old, but he was no fool. He certainly had no illusions. Maybe Sam was a better person, but even in death, Mr. Becker had taken no chances. Or maybe it was his sister? Either way, there was a good chance Sam would get through the next six months. After that, how would she manage him? By loving him. Yes, by loving him. That was all she would have. She hoped it would be enough.